THE HOLLIS TIMEWIRE SERIES
BOOK 2

THE UNSEEN ONES

DANIELLE HARRINGTON

FROM THE TINY ACORN...
GROWS THE MIGHTY OAK

The Unseen Ones

First Edition
Copyright © 2020 Danielle Harrington

Book interior design and digital formatting by Debra Cranfield Kennedy.

www.acornpublishingllc.com

Library of Congress Control Number: 2020920450

ISBN—Hardcover 978-1-952112-25-6
ISBN—Paperback 978-1-952112-24-9

I THINK WE ALL HAVE MAGIC IN OUR BLOOD.

IT JUST COMES OUT IN UNASSUMING WAYS.

I

I'M DYING, AND THE DARKNESS OF THE NEXT WORLD SMELLS of blood.

My feet slam into concrete, and I crumple forward, smacking my hands against something hard. Pain shoots up my left arm, causing it to spasm.

Blood. There's so much blood. My hands are covered in it.

Fluorescent lighting attacks my senses, and for a moment my brain refuses to function. What happened? Where am I? What's going on? I don't know . . .

I reach for my chest, jittery fingertips clawing at my clothing. Is this my blood? It must be, but I can't feel anything. No pain in my body explains this. Then a chilling cry reaches my ears, and all the blood makes sense. My best friend, Tiffany, is lying next to me, pale-faced and convulsing, a deep crimson stain spreading across her sweater like ink spilling from a bottle.

My heartbeat drops into my gut, and everything comes back

to me in one clarifying moment. My ability attacked Ashton Teel, that blond-haired, antagonistic bully, and I almost killed him. I forced Tiffany to teleport me to the Area 19 Testing Center. The secret weapon of a hundred years ago is real. The military men are on their way. And the gun. There was a silver handgun.

As I take in my surroundings, recognition twists my stomach into a knot. I'm back in the underground compound, I'm in my room, and Tiffany's been shot.

"Tiffany!" I cry, crawling to her. "It's okay! You're okay!"

I press my hands to the source of blood to staunch it. Tiffany shrieks. She fights my grip, and in her spasms of agony, she nearly throws me off, but I double down. I straddle her, placing the full weight of my petite body on the wound and looking around for help. The concrete walls of the small room appear to shrink in on us, and all I can think to do is scream.

"Help! Somebody help us!"

The sound rips through my throat like I'm an injured beast. This can't be happening. This can't be real. Adrenaline thumps in my ears, and my body begins to tremble. Blood springs up over my fingertips, bright and fresh. The color nauseates me.

Footsteps echo down the hall. Someone is coming.

"It's okay, Tiffany," I say, whimpering. "Someone's here. It'll be alright. Just hold on. Do you hear me? You'll be okay."

She shudders, and then all at once, four people spill in through the cramped doorway. Everyone gasps. Tiffany's blood is smeared across the floor—and all over me. It looks like I've attacked her, but nothing could be further from the truth. To my relief, Jonah Luxent, my ability teacher, is among them. I meet his somber brown eyes.

"Help me."

"What happened?" He drops to his knees beside me, brushing a hand over his dark brown hair and stubble beard.

"She got shot," I say, and my voice cracks. "Please, help me."

"She got shot?" Jonah repeats.

His face develops a nasty hue of grey, and he turns to the trio in the doorway. The first two men I've only seen in passing, but the third I recognize: Keith Keaton, the boy I had been falling for. His shocked look plunges regret into my gut.

"Keith," Jonah says over Tiffany's cries. "Get Liz Engel in here now."

"Yes, sir."

There's a scuffle of footsteps, and Jonah moves his hands to mine.

"It's all m-my fault," I stammer, stricken. I'm gasping for air, and stars begin to pop in and out of my peripheral vision.

"Hollis," Jonah says, his tone firm. "Move your hands. Let me hold pressure."

"It's all my f-fault."

Jonah's hands are vice-like upon mine. "Hollis, listen to me, you need to move your hands. Let me help you."

"She got shot," I say, wide-eyed. "Jonah, she got shot!"

"Hollis!" Jonah squeezes my wrists, and this small act grounds me. "It's okay. Move. Let me do it."

I obey him, sliding sideways off of Tiffany's seizing frame. Her long black hair is fanned out around her, drenched in blood, and her olive skin is perspiring. As Jonah trades places with me, he presses down on the bullet wound. I'm numb, unable to think. Tiffany is convulsing. She's going into shock. She's dying. I begin to hyperventilate, and my words come out in a jumble.

"I w-went back to the Testing Center to find the secret weapon. I m-made Tiffany take me."

"You what?" Jonah's horrified tone pierces me.

"I made her take me there," I say. "And then I ordered her to teleport herself back to the compound—with my ability— but she . . ."

I trail off, clawing at my chest. I can't breathe. I suck in huge gulps of air, but this only makes me dizzy. Panic is drowning me in a sea of fear, and my vision begins to black out.

"Hollis," Jonah says, staring intently into my face. "Look at me. Tell me what happened."

I fix my eyes on him.

"After I sent Tiffany away, she came back for me," I say. "They were going to shoot me, but she teleported back for me and now . . . now she's been shot." My eyes burn as the weight of what I've done crashes over me. She was shot in my place. But before Jonah can say another word, a stark realization hits me, and I yelp.

"The tracker!"

My bloody fingers fumble with the folds of Tiffany's sweater, and then I find it—silver and small—my terrible mistake. This, my betrayal. I pull the pea-sized bug off of her and jump to my feet, smashing it under the heel of my burgundy laced boot.

"They're coming!" I say, hysterical.

The two husky men loitering in the doorway appear confused, but Jonah understands, and his eyes turn sharp. "Hollis, you better speak quickly."

"Jonah, the government is coming. They know there are more of us, and they know where we are! I'm not sure how much longer we have!"

I take heaving breaths. My head is pounding in a sickening rhythm, but my mind is on fast forward. How long has it been since the woman gave the military the order? How long until we die?

"Jonah, we have to get everyone out of here!" I screech. "Now!"

Jonah's face turns, if possible, even paler. "Hollis, are you absolutely sure they know?"

"I'm positive." I hold up the remains of the smashed bug. "The woman at the Testing Center put a tracker on Tiffany. I didn't know at the time. I swear! And when I forced Tiffany to teleport herself back here . . . they know."

Jonah turns to the men. "Peter. Michael. Sound the evacuation alarm. We need everyone out. Tiffany can't teleport us. Tell everyone to take the East tunnels like we've practiced, and get everyone to the forest. Now."

The two men nod and dart into the hall. Jonah presses on Tiffany's wound, but his eyes don't leave mine.

"You have a lot of explaining to do," he says sharply. "I don't know what's happened here, but now's not the time to discuss it."

"Yes, s-sir."

"Hollis." Jonah's eyes bore into mine.

"Yes?"

"I need you to use your ability to control these men. Do you understand me? Freeze them. Don't let them come near the compound. I know you can't hold them off indefinitely, but it will buy us time to evacuate."

Fresh tears blur my vision. I hang my head, ashamed to utter the one thing I've wished for all this time. "Jonah, I don't have my ability. I'm not a puppet master anymore."

His brief silence sears a hole through my insides.

"You don't have . . . you don't what?"

I look up at him, shame dousing me. "The government took it away," I say, constricted. "I let them take it away. That's why I went to the Testing Center. After I accidentally hurt Ashton with my powers, I couldn't stay here. I was so scared that my ability would force me to hurt someone else. It just took over. I couldn't control it. I had to know if the secret weapon was real because I . . . I just wanted to be normal. I wanted to go back home."

Jonah's sober expression deepens. It isn't a shaming look, but rather, one of profound sadness. He understands the decision I made, and why I made it. I can see it in his face.

Shrill alarms explode through the compound and I jump, electrified by the noise.

"Hollis—"

But before Jonah can say anything else, a squat little lady with short black hair bursts through the door with a large medical bag in hand. She squeaks. "Dear Lord!" Her eyes move to Tiffany's bloodied wound. "Jonah, what on earth happened here? And why are the evacuation alarms going off?"

"Tiffany's been shot. We've been found out, Liz," Jonah says.

"Goodness . . ." Her pudgy face drains of all color. "Are you sure?"

"Yes."

"Very well then, first things first," she says, moving to examine Tiffany. She places her stubby fingers around the wound. "Damn. The bullet is still in her shoulder."

Tiffany whimpers as Miss Engel presses firmly near the bullet's entry.

"Can you fix it?" Jonah asks.

She clicks her tongue at him. "My ability can do plenty, but I need to get that bullet out before we move her, and I need to stop this bleeding." She shuffles through her bag, extracting a pair of long, silver tweezers and a white cloth.

Tiffany's face is growing paler by the second, and I back away from her, shaking my head.

"Put this in her mouth," Miss Engel says, holding up the white cloth. She chirps at me. "Quickly now!"

I snap out of my trance and kneel beside Tiffany's head, taking the cloth in hand. "What's this for?"

"The pain," she says. "This is going to hurt like hell. Prop her head up on your lap. Hurry now."

I obey, placing the cloth between Tiffany's teeth. "Now what?"

Miss Engel rummages in her bag again, removing a pair of scissors and a small vial with dark green liquid in it.

"Jonah, you and Hollis need to hold Tiffany still while I do this. Do you understand me? She'll pass out from the pain, but before then, she'll put up a fight."

"Okay," Jonah says. He steps over Tiffany, holding her legs down. "Hollis?"

I meet his gaze for a fraction of a second. "I'm good." I brace myself on Tiffany's uninjured shoulder.

"Right," she says. She looks between us. "Absolutely still."

With uncanny speed, she wields the scissors and cuts Tiffany's shirt open with one long snip. Uncapping the vial, she inverts it, dumping the contents around the bullet hole. The green fluid sizzles, mixing with the blood. Then, with expert precision, she inserts the metal tweezers into the opening of the wound.

Tiffany's strangled scream cuts into me like a hot, fiery knife.

"Pass out," I whisper. "Please, pass out."

"Hold her still, Hollis!" Liz Engel barks over the alarms.

I push my weight over my palms. I'm quivering as tears stream down my face, and I bow my head over Tiffany's. "It's going to be alright. I'm sorry. I'm so sorry. I was wrong and selfish. I'm sorry."

After several seconds of writhing, Tiffany's eyes roll back, and she stops moving. Miss Engel probes a moment longer before extracting the tweezers.

"Got it!"

She holds the fragment up to the light, and I grimace. There it is—the bullet that was meant for me—clutched between the blood-stained, pincer-like ends of the silver instrument. She discards it onto the floor, and the distinct clatter of metal and concrete sends chills down my spine.

"Is she okay?" I ask.

Miss Engel ignores me and turns back to her bag. She delves within and removes another cloth. Dabbing off the green liquid, she places her palms over the streaming wound.

Without warning, her fingertips begin to glow, and I gasp. A strange, purple substance flows from her, seeping into Tiffany's shoulder. I watch, mesmerized as the purple snakes around the wound, hovering there and then tucking itself under Tiffany's skin, like a creature retreating into a burrow.

"That's the best I can do for now," she says. "She's still critical, and she's lost a lot of blood, but I've stopped it."

Jonah and I let out a collective sigh. It's a small moment of shared relief. I meet his eyes, and I'm overwhelmed. The bleeding has stopped. It's a minor victory, but a victory nonetheless. Tiffany is okay, and the bullet is gone.

Boom.

An eruption of sound rips through the air, and an explosion echoes about the concrete, tearing the earth askew. I'm lifted from my feet and thrown sideways as the floor beneath me trembles. My hands smack against the wall, and I hear a distinct pop. Blinding pain shoots through my left arm, paralyzing me for a beat.

Another violent shudder shakes the room and I scream,

crumpling into a heap on the floor as bits of concrete and dust shower over the four of us. I throw my hands up to shield my head.

"We have to move! Now!" Jonah says, hoisting Tiffany over his shoulder and standing to brace himself against the entryway. Liz Engel snatches up her medical bag, tottering as another bang shakes the foundations of the room.

For a split second, I can't move. I'm frozen in place, wracked with fear. The realization of what's happening is too much. I can't process it.

"Hollis, we have to go!" Jonah shouts.

I fumble with the wall to keep my footing. I have to get to the door.

Another explosion wrenches the ceiling apart, and I'm thrown to my knees, scraping my skin against the jagged stone. Cold sweat drenches my shirt, and my mouth turns dry. The government is here, the raid has begun, and everyone is going to die . . .

What have I done?

2

I'M SPRINTING DOWN THE LONG, CONCRETE HALLWAY. Jonah is ahead of me, supporting Tiffany's limp body in his arms. Liz Engel stumbles behind us, huffing madly, her large medical bag stuffed under her thick forearm.

"Hollis, the door!" Jonah says. "Get the door!"

I charge forward, running past him, but the instant I reach the metal handle, a violent bang rips it from my grasp. I'm thrown to my hands and knees with a hard smack. Smoking debris showers the floor around us. I shield my face, and a singular thought consumes me: the door. I have to open that door or we're all going to die. I spring to my feet, grab the handle, and swing it open.

Jonah makes it to me in two more strides. Holding Tiffany like a lifeline, he jumps onto the rickety metal platform clinging to the side of the massive common room. I follow suit.

"Liz, hurry!" he shouts.

I look over my shoulder, and, as if in slow motion, I catch

the last glimpse of the squat little lady running down the remaining stretch of hall . . .

I'm slammed into the handrail as the next bomb detonates. All of the air is sucked from my lungs. White-hot color blurs my vision, and pain attacks me. I try to breathe, but my chest refuses to comply. Blood pools in my mouth, and ringing fills my ears.

I can't move. I can't breathe. I'm dead. I must be dead.

Adrenaline is working to restore my senses, and as I sit up, my terror climbs to new heights. The hallway behind us is gone, and Liz Engel is nowhere to be found. Blood drips from the side of my face. I place my hand to it, and the slippery, warm sensation makes me vomit. I turn over, spilling the sick to my left.

Someone is shouting at me.

I wipe something hot from my mouth.

Someone is shouting my name.

I stare at my hands, my vision blurring in and out of focus.

"Hollis? Hollis!"

Firm hands grip my own, and I'm pulled to my feet. The second I'm up, a fresh spike of panic brings me out of the fog.

"Jonah." I cling to him to stay upright as another boom shakes the flimsy metal stairway.

"Move!" he says. "Down the stairs. Quickly!"

I grab the handrail and begin the descent into the massive room.

Darkness overwhelms us as we drop lower into the chaos. Concrete and earth litter the floor below, and as we move deeper into the belly of the compound, the smoke and dust thicken, like the brewing of an ocean before a great storm.

I clutch the railing, squinting through the tumult. Chunks of the vaulted ceiling are missing, and the night sky, littered with stars, twinkles above us—as if freedom were at our fingertips, taunting us with an escape that's just out of reach. The truth is, everyone is stuck in the pit. Everyone is trapped, and the roar of military jets and the screaming of frenzied people stab at my bleeding ears.

We make it to the bottom flight just in time. Another quake rocks the foundations of the room. I leap from the twisting metal as it peels away from the wall, folding in on itself and crumpling to the cracked earth.

Jonah hoists Tiffany over his shoulder and forges ahead.

"Jonah!" I scream over the uproar. "What do we do?"

"Run!" He points across the war-torn and burning room. "To the tunnels. Follow everyone else."

"What about you? What about Tiffany? Let me help you!"

"We'll be fine. I'm right behind you. Go!"

I hold his gaze for a split second longer and then nod. "Okay."

I begin the trek, heartbeat pounding in my throat. The dust is so thick I can barely make out what's in front of me. I hold my hands out like I'm blind, but before I can take another step, a massive burst of blue light illuminates the space. I look around, tripping over a chair. It's emanating from the center of the crowd, and its intensity is overwhelming.

I shield my eyes. "What the—"

Boom.

I fall to my stomach, and dirt showers me from above. The blue light shoots upward and spreads throughout the room, covering the entire ceiling like a vast umbrella. It pulses with the force of an electric storm, creeping across the sinews of the shattered compound.

I look around for its source, and a moment later, I find it: a scrawny, dark-skinned girl, standing on a stack of overturned tables with her arms raised above her head. She's trembling, pouring the blue light into the open sky.

My eyes widen, and hope flutters in my chest. A force field. She's creating a force field with her ability. I jump to my feet, sprinting through the twisted ruins. The tunnels. I have to get to the tunnels. But another bomb sends me reeling forward, the corner of a chair gashes my head, and blackness invites me into its arms . . .

I'm staring into the vibrant blue eyes of Keith Keaton. His dark hair falls disheveled across his forehead, and his boyish smile sends flutters down to my stomach. We're sitting on the ledge of the cave in the ceiling, watching over the peaceful compound below. Those beneath us stroll about, unaware of our dangling feet.

It's our spot. Our little secret.

Keith takes my hand, and the scent of his skin draws me in. His lips brush mine, and we sink into a wonderful moment of bliss. Everything about this feels right. I'm home, and the hands that twist through my hair make me feel alive. It's better than any ability's tingling touch.

When we break apart, warmth prickles across my body. Keith places his arm around me, and I lean my head on his shoulder. We don't say anything to each other. We don't need to. In this moment, I'm safe. It's Keith. He makes me feel like I've always known this kind of acceptance. I don't have to pretend around him. I don't have to fight, or struggle, or fear. I can be me.

His strong hands give me a gentle squeeze, and I close my eyes, breathing him in. He smells of sandalwood and summer—sweeter than honey. It's intoxicating.

But something isn't right. With each new breath, sour arises, and his aroma turns pungent as smoke fills my lungs. A bitter taste spoils my tongue, and I come to, surrounded by the wreckage of the burning compound. The bombing isn't over.

My head throbs hot with blood, and the stitch in my chest stabs at me.

Get up. I have to get up.

Floundering, I find my bearings a few seconds later, and I grip the edge of a splintered table. I have to keep moving. I press forward, closer to the exit. The girl with the blue light force field is directly in front of me. Blood seeps from a gash in her leg, and tears smear her face as she strains to keep the remains of the compound from caving in.

Just then, a huge rock tumbles through the chasm above, but instead of falling to the floor, it shatters at the edge of the blue light. The girl falters, and the force field flickers, but it doesn't vanish. Her face is strained, and even though blood trails from her nose and ears, she remains upright, dumping her power into the protective shield.

I take off again, weaving my way through the throngs of scattered people. The shrill sounds of crying reach my ears, but I push it away. I'm searching in the near darkness for a clear path of escape.

A group of people sprints past, knocking me into one of the tables. I inhale sharply as the corner of the wood scrapes my stomach, but I push off of it, scurrying after them. They're moving toward the back corner of the compound. I squint ahead. Through the cloud of debris, the faint, black outline of the tunnel looms into view. I'm almost there.

Running at breakneck speed, I launch myself over chairs and chunks of broken ceiling. My chest heaves and my arms shake, but I keep going. I make my way to the end of the common room and fall in line behind the mass of frightened souls, all shoving their way through the entrance of the pitch-black hole in the rock.

The compound groans with the force of another blast, throwing the crowd to its knees, but instead of screams, a tumult of voices cry out, almost in unison.

"Look!"

I stare up at the ceiling, my eyes following the dozens of pointing fingers. The blue light of the girl's force field has extended its way into the tunnel, snaking around the walls and enveloping the floor. It charges forward like a steadfast guardian, and the crowd cheers, pushing toward freedom.

Hands claw at my back, and sweaty bodies press in on me from all sides. I almost lose my footing. People shove past me, running up the incline. My heartbeat is bursting. With a strangled yell, I continue on, racing up the slope with all the strength I can muster, hoping against hope that we will make it out. We have to make it out. All of us.

The tunnel stretches on, twisting and curving up. The earth crunches beneath the pounding of hundreds of feet. The blue light pulses, holding the tunnel intact, but with another resounding bang, it flickers and then dies, extinguishing us into complete darkness.

Shrieks come from all around me, and someone pushes me down in the hysteria.

I fall to the ground, and the stampede swarms. Feet stomp onto my arms and legs, stabbing me over and over again, and I scream. I try to climb to my feet to fight the tide, but I'm pushed down again by the chaos. I'm going to be crushed.

Numbing pain coats me, creeping up through my chest and into my face. Stars are dancing across my vision. My body is tingling from the impact of so many people. I'm going to be trampled to death . . .

Someone's strong hands grab me, and I'm hoisted to my feet. I know those hands.

"Keith?" I yell into the darkness, clutching onto him.

"Hollis?"

My heart leaps. I'm vice-like upon him. "You're alive!"

"I'm okay," he says, squeezing my hand and pulling me back into the disarray. "We're almost out. We're going to make it!"

"Okay," I say under my breath.

I want this to be true. This has to be true because this is my fault. We have to make it out.

Another violent tremble almost knocks me over, but Keith holds me steady. A faint light glints ahead of us. The stars. We are nearly there.

Keith pulls me forward, and after ten more strides, we leap from the tunnel and into the open. The crisp breeze catches my hair, whipping it across my face, and the cold bites my nose and cheeks.

An earth-shattering roar explodes from the heavens. I look up, horrified, as dozens of small planes dive, one by one, over the top of the compound, emptying their deadly contents onto the writhing people below.

"We need to get to the trees!" Keith shouts, pointing to the shrouded line of forest opposite the burning carnage. "Let's go!"

I stare across the vast expanse of ground. My first thought is we'll never make it that far, and an urge to help more people overwhelms my desire to run.

"Keith, wait. We have to help!" I cry, charging across the dirt in his wake.

"If we stay, we're going to die!"

The night sky lights up as a jet of fire expands into the darkness, hitting one of the bombers dead on. The screeching of hot metal pierces my eardrums, and the plane plummets to the earth with a resounding thud, sending bits of shrapnel everywhere.

"Candice!" Keith roars. "It's Candice!"

He turns back toward his sister, pulling me against the tide of scattering people with surprising strength. Candice's brown hair whips around her shoulders as another burst of fire illuminates the night.

"No! Candice, we have to go!" Keith yells. "Get out of there!"

"Keith, watch out!" I yelp, pointing up to one of the planes. It's hovering in mid-air, caught in the midst of a tornado-like wind. The spiral of air vibrates around the aircraft, gripping it with animalistic fervor, and then, without warning, the tornado slams the plane into the ground. The dirt beneath us gives way, and Keith and I are thrown backward.

We hit the ground. Hard. So much dust fills my lungs that I'm suffocated. Coughing, with my eyes streaming, I manage to find my footing. Keith's hand is clamped over mine, and he drags me forward, closing the gap between us and his sister. The heat from the scorching metal sears my skin, and the caustic smell of burning flesh makes me gag.

"Come on," Keith says, pulling Candice away. "We have to go. Now!"

He is struggling with her, fighting her, and his grip on my hand vanishes. He pulls Candice away from the flaming wreckage.

"No!" she screams, yanking herself from her brother's grasp. "Let me go! I can take out the planes. I can help him!"

She points to a burly man a few yards off. Wind is swirling around him as another tornado bursts from his palms, rocketing up toward the next plane.

"Candice, no! We have to go! I'm not letting you die!" he roars.

Keith arrests her arms, physically picking her up, but she kicks out at him, pulling herself free again.

"Get off of me!" she shrieks. "I can help. I can stop them! Will you let me—"

"Wait!" Keith spins around, grabbing my hand, a wild look painted across his dusty face. "Hollis. You can take down all of the planes!"

My heart leaps into my throat. I shake my head. "I can't."

He squeezes my hand so hard it hurts. "Yes, you can. You can do this. Just freeze the pilots, and all the planes will go down. You can save us!"

My voice breaks. "Keith, I can't. We have to go. Please. I can't do it!"

Tears are streaming down my face, and I'm starting to panic. I pull at his arm.

"What are you talking about?" He shakes his head. "Just freeze them. Use your power—"

"I don't have my power. It's gone. We have to go. Please!" My throat closes. I can see the confusion etched across Keith's features. "We have to get out of here!" My eyes plead with his. I'm shaking so badly I can barely keep hold of him.

"Okay," he says, without questioning me further. He turns to his sister and grabs her arm. The wind of the tornado picks up once more, buffeting us back. "Candice, we're leaving. Now."

"But I can help!" she shouts, trying to pull away from him once more.

"This isn't a request! We're leaving!" he says firmly, and

without warning, the three of us are lifted into the air. I grip onto Keith until my knuckles turn white. We're flying, and the frigid air rushes about us as we soar higher and higher, away from the terror below.

3

WE TAKE COVER IN THE TREES. HUNDREDS OF US SPRINT over the broken earth, desperate to flee the fire and shrapnel of the attack. It takes everything in me to keep running. The black forest hums with the unknown, but the planes haven't stopped searching for us.

Bullets spray the pines, and Keith dives for the ground, taking me and Candice with him. As we roll in the dirt, wood chips fly from the trunk directly ahead.

Before I can process the pain of slamming flat onto my chest, a new sound arrives. A creaking, roaring, groaning sound. The pine trees. They begin to bend and twist, like a giant monster stretching from a thousand-year slumber. I gasp when the thick wood envelopes us as a snake would a mouse, herding everyone into a tightly-knit group.

"Keith, what's happening?" I cry.

"It's Libbie Lizette!" he shouts. "She can move the trees!"

The forest continues to wrap itself around the survivors, and I'm shoved forward. It's impossible to tell whose hands are on me—except for Keith's. His hand holds mine like a promise, and as the last bit of starlight is stamped out by the coiling forest, I cling to him.

Darkness.

We stay in that darkness for a long time, and one by one, the planes are struck down. The very earth beneath us is unhinging itself to thrust the military into the dust—one shriek of hot metal after another . . .

The next day arrives in despair. We're hidden in the depths of the intertwining wood, and the pungent smell of burned flesh suffocates me. I can't breathe in this tangle of packed human bodies and stale air.

Someone tells me to walk—a gruff, mean someone with rough hands. I can't move properly, but I obey, and after I start, I don't stop. My legs slip into a rhythm all their own.

We walk for miles on end, the enchanted trees guarding us from the threat above. It's all-consuming and never-ending, and the rests we take aren't enough. We march for so long that my feet become numb, and all the while, the only thought coursing through my mind is the crushing reality that none of us know who's alive . . . and who's dead.

Keith keeps by my side. For two days, he never leaves me. Even though we can barely see each other, I can feel him. His presence is the only thing I have. His strength. His words. The tone of his voice. He makes me believe we'll be alright.

My legs burn, my stomach is empty, and my feet are on fire.

Every muscle in me begs for relief, but no one stops. The trees continue on, gently prodding us forward, and my mind turns over and over with a torturous mantra.

Who is dead? Who is gone? Who isn't here with us? We'll know when we stop . . .

When the trees halt everyone, my heart skips a beat. Like a bad dream, the trek is finally over. Libbie's hands, however, continue on, and a massive dome takes shape from the forest. It arches high above, expanding and twisting itself into a home by the grace of her dancing fingertips. Hundreds of cots and dozens of room outcroppings burst from the ground—a brand new compound made from nature herself.

We're safe . . . for the time being.

I shake my head, rubbing my eyes and staring around in awe at the structure Libbie created. I can see clearly for the first time in two days, and in some ways, it's more frightening than the dark. As everyone adjusts to the light, the atmosphere turns gloomier than the two-day journey. People are crying for their loved ones, and their voices stab at my heart.

A woman calling for her son. A boy calling for his sister. A man calling for his wife. Not everyone made it out.

I release Keith's hand. "I have to find Jonah."

It's all I can manage to say.

To my relief, I don't have to look for long. The moment I see him, I crumple at his feet, sobbing. He's alive. I must confess everything to him—every excruciating detail. It can't wait any longer. Today, I answer for my crimes. Judgment is inevitable.

4

"ORDER, PLEASE! ORDER!"

I'm bound to a wooden chair crafted from the trees. Cuffs tie my wrists and ankles in place, and it reminds me of the metal throne in the Testing Center.

A semicircle of twenty Council members sit before me, all chattering behind a makeshift, curved desk that sits on a raised wooden platform. Pine trees surround us, twisted into a domed room that comfortably fits thirty people. The door, which is more like a large piece of driftwood, sits closed, creating a stifling atmosphere.

Eli Stone, the lead Council member, squares his shoulders and peers down at a tattered notebook through his cracked glasses. He's an older man with a wildly greying beard and deep wrinkles.

He clears his throat. "Brothers and sisters of the Council, we are here to address the serious repercussions of Miss Timewire's actions. It is our duty to come to a verdict on her place here. As such, we must determine the proper disciplinary course of action," he begins, pushing his glasses up the bridge of his nose. "Tonight we discuss Miss Timewire's fate."

There's a disgruntled muttering that carries across the small room. My heart is pounding, and I clench my sweaty palms into fists. I shift within my restraints, trying to find a comfortable position, but the wooden cuffs are abrasive on my skin. I swallow a knot, fighting the urge to be sick.

I look up to the only kind face in the room: Jonah. But he's making notes on a crumpled piece of paper and doesn't see my silent plea for his attention. I know I deserve to stand trial for what I've done. I've only known these people for a short time, yet I've managed to uproot and destroy their entire way of life. How can I even begin to express the depths of my repentance?

Eli Stone gazes at me with watery, grey eyes. "Let's begin. I give the floor to Mr. Caleb Stuart."

Mr. Stuart stands, and I can't help but notice the deep gash above his right eye. He leans over at an odd angle, brushing his peppery grey mane from his face and adjusting his singed vest.

"Miss Timewire," he says, and his fierce expression sends a squirming sensation down to my toes. "We have been informed by Mr. Jonah Luxent that, on the night in question, you used your ability to force Miss Tiffany Chang to teleport you to the Area 19 Testing Center. And you did so against her will. Is this correct?"

"Yes, sir," I say.

"Speak up, girl."

"Yes, sir," I say, a little louder.

"And on this night, you sought out the Chief Overseer of the facility, and through your actions, a tracking device was placed on Miss Chang?"

"Yes, sir."

"And then you used your ability to send Miss Chang back to the underground compound?"

"Yes, sir."

"Well," Mr. Stuart says gruffly, throwing a hand up. He glances around the semicircle. "The girl has confessed. I don't see any reason to prolong these proceedings. It's clear that she's responsible for this."

"I agree."

My eyes dart to a scrawny-looking, older woman. She wears a begrudging look, her face pressed in and her brow furrowed.

"She's exposed us after a hundred years of hiding."

There is a general murmur of agreement. My stomach tightens, and nausea overwhelms me. I glance at Jonah again, but he doesn't look up. He's still making notes on his sheet of paper.

"Miss Timewire," Mr. Stuart says, bringing my attention back to him. "Did you go to the Testing Center to expose us?"

My eyes widen. "No!" I say, half yelling, half fighting the impulse to cry. "No, sir!"

"Would you please tell the Council *why* you decided to go to the Testing Center?"

I open my mouth, but nothing comes out. I survey the men and women before me, a deep sense of dread collecting in my gut. What do I say to them?

"Miss Timewire, you are obligated to answer any and all

questions directed to you," he says, rather sharply.

"I . . . I went there because . . ." I falter. Everyone is staring at me, and heat rises in my cheeks. I feel like I can't breathe properly. I swallow, the skin at the back of my throat sticking together. "I went there to get rid of my ability."

There is an audible gasp that flies about the room, and a few people stand to their feet. I'm met with about a dozen looks of pure disgust.

"We must decide what to do with her," someone says.

"We should turn her in!" a husky-looking, bald man shouts.

I shudder, pulling at my restraints. Splinters from the armrest stab my skin. "No! Please. You can't turn me in. I didn't know there was a tracker. I didn't know that—"

"Silence!" Eli Stone yells. "Miss Timewire, you will speak only when spoken to, and if you cannot hold your tongue, then we will remove you from this disciplinary hearing. Is that understood?"

I stare blankly ahead, trying to keep myself from becoming hysterical.

"I said, is that understood?"

"Yes, sir."

"Miss Timewire," Caleb Stuart continues. "You went in for your Test five months ago on your sixteenth birthday. Am I correct?"

"Yes."

"And isn't it true that the people in that facility attempted to kill you when you tested positive for the biomarker?"

"Yes, it's true."

"And isn't it true that upon making it out of the Testing Center, your parents proceeded to turn you in to the authorities?"

"Yes, but—"

"And isn't it true that Miss Chang saved you by teleporting you out of your home at the risk of her own life?"

"Yes, sir. It's true. But—"

"And didn't we take you in? Give you a place of refuge? House you? Feed you? Provide work for you?"

"You did!" I say, my frustration rising. "But, sir—"

"And didn't Mr. Luxent give you countless hours of private lessons, teaching you how to use and hone your ability?"

I glance over to Jonah again, desperate for a hint of eye contact, but he still hasn't looked at me. I clear my throat, my resolve failing. "He did."

Mr. Stuart glares at me. "Then what on earth could have possessed you to return to the people who have been lying to you your entire existence? The *same* people who tried to kill you five months ago?"

"I . . ." My voice cracks. It's time for me to speak up. I have to say something. I must explain myself. I need to make them understand that I never meant for this to happen, that I only went back to the Testing Center to get rid of the monster inside of me, that I nearly killed Ashton Teel because I lost control of my power, that I only did this to protect everyone from my own ability . . .

But I hang my head because nothing I say can bring back the dead, and nothing I do can turn back time.

"Brothers and sisters of the Council," Eli Stone says. "It's clear that all of us want justice for the terrible events of two nights ago. I will open the floor for suggestions on what is to be done with Miss Hollis Timewire. We must come to a unanimous decision."

The same husky-looking, bald Council member speaks up again. "We need to turn her in."

I look up at him. He's hunched over, supporting a mutilated left arm. Dried blood is caked onto his clothing, and he looks like he hasn't bathed in a week.

"Mr. Thomas, can you—" Mr. Stuart begins, but he's cut off.

"I say give her to the government and be done with it," he snarls.

Blinding panic shoots through me, and my blood runs cold. Give me to the government? I open my mouth to say something, but another Council member beats me to it.

"What good will that do?" a mousy-haired woman says. It's Libbie Lizette. She hugs her thin waist with delicate hands, scowling at the man with the mutilated arm. She turns her button nose upward, shaking her head. "We would be giving the government the victory. If we hand Miss Timewire over to them, they will kill her publicly and that won't help anyone. Killing the leader of the second Terror War would be an undeniable blow to the remnant of us left."

I stare at her. The leader of what? What is she talking about? I start to speak, but I stop myself. Eli Stone's cold eyes are hovering on mine. I'm completely helpless—silenced and bound to this dreadful chair.

"Then what do *you* suggest we do with the 'leader of the second Terror War,' Libbie?" Mr. Thomas spits, throwing his good arm into the air.

"Excuse me," a familiar voice says.

My heart nearly jumps out of my chest. I clutch the armrests, and my knuckles turn white. Jonah has finally paused from his notes. I hold my breath, hoping that he'll also protest the idea of handing me over to the government.

"I'm sorry to interrupt your discussion," Jonah says, "but I'm afraid Miss Timewire has not seen the footage you're referring to. Considering its content, I think it's appropriate for her to view."

Several people nod, and hushed voices break out across the panel.

"Mr. Luxent has an excellent point," Eli Stone says. He adjusts his glasses. "Libbie, would you mind setting up a playback of the feed?"

"Of course," she says, shifting in her seat to rummage in a tattered duffle bag. After several moments, she rises gracefully, clutching a thin tablet. She taps on the screen, whispering to herself. "Here it is."

She moves out from behind the curved table and approaches me, holding the tablet up so I can see. Part of the screen is broken, but the feed still plays.

A muted, chic-looking reporter woman in a shiny silver pantsuit addresses the camera. Her societal look holds a glint of contained elation. My stomach turns. I've seen this look before. I've seen it in the eyes of the wolfish woman with the gun when she pointed it in my face the moment I betrayed everyone.

"Behind me you can see the extent of this vicious attack," the reporter says, gesturing to the studio screen, her teeth bared. She steps back to allow the cameraman to zoom in. "Here is the raw footage."

I watch the tablet, horrified, as a jet of fire spurts from the ground, lighting up the screen. The cameraman capturing this is seated on one of the planes, and his view is directed at Candice. Another spurt of fire bursts into the air. It arcs into the belly of the adjacent plane, and the shriek of hot metal that issues from the audio makes my hair stand on end. The plane plummets to the earth with a thunderous boom.

The camera angle shudders, and the footage skews as a gust of swirling wind envelopes it. The video trembles and then cuts to black with the sound of screams.

Another feed pops up, and the pixels turn brilliantly blue as the image zooms in to the top of the decimated common room. The dark-skinned girl is emptying the blue light force field from her hands into the sky. It expands, and the plane vibrates, buffeted back by the intensity of the shield. Cries echo with the howling wind, and the camera angle tosses back and forth.

"We regret to inform the world that there are more Diseased Ones," the reporter says. "They've been in hiding, biding their time, waiting for the opportune moment to attack. And it seems that they will stop at nothing to reignite the terror of one hundred years ago."

My mouth is half open, my eyes glued to the reporter

woman. Her sleek brunette bun shines in the artificial lighting of the news studio.

"The attack occurred during a peaceful military fly-over drill. These monsters hit our planes with deadly force, and we lost forty men," she continues. "Their leader, Hollis Timewire, was spotted a mere hour before the attack, infiltrating the Area 19 Testing Center to announce the initiation of the second Terror War."

An additional feed crackles to life, and my hands turn to ice. There, on the grainy footage, is the white room with the large, curved desk—the room where I met the wolf-like woman, the room where I lost my power, the room where I made my lethal mistake . . .

Helpless to do anything but watch, I see myself charge in, forcing all of the military men to their knees with my ability.

"No . . ." I whisper, angry tears blurring my vision.

"And now, a word from our world leader, President Alvaro Camille."

A vast presidential suite appears. Cameras flash, and hushed silence ensues. Alvaro Camille stands at an ornately carved podium, his spindly hands grasping at the edges. His face is downcast and reserved, but perfectly controlled. His jet black hair, trimmed and gelled down, matches his clean-shaven beard. And his white suit is blinding.

"Citizens of the world, it is time we stand up and finish this atrocious race. Regrettably, the Diseased Ones are alive and well, and they will continue to fester and multiply until they've murdered us all. This horrid mistake of evolution is a virus that threatens to kill, and we must face the reality that we live in a world that will never be safe—not as long as there are Diseased Ones."

The President adjusts his silver tie, his brow knitting together ever so slightly.

"Tonight, I urge you to reach out to those who have suffered such an egregious loss. I urge you to come together in camaraderie and stand as one world—a united order against a common enemy. Tonight, we will bury our dead. But tomorrow . . . tomorrow is a new day."

The President's posture elevates.

"Tomorrow the sun will rise on a world that is ready to end this terror. The sun will rise on a world of bravery. Tomorrow is the day that we declare war on injustice, hatred, and senseless death. Tomorrow is the day we declare war on the Diseased Ones."

Alvaro Camille grips the podium, and his dark black eyes stare into the camera.

"And now I speak directly to you, Hollis Timewire, leader of the second Terror War. I only have one thing to say: we will not lose."

The footage cuts to black, and the tablet glitches in the static of the feed.

5

I STARE AT THE BLANK SCREEN, MY MOUTH DRY. THIS CAN'T be happening. Me? The leader of the second Terror War? This is a mistake.

My voice trembles. "But I'm not."

"You're not what?" Eli Stone asks.

"I'm not the leader. I'm not. I . . . I didn't mean for this to happen. I didn't—" I sputter, my eyes still fixed on Libbie's tablet.

There's a pointed scoff that reverberates through the shrouded trees.

"Yes, Miss Timewire, we are quite aware of the fact that you are *not* our leader," Caleb Stuart says, his thin mouth pressing into a line. He towers over me, bearing down with a look of pure disgust.

"Fine then," Mr. Thomas pipes up, cradling his mangled arm. "If we don't turn her in, then what do we do with her?

We certainly can't let her go. She could turn us in all over again!"

"No!" I shout, pulling against my restraints. "I wouldn't turn any of you in. I never did in the first place!"

Eli Stone stands to his feet, slamming his hand against the wood of the table, and I jump. He speaks in a dangerous tone. "Miss Timewire, you will control yourself. You are not to speak unless spoken to. One more outburst and I'll have you removed. Do you understand me?"

I clench my jaw. I'm panting, frustrated, and completely out of sorts. But I catch sight of Jonah. He's watching me. We lock eyes, and he gives me the slightest nod.

I turn back on Eli Stone. "Yes, sir. I understand. It won't happen again."

Mr. Stuart scratches the back of his neck. "You're right, Mr. Thomas. We will not be releasing Miss Timewire to her own devices. That is out of the question."

"May I suggest something, Caleb?" Libbie says, raising her delicate hand.

Mr. Stuart nods. "Of course, Miss Lizette. The floor is yours."

Libbie stands, turning to address the semicircle. "First, we must consider everything that's happened." Her green eyes are somber, but her tone is firm, almost angry. She speaks in a directed manner. "Miss Timewire's deliberate actions have caused the destruction of the compound, the re-exposure of our kind, the start of a war, and the deaths of over a hundred individuals. A quarter of our brothers and sisters. Gone."

My stomach squirms, and the quiet of the small forested room beats against my eardrums. I'm ashamed. How could I have done something so horrible to these people? The carnage I've caused makes me feel like the monster I was afraid of becoming.

"Taking this into consideration, I believe that the most viable course of action is execution. As far as I'm concerned, it's the only punishment suitable for her crimes."

Voices explode across the panel as Libbie Lizette takes her seat. I can feel the blood drain from my face, and my mouth turns to ash. Execution? I don't want to die. I look over to Jonah, desperate for him to speak, but to my horror, he's returned to scratching down notes.

My breathing turns shallow, and I begin to panic, clutching the armrests of my chair for support. I want to say something, but Eli Stone's severe warning lingers in the back of my mind. I have to stay. I can't be removed from this trial. I need to hear what the other Council members think.

"I agree," Mr. Stuart states.

"What is your opinion, lead Council?" Libbie asks, turning to Eli Stone.

"Execution may be a practical option," he says. "I will open the floor for discussion."

"Does there need to be a discussion?" a younger-looking Council member says. He's a little overweight and sits tall. He points at me. "She's clearly guilty, and barring the options of releasing her or turning her over to the government, I'd say we have no choice."

"I second this," another woman adds.

"Execution!" Mr. Thomas thunders, a sick look of glee plastered across his crooked face.

"Shall we put it to a vote?" Mr. Stuart asks, looking around.

Everyone agrees to this with muddled voices, and the room grows louder.

"Wait . . ." I say, inaudible.

I sound strangled. No one can hear me. They are all talking amongst themselves, leaning in and whispering to each other. My heart thuds in my ribcage like the beatings of a frightened bird attempting to flee for its life.

"Jonah," I whisper, looking up to my mentor. I'm petrified. He's still fiddling away at his notes, as if unaware of what's just been suggested. What is he doing? What is he writing? Why isn't he saying anything?

Mr. Stuart squares his shoulders. "Can I see a show of hands?"

I watch, powerless, as arms raise all about the panel. A few stragglers move their hands gingerly into the air, finally resigning themselves to the pack.

I can't breathe. This isn't happening. I don't want to die. Stars invade my peripheral and I start to hyperventilate. I search the faces of the Council in desperation, hoping that someone will protest—that someone will say something on my behalf.

"Very well then," Eli Stone says, adjusting his collar. "The Council rules in favor of the execution of Miss Hollis Timewire for her crimes against—"

"Excuse me, lead Council, but I do believe you said we need a unanimous ruling, do we not?"

My heart skips a beat. Jonah.

"I'm sorry?" he says, raising an eyebrow. He rubs the bridge of his nose. "Weren't all hands accounted for?"

"I did not raise mine," Jonah says matter-of-factly. He leans back against his seat. His calm demeanor is disconcerting.

"You are *not* in favor of Miss Timewire's execution?"

"I am not."

I can scarcely contain myself. Jonah is coming to my defense, and I'm overwhelmed with relief. My back props against the chair for support, and I hold my breath. My heart is beating so loudly that I'm surprised Eli Stone hasn't demanded my silence again.

"May I ask why?"

Jonah takes a moment to collect his notes, tucking them into a neat stack before standing from his seat. He walks down to the floor to face the Council, placing himself directly between me and my accusers.

"I would like to take full responsibility for Hollis Time-wire."

There is an immediate outcry at this statement. Half the Council jump to their feet, shouting and shaking their fists. The other half appear shocked, bearing looks of disgust, even slight pity, as if poor old Jonah had finally lost his mind.

"Order!" Eli Stone barks, waving his hand. "I say order!"

The room dies down, shifting back into their seats.

"Jonah, are you suggesting that she be allowed to stay here?"

he asks, his hands pressed to either side of his worn face.

"That is precisely what I'm suggesting."

"This is ridiculous!" Mr. Thomas snarls. He turns to the group. "Are we supposed to let one unraised hand stop us from doing what needs to be done? She's a criminal. She deserves to die! A hundred people were blown up or crushed to death! Our home was destroyed! What kind of joke is this?"

A smattering of applause follows this.

"Mr. Thomas—" Eli Stone begins.

"And aren't you her teacher?" Mr. Thomas asks, pointing a thick finger at Jonah's chest. "You're biased. You shouldn't even be on this Council."

"Mr. Thomas!" Eli Stone says, cutting in with venom. "Jonah is a highly esteemed member of this Council and I will not have you questioning his place here. He isn't the one on trial. Now please, *lower* your voice."

Mr. Thomas looks taken aback, his mouth suspended in a mildly dumb-looking 'O.' He folds himself up, knotting his arms together.

The lead Council member turns his attention back to the floor. "Jonah, you can't be serious."

"I am." He directs himself to the semicircle. "I will take full responsibility for Miss Timewire. I understand the gravity of what has occurred. I know that all of us have suffered a tremendous loss. However, I also know that we are a remnant with incredible abilities, and who we are, as a people, is not execution."

Jonah begins to pace as he speaks, walking the length of the panel.

"For one hundred years we've sought out those with abilities and invited them in. We've given them a home, extinguishing the constant presence of fear. We've provided hope where there was none." He pauses. "And we did the same for Miss Timewire."

"Must we recount this little history lesson?" Mr. Stuart interjects, rolling his eyes.

"I believe we must," Jonah says brusquely. "We cannot forget that Miss Timewire came to us from a completely unique set of circumstances. She is different than anyone else we've brought in. She comes from a world where people like you and me are considered to be evil and murderous."

"Yes, but Jonah—"

"This is all she's ever known—all she's ever been taught— and for sixteen years, she was indoctrinated."

Jonah continues to pace, all the while keeping his back to me.

"Five short months ago, we rescued her from the government, and though she hated us then, and would have gladly turned us in if she had the chance, she experienced something that she'd never known before: love and family. True family. She experienced what it was like to feel things deeply, and for the first time in her existence, she was allowed to cultivate her emotions."

Jonah stops walking, his demeanor subdued. He faces Mr. Thomas.

"Yes, I am her teacher, and rightly so because of my ability. I worked with her and helped her craft her power. I even learned from her power myself. I sensed its vastness, volatility, and danger . . . and that is an oversight I take full responsibility for."

Jonah appears to take a moment to himself, and my heart breaks. I know what he's talking about. He blames himself for letting my power consume me. But it's not his fault. It's mine. He shouldn't bear the blame. *I* made the mistake. *I* betrayed everyone in the compound. *I'm* the reason we're exposed, homeless, and laid bare to the cruel world outside.

"We could not possibly have guessed that the culture shock, emotional overload, years of propaganda, and indoctrination could have led Miss Timewire to act as she did, but I do believe with all of my heart that she did not bring about this tragedy on purpose." Jonah holds his hand out to the Council as if inviting them in. "She bought the lie of history. It's as simple as that."

I'm struggling with myself as I push to keep my emotions at bay, but I can't. Hot tears roll down my face in shame.

"And I implore you, brothers and sisters of the Council, to look at the outcome of this hearing as a means to define us as a people," Jonah says. "We are not a people of execution. We are not a people of hatred or death. We are a people of everything the government stands against: one of courage and hope, of tenacity and resourcefulness. But most of all, we are a people of second chances and grace."

And for the first time since Eli Stone opened the floor, Jonah turns to me and looks me full in the face, deep compassion filling his features. "I take full responsibility for this, and I propose that Miss Timewire be allowed to remain here with us as a prisoner under my care. I will accompany her any time she needs to leave her cell, and I will provide a useful place for her in our community."

No one speaks for what feels like an eternity. I watch Eli Stone's face as he pours over a piece of paper. It's so quiet I'm afraid I'll disturb him with the slightest movement.

"I suppose," he says, looking around, "that Mr. Luxent has made several valid points. I am willing to suggest to the Council a thirty day probationary period in which Miss Timewire must prove herself to be a model citizen. I will open the floor for discussion."

I'm sweating profusely, my clammy hands slipping on the chair. I can't believe what I'm hearing. A probationary period? It's more than I could have ever hoped for.

"Jonah." Libbie Lizette rises from her seat, arms crossed. "Are you suggesting that the girl should not take responsibility for her actions?"

"Not at all," he says. "She is fully aware of what her actions have brought about. You said it earlier. She is responsible for the destruction of the compound, the re-exposure of our kind, the ignition of a war, and the deaths of over a hundred people."

I want to melt into the floor and vanish without a trace. Every word singes me like the branding end of a cattle prod.

"She is well aware of this and has already come forward to me," Jonah continues. "That's why we're here this evening. I am merely saying that we must consider what the outcome of an execution will mean for us. Are we ready to kill one of our own?"

Mr. Thomas scoffs, cradling his wounded arm. "But she doesn't even have her ability anymore. She's not 'one of our own.'"

"Regardless of her current state, Mr. Thomas, Hollis Timewire *had* an ability and is now and forever considered a member of this people," Jonah says in an alarming tone. "No action of hers or any other human being can change that."

"Jonah, you've made your point," Libbie says, waving her hand. "If you're willing to fight this hard for the girl, then I suppose I'm willing to concede to a thirty day probationary period, but *only* because I respect you."

Jonah gives Libbie a stiff nod.

Eli Stone readjusts his glasses, examining me. "Does anyone else have something they wish to add?"

"I don't particularly like it," Mr. Stuart says, scratching the bottom of his chin.

"Well, I think it's fair." The younger-looking Council member who spoke before raises his hand. He swivels in his seat. "Jonah has given us another option. And what he said is true. I don't think we're ready to kill one of our own. We aren't like the government, and I hope to God we never become like them. We *are* a people of grace."

Hushed whispers erupt across the panel. Eli Stone speaks up again. "Jonah, are you really willing to take responsibility for this? To risk your place here? If the girl fails—if we have to reconsider this decision . . . what will people think of you? Your capabilities? Your mental state? I'll have no choice but to terminate your position on the Council. You know this. Are you honestly willing to speak for her and take this on yourself? If we must execute the girl . . . I won't be able to defend you *or* your reputation. Jonah, please. People will demand that you step down."

I can hear the concern in his voice. He leans across the flat of the table, giving Jonah a troubled look, begging him to reconsider.

Jonah walks over to me and stands by my side. "I am willing."

I look between Jonah and Eli Stone, and my brain clicks. I understand now. If I fail, Jonah's character will come into question. He'll be seen as inept, unable to make sane decisions for his people, kicked off of the Council, and possibly stripped of his teaching role. Vouching for me is as good as taking the blame himself. For how could he truly remain impartial if they were to execute me? And how could this community ever put their trust in someone who would side with the one responsible for their suffering?

I shake my head. "No. Jonah, you—"

But he places a hand on my shoulder, and his sudden touch stops me.

Eli Stone sits back in his seat. "Very well then," he says. "I will need you to swear it before this assembly."

Jonah nods. Eli Stone hesitates, but then sighs.

"Jonah Luxent, do you swear before the members of this Council that you will fulfill your duty as caretaker of Miss Timewire?"

"I swear."

"And do you acknowledge that by taking responsibility for Miss Timewire, you are placing your own standing on this Council at risk?"

"I do."

"And should Miss Timewire fail to be anything short of a model citizen, do you understand that you will no longer have a place on this Council, as we cannot have you participate in any further decision-making for this community?"

"I understand."

Eli Stone turns his weary face to the room. "Then let's put this to a vote. All in favor of a thirty day probationary period for Miss Hollis Timewire, please raise your hand."

I glance around, my pulse thumping erratically. For several seconds, nothing happens, but then I see it. Hands spring up across the semicircle, some more reluctantly than others, and hope flutters in my chest. Only one hand remains fixed on the table.

"Mr. Thomas?" Eli Stone says, raising an eyebrow.

He glares at me with malice. His cold eyes burrow into mine, and I shift myself in the restraints, trying my best to keep calm. He slowly lifts his good arm. "You get thirty days, girl," he growls.

"Very well." The lead Council member slams his palm against the table, and it startles me. I wince as the wooden cuffs bite into my flesh. "The Council is in agreement. Miss Hollis Timewire shall be granted a thirty day probationary period in which to prove herself to be a worthy citizen of this people. Mr. Jonah Luxent has volunteered himself to take full responsibility for her at the penalty of his own standing on this Council. We will reconvene at this period's termination. Libbie, you may release Miss Timewire into Jonah's custody."

I let out a soft whimper as a single tear slides down the side of my face and into my mouth. I can taste the salt. I try to wipe it away with my shoulder. I don't want Mr. Thomas to see me cry. I don't want any of them to see me cry. I deserve far worse than what's been decided, so I must show them my gratitude, not my tears. I can't appear weepy when my life's just been spared.

Libbie Lizette stands gracefully and moves her thin fingertips into a beautiful arc. My cuffs fall away at her ability's command, slinking back into the woodwork of the chair as if they were never there.

I rub my wrists and stand to my feet, trembling. I can't bear to look up. I keep my view trained on Jonah's feet.

"Hollis." Jonah's soft voice coaxes me to his side. "It's alright. We're done. It's over now. You can follow me."

I walk delicately in my teacher's wake, feeling the staring eyes at my back with every step.

6

MY PRISON CELL IS MADE FROM THE TREES, AS IS everything else here. I sit on the ground, a small cot to my right and a bucket to my left. I pull my knees up to my chest, feeling winded and unable to breathe. Cold tears smear my face, and I wipe them away with the flat of my hand. I grasp the fabric of my jacket, attempting to ground myself to something real as the thunderous cascade of a thousand torturous thoughts assault me.

All that permeates my mind is the metallic scent of blood, the darkness, and the rotting air. It was terrifying—the planes and bombs atop the burning wreckage. All of it sucks me back into the horror of escaping the government's brutal slaughter.

I close my eyes, trying to block out the onslaught of images, but all this does is fixate me on the events. The memories sharpen, like a waking nightmare, and I'm plunged into the moment all over again.

Two days of sensory deprivation. Two days of no food. Two days of walking with no end in sight. I shudder. Even those of us who fled the bombers didn't know if we'd make it out alive.

I sit in my cell, shaking. Tears stream down my face, and this time, I let them fall. I'm trembling in the dirt, unable to move. What have I done? I still don't know who's gone. I never had time to look properly because I was placed into the custody of the Council immediately upon my confession to Jonah.

My teeth begin to chatter. This is my fault—my betrayal. I can't think. My brain is shorted out. This doesn't feel real. I'm supposed to be Hollis Timewire, the perfect society member, blended into the world, nameless, faceless, a nobody. But somehow, I'm Hollis Timewire, the leader of the second Terror War, an atrocious mistake, an infamous criminal—and everyone in the world knows my name.

Jonah sits on a rock just beyond the wooden bars. He leans against the side of my cell, clearly exhausted. Deep bags hang under his soft brown eyes, and he looks like he hasn't slept in days.

"Jonah," I whisper, clutching my knees. I rock myself back and forth, cowering on the ground. He turns to me, placing his hands on the bars that separate us. "Why did you speak for me?" My voice is laden with grief, and my throat closes. I can't bring myself to look at him. "I don't deserve this mercy. You could have voted with the others. Why didn't you?"

He doesn't respond. His brow deepens, and his gaze drops from me to the base of my prison cell. He releases the wooden bars and rests his elbows on his knees.

"I want you to know something, Hollis," he says. "And I want you to listen carefully to my words."

My lower lip trembles, but I nod.

His eyes travel back up to mine. "As terrible as this is, I understand why you did this. I understand why you went back to the Testing Center."

His look grieves me. I can see the loss and pain welling beneath the surface of his countenance. I shake my head, unable to comprehend.

"Jonah—"

"Hollis, my power doesn't just give me the ability to take on another person's power. It gives me the ability to connect to their feelings and read into their emotions." He pauses, clearing his throat before continuing. "I sensed a great danger in you."

A pit forms in my stomach.

"And I was too foolhardy to pursue it." Jonah bows his head, and his tone deepens. "I was fascinated with the intensity of your ability to a degree that caused me to ignore the most fundamental portion of my *own* power. I saw a hunger in you—a deep, primal longing, and I ignored it."

Jonah's face changes, and something I've never seen creeps across his features. It's more than sadness. It's misery, as if he were sickened with himself.

"I understand." Jonah holds his head in his hands. "You had a monster in you, you didn't want to hurt anyone else, and you were convinced that somehow you could be reintegrated into society if your ability was removed... and I was too caught up in the excitement and depth of your ability to teach you properly. I let it blind me."

"No," I whisper, shaking my head. I'm choking on my tears, trembling from head to foot. "Jonah, no. You were a good teacher. This is my fault. I couldn't see the lie. I couldn't see it. I was foolish. This has nothing to do with you. It was my monster—*my* mistake!"

Jonah stares at me, tilting his head to the side. His face is ashen, as if he bore the weight of a hundred years of turmoil. "I want to apologize for not teaching you as I should have. You were my responsibility, new to our society, infant in your power, and I let that get away from me . . . and for that, I am deeply sorry."

"You were a good teacher!" I say again, clinging to my jacket to still my shaking hands. "I'm the one who should be apologizing. I was stubborn and obstinate. I didn't listen to you. I didn't practice what you asked me to. I didn't learn from you like I was supposed to. You shouldn't have to teach a student like me."

My tone constricts, and I stop. I bite my lip, staring at the dirt, unable to compose myself.

"I don't deserve a teacher like you . . ."

These words gut me, but it's true. I haven't earned Jonah's help or compassion. I didn't earn what he did for me tonight.

Jonah's sorrow makes the knots in my stomach turn from unpleasant to awful. I feel sick. There's nothing I can do. I've lost everything, and because of me, so has everyone else. I stare at the dirt, weeping, my eyes puffy and my nose running, but I make no attempt to wipe my face. I deserve to feel like this.

"I would still like to be your teacher, if you're willing to be my student."

I blink, sniffling. "What?" I look up, thinking I may have misheard him. "But . . . Jonah, I don't have my ability anymore. I'm nothing."

"Hollis, your ability doesn't define you. It never has," he says. "It is the content of your character, and the choices you make that shape who you are."

I whimper, cradling myself in my arms.

"I will say this, you can do nothing to change the past," he says, looking at me with empathy. "You've been given an impossible set of circumstances. The whole world is against you, and those of us left will be watching you, but that is all the more reason to have courage." The intensity of Jonah's gaze brings his words into sharp focus. "No one will expect anything from a sixteen-year-old girl, but it's your decision to prove them wrong. It's what you choose to do now that will define who you become."

I'm speechless. I can't seem to wrap my mind around the grace of this man. How can Jonah, despite everything I've done, still look me in the eye and tell me to have courage? How can he truly mean that? I'm baffled to my core that he would accept me—that he would still teach me. But something tells me not to question it—as if the inklings of my lost ability still have a hold over my mind.

"Okay," I say, brushing the stray wisps of blonde hair from my dirt-smudged face.

Jonah nods. "Okay."

"I'd be honored to be your student."

"Then you have yourself a teacher."

My mouth quivers, and I bite down to stop my teeth from chattering. Without my power, I don't know who I am or what Jonah could possibly teach me, but I have nothing left to do but trust him. He's the one who stopped my execution, and the only one who spoke for me.

"Hollis."

"Yes?"

"I . . . I have to tell you something."

Jonah's words send a wave of dread to the ends of my limbs. I peer at him, a horrible feeling washing over me.

"What is it?"

He bows his head, taking a moment to breathe. Something isn't right, and the silence that extends between us terrifies me.

"Jonah, what is it?"

He looks up at me, eyes watering, and places his hands back on the bars of my cell, as if bracing himself.

"Hollis . . . in the forest, when we were traveling here—"

An eruption of noise shrieks at my ears, causing me to jump up. Something dark and huge hurls itself at the bars of my cage, and the force of it shakes the foundations of the wood. Jonah, completely taken off guard by this flash of movement, dives sideways to avoid the figure.

I gasp, my hands folded at my chest.

An angry voice screams at me as its owner pounds on the side of my cell with hot rage. "What did you do to me?"

It takes my brain time to realize who I'm staring at. Ashton Teel, eyes blood-shot and mouth parted, slams his body into the wood, shoving his hands through the bars. His dirty blond hair matches his wild demeanor. I retreat, tripping over my feet and falling backward on the uneven ground.

"Ashton!" Jonah yells, jumping up and grabbing him by the upper arm. He pulls him away from me, and I watch as the two of them struggle.

"What did you do to me, you witch!" Ashton bellows, furiously fighting Jonah's grip. He wrenches himself free and flies at me once more, striking his fists into the bars over and over again. My pulse thunders in my ears as I meet his crazed look.

At this point, a smattering of people have gathered, keen to know what all the commotion is about. They stand a few yards off, their curious eyes darting between me and Ashton Teel.

"Ashton!" Jonah arrests his arms again, dragging him back. He holds the writhing boy. "What do you mean?"

"My ability doesn't work anymore!" he shrieks, livid. He rips himself out of Jonah's grasp, diving toward the bars anew and trying to push himself in between them.

"You—"

"That's enough!" Jonah roars, yanking him away. I stand to my feet, quaking.

Ashton takes a swing at Jonah's face, and I scream. The sound of flesh connecting with flesh is nauseating. The two of them tumble to the dirt, struggle hand and fist. Dust kicks up around them, and several more blows echo through the forest.

"Jonah!" I screech, running forward and grasping the bars of my cell. My hands tense, but I'm helpless to do anything. My power is gone. I can't stop him. Shouting ensues, but the bout is over quickly as two larger men come to Jonah's aid, dragging Ashton off of him. They pin Ashton's arms down and hold him back, keeping him firmly in place.

Jonah stands gingerly, wiping his bleeding lower lip with the back of his hand. He spits onto the ground. "I said that's enough."

"You're defending her?" His eyes bulge as he struggles against the men restraining him. "She turned us in!" He looks around the sizable group gathered. "She's a psychopath! She gave us to the government. She attacked me!"

Murmurs sizzle through the crowd.

Jonah approaches Ashton, holding his hand up to quiet the onlookers. "What do you mean your power isn't working? What's wrong?"

"It's gone. That's what's wrong. I can't suppress anyone's ability!" He spits his words, glaring at me over Jonah's shoulder with venom. "She did something to me."

My hands are shaking so badly that I can scarcely keep a hold of the bars.

"She attacked me!" he bellows. "In the common room. Two days ago. She tried to kill me! Right before she betrayed us all."

Everyone is standing in a semicircle around my cell. It's like I'm being sentenced all over again. Ashton stares me down, like a predator waiting for the kill. He's still fighting the strong grip on him.

"Ashton, you need to calm down," Jonah says. "We will figure this out."

He sneers at Jonah, but his watery grey eyes never leave mine.

"I'm sorry," I say, barely audible. I can't help myself. I know I shouldn't say anything. There's nothing I could possibly say to rectify this, but the words slip from me.

"You're sorry?" Ashton cackles, throwing his head back. "Hey everyone, you hear that? She's sorry! I guess it's all good now."

His words feel like fiery darts.

Ashton lunges forward again, causing the men holding him to stumble a bit. "You took away my ability! You killed all of us! You—"

"Enough!" Jonah shouts, cutting him off. He motions to the two men. "Let's take him to the Council room."

Ashton glares at me, a demented look coming across his face. "This isn't over, Timewire." The men start to pull him away from me, but Ashton is relentless in his aggression, a look of violent rage and grief dominating his features. He speaks with spite in his tone. "By the way, Tiffany is dead. Congratulations, hero."

My hands slip from the bars as an icy numbing sensation douses my face and limbs. I stumble backward, grabbing my chest. It's as if the monster of my ability is back, its dark hands around my throat, slowing suffocating me into oblivion. My vision turns black. My knees begin to tingle, and hot skewers of pain stab my skin.

I fall to my knees and vomit into the dirt. My ears are ringing, and in the following moments, reality drifts away from me into the cold, unendurable arms of darkness.

7

I LIE IN MY COT. I DON'T KNOW HOW LONG I'VE BEEN here, but I haven't moved, and I haven't eaten anything. My whole body is numb... tingling. It reaches my fingertips, lingering there—taunting me—a broken whisper from the ability that no longer exists.

Tiffany was my best friend. She rescued me five months ago and saved my life. She befriended me when I was obstinate and hateful toward her. She sat with me in my concrete cell and stayed by my side, laughing and encouraging me through the difficulty—and despite my hideous betrayal, she came back for me. Now she's dead, and I never got to say sorry. It should have been me...

"Hollis, you need to drink some water."

The door to my cell creaks open, scraping across the dirt. Jonah is here, but I don't move. I've been staring at the ground for so long my eyes have glazed over, blurring my vision. I'm freezing, but I make no attempt to pull the thin blanket over me.

"You need to drink," Jonah says again, kneeling by my side. "Sit up."

I can't. A weight heavier than the world is pressing itself on my chest, as if I were bound under my own power, trapped by the crushing reality of Ashton's words: "By the way, Tiffany is dead. Congratulations, hero."

"Hollis, sit up."

Jonah's tone isn't angry, but his inflection prompts me to obey him. He leans by the edge of the cot, patiently holding a tin of water. He offers his hand to me, and after a few seconds, I take it.

He pulls me into a sitting position. "Drink."

The instant the icy liquid touches my lips, I gulp it down. I breathe deeply, savoring the crystal clear taste of the stream before wiping my mouth on the sleeve of my jacket. I hand Jonah the empty cup, and turn away from him, staring at the ground once more. I hug myself, trying not to shiver. Tiffany surges to the forefront of my thoughts, and I bite the inside of my cheek, stifling the urge to sob.

Jonah doesn't say a word. He simply bows his head and folds his arms across his chest.

I don't know how long we're in each other's company, but my grieving heart urges me to speak. My vocal cords crack from the lack of use.

"She came back for me . . ."

These words strangle me, attacking my throat. I swallow,

and a painful lump travels down into the pit of my stomach. The raw emotion coursing through my body sends shock waves to my limbs. I'm lightheaded and my forehead is throbbing.

Jonah nods. "I know."

It all crashes over me once more, and I clutch my sides, leaning forward as if I were going to be sick again. I don't know if I can do this. I don't want to bear this. It's too much. The idea of having to feel the pain over and over again, every day, is tearing me to pieces. My thoughts are torture—relentless in their charge to break me.

"That bullet was meant for me," I whisper. "I was supposed to get shot."

Jonah's silence is chilling, and the tears I'd been holding back slide down my numb cheeks.

"I should be dead . . ."

Jonah puts his hand on mine. "But you're not."

I can't bring myself to look at him. "Is Tiffany really dead?"

"Yes."

I never knew that one word could burn a hole right through my chest. "Then why didn't anyone say anything? That whole time!" My words come out in anger. "During the trial, they were talking about her. And they knew. All of them knew!"

"I requested that the Council not mention it to you."

I shake my head in disbelief. "Why would you do that?"

"Hollis, it wasn't the time or the place," Jonah says softly. "I wanted to tell you later, in private."

I bury my head in my arms.

"I'm sorry, Hollis." Jonah's tone is pained. "The damage from the bullet was extensive. Even with Miss Engel's help, she lost too much blood, and then . . ."

The image of the concrete hallway blowing apart twists my stomach into a knot. One moment the squat little lady was behind me, and then she was gone. I killed their healer.

"I didn't m-mean for this to happen," I say, gulping the air. "I was s-stupid. I couldn't see the truth. I was wrong. I'm so sorry."

I'm still hidden in the folds of my jacket. My words feel meaningless—less than nothing—so I close my mouth, hating myself for even attempting to justify this. I'm disgusting, but something deep within me is alive with the urge to explain—even if it feels hollow. Nothing I say can mend what I've done. I know that. It won't fix this, but Jonah's presence brings back his words: "No one will expect anything from a sixteen-year-old girl, but it's your decision to prove them wrong. It's what you choose to do now that will define who you become."

I lift my head, determination prodding me upright. Whatever is to become of me in this forest, I owe my friends an explanation—however vain the attempt. I need to tell them I'm sorry. I have to express my regret. They should know the truth behind my intentions and my horrid plan. If I'm ever going to have a chance at redeeming my friendship with them, they need to hear this from *me*, not from others. Rumors of what I've done will spread quickly, and everyone will have something to say. I'm sure my friends have already heard appalling things about me, but I want them to know that I regret what I've done. It's the least they deserve.

"Jonah, I need to see my friends," I say, hiccupping as a burning sensation enters my chest. I turn toward him, kneeling on the ground and wiping my face with my dirt-stained hands. "Please? I need to see them. I want to apologize. If nothing else, I owe them that. And I know it won't undo this. I know that, but please?"

I try to read Jonah's face, but nothing comes of it. My heart falls. I don't know if I'm allowed out of my cell . . .

"I will find them and come get you."

I look up at him, and for a moment, I don't feel the sickening pit in my abdomen. But it returns, and with it, the horrifying reality of what I've asked Jonah to allow me to do. I'm going to speak to the people I've betrayed. I'm going to look them in the eye and own up to what I've done.

Anxiety thunders through me as Jonah stands and walks to the door of my cell. He slips through, the wood closes with a shudder, and Libbie's enchanted branches snake back into place.

I sit on my cot and grab the thin blanket, wearing it like a shawl. A breeze causes my blonde wisps to dance across my face, so I hug the blanket tighter. The forest's chill is unforgiving. I stare at the pine-littered dirt, my mind zooming at unsettling speeds. If I'm going to do this, I need to calm down, but it's proving impossible.

I want to tell them that this wasn't supposed to happen—that I only did it to keep them safe from my ability. My heart aches. I so desperately need them to know that *they* are my family. I wanted to stay. In the end, I chose *them*. I decided to join their world ... but when my power possessed me, I couldn't do it. The monster under my skin could have killed them. In that moment, there didn't seem to be a choice.

But as I mull this over, guilt infests my mind. Stupid girl. Naïve, brainwashed society member. I could have gone to Jonah. He could have helped me. I could have listened to Tiffany. I could have done *anything* other than what I did.

Keith's disappointed face comes to mind, and my body stiffens. What can I say to him? I'm so grieved by what I've done that the thought of seeing him again terrifies me. How can I tell him how sorry I am? What I can possibly do?

Nothing. That's the short of it. Absolutely nothing.

"Hollis."

I jump, turning toward the door of my cell. Jonah is standing there, his brow wrinkled. He unlatches the wood, and the branches slink back.

"Follow me."

I move to his side, stepping free of my new confinement. It reminds me of the first time I stepped out of the concrete cell back at the old compound. I'm overwhelmed. How am I back here? I'm a prisoner all over again.

I follow in Jonah's wake, staring up at the vast dome of twisted trees that canopy the ceiling of our new home. The height is easily three stories, the branches of every pine interlocking together from the ground up, sealing us in to create one large space. Libbie's handiwork looks a lot like the old compound, but with much more color. I gaze around, taking it in. Peppered along the earth are dozens of wooden alcoves, all facing the center of the dome so that they form one large ring. The space is easily a hundred yards long.

"Before I take you to them, I want to let you know that Audrey is gravely injured," Jonah says, scratching the bottom of his stubbled chin.

My hands begin to shake, but I curl them into fists, stuffing them under my armpits. I can't fall apart. I have to stay strong enough to do this. "What happened?"

"A piece of the ceiling fell on her leg," he says. "It was crushed from the knee down, and we had to amputate."

I inhale, tears choking me, but I dig my fingernails into my palms and grit my teeth. "How?"

"We were able to bring some emergency medical supplies with us from the compound during the attack—ready packs with food, blankets, tools, and some technology in case of an evacuation—but given our lack of resources, it wasn't as clean-cut as we hoped."

Ready packs. My stomach churns. That means they were prepared for something like this. I don't know if that makes me feel better or worse.

"Audrey will recover," Jonah continues. "But I must warn you. I don't know how kindly your friends will take to you right now."

I nod, concealing my fists deeper into the folds of my jacket. I'm shivering, but I bite down to keep my teeth from chattering. The cold of the forest stings my cheeks, making the hairs on the back of my neck stand on end.

We trek across the open expanse of the dome, and I keep my gaze on Jonah's back, not daring to look up. People are staring at me. I can feel them—their accusing eyes tracking my every move. I can't face them. I can't stand to see their anguish or their labored looks.

"This way." Jonah stops at one of the last alcoves on the right. He turns to me. "They're in here. You have five minutes."

"Yes, sir."

I can't breathe. Five minutes. I have five minutes . . .

I untuck my arms and step through the curved opening into the dark room. Jonah follows me. Two candles sit on a makeshift stool, flickering erratically.

Audrey lies in a cot in the center of the alcove, and my blood runs cold when I see her complexion: ghastly white, clammy, and disheveled, with blackened bits of grease running through her mousy brown hair. I know she's alive, but her short frame looks more like a shell than anything else. Darren is kneeling next to her, grasping her hands and looking utterly beside himself. His black hair is just as unkempt as Audrey's. He looks different—wild—like he's no longer the stoic boy who phased his fist through the training mat to show me his ability during the marble game. Ben, standing lanky and tall, is off to the side of the room with his arms around Candice. And Keith is sitting in the corner, head bowed so that his dark brown hair shields his eyes.

The group turns when we enter, and as if in slow motion, every eye meets mine.

Darren leaps to his feet with a poisonous look that rivals

Ashton's, and I slink back against the wall.

"What is she doing here?" he demands, pointing at my chest and glaring at Jonah.

"Hollis would like to speak to you all," he says, his demeanor calm and collected.

"Well, I don't want to hear it," Darren spits.

I stand there, trying to find my voice. I peer around at the group of people in front of me—my former friends—and I can hardly bear it. My knees begin to tremble, and my limbs turn to ice. I want to disappear, but I have to speak to them. I must push through the violent urge to run away.

"I want to tell you what I did," I begin, my lower lip quivering, "and why."

Darren scowls at me. "We know what you did. And I don't want to hear it. Get out!"

I catch Keith's blue eyes and his sadness nearly tips me over the edge, but I turn my attention back to Darren. "Please, I need to—"

"You exposed us!" he says, cutting me off and taking a step toward me. "You went back to the Testing Center and betrayed us. You're a traitor! So I don't give a damn about what you have to say!"

His words cut through my resolve, and my arms go limp. What he's said is true. I am a traitor.

"You're right." I'm trying not to cry. This group of amazing human beings deserves to know exactly how I failed them. "I did go to the Testing Center, but I didn't go there to expose you. I would never do that."

"Hollis?" Keith rises from his seat with a disturbed look. He tilts his head to the side. "Why did you go there?"

"I went there because . . ." I clear my throat, stuffing my hands under my armpits again. My head is starting to spin. "I went there to see if the secret weapon was real. I went there to get rid of my ability. I didn't want it anymore."

"What?" Ben, still hugging Candice, shakes his head, and his posture stiffens. "Why?"

"I . . . I thought that if the secret weapon was real, then I could get rid of my ability and go back home," I say, my voice breaking. "When I first got here, I wanted to leave. I didn't believe you. I thought you were evil, and that the government was right. I thought that you were monsters."

I'm crying again. Salted tears make their way into my mouth, and snot mixes with my saliva. No one says a word, and my sorrow spurs me onward.

"But you were all so kind to me. You showed me what it was like to feel—to express myself—to . . . to be someone I never thought I could be. I didn't expect that. And I was blind. I was so caught up in what I'd been taught—in the history I'd been raised to believe—that I couldn't see what was staring me in the face. That you were good. That you were *right*, and that I was wrong."

My whole body is trembling.

"And when you talked about the rumors of the secret weapon, I decided to see for myself. I started training. I was so caught up by the idea that my life could go back to how it was before. I wanted to escape. I felt like a prisoner in your world, but I know now that it wasn't true. I was never a prisoner. In the end, I didn't want my power . . . and that's why I went."

My eyes begin to tingle and burn. I gulp, sucking in uneven breaths that wrack my chest.

"My power was too strong. It felt unbearable—like I had the brain mutation I was raised to believe in. And when it almost made me kill Ashton, when I attacked him, when I couldn't control myself, I left. I forced Tiffany to teleport me back to the Testing Center because I thought it was the only way to protect everyone."

To protect everyone . . .

My stomach seizes. It's getting harder to breathe, but I push through the choking sensation in my lungs.

"And when the woman offered me a chance to go home . . . when she gave me a chance to get rid of my ability . . . I took it, and I was wrong."

My skin turns clammy as I continue.

"And Tiffany came back for me. They were going to shoot me, but Tiffany came back for me. She saved me."

Leaning against the wall for support, I turn to Keith. My legs feel heavy as an overwhelming weight bears down on me.

"Keith, I wanted to stay. I did. I wanted to make the compound my home." I look around the small alcove, speaking barely above a whisper. "You're my home. You're my family. And I was wrong. I never meant for this to happen. I never wanted to hurt anyone, and I'm so deeply sorry for what I've done."

The air in the room turns stale, and the only sound I can

hear is my ragged breathing. Candice turns her face away from me, burying her head in Ben's shoulder. Her muffled cries pierce the quiet of the room. Ben pulls her into an embrace, patting the back of her head.

Grief rips into me like a wildfire.

Keith's eyes meet mine. "Did you know about the tracker?"

"No." I wipe my face with the flat of my hand. "I swear to you I didn't."

Out of nowhere, Darren advances on me, his eyes narrowed in disgust. Jonah stiffens, as if he were contemplating the need to intervene, but Darren stops a foot away from my face. His countenance is eerily calm, and he speaks with deadpan hatred in his voice.

"You're a traitor, and Tiffany is dead because of you. We're not your family, we're not your home, and we don't forgive you. Now get out."

I glance at Keith, and my heart sinks. He's not looking at me anymore. He's staring at the ground, sadness etched across his strong features. I don't blame him. I wouldn't want to look at me either. Back in the darkness of the forest, he held my hand for two days, but all he knew at the time was that I didn't have my power. He didn't know the bombing was my fault. He didn't know that I was a traitor. And now that he does, I fear I've lost him for good.

I point to Audrey. "Will she be okay?"

"Leave!" Darren hisses. He grabs my upper arm and shoves me. I gasp, tripping over the uneven earth.

Jonah takes a step forward, placing his hand on Darren's

chest to hold him at bay. "That's enough."

The sides of my vision blur out. It's as if I'm looking through a narrow tunnel. I turn to Keith again, hoping against hope that he will say something more. Anything.

"Keith?" I say.

He shakes his head, waving his hand at me as if brushing me off. "I think you need to leave now."

His words burn me, but the vicious thoughts circling in my head say I deserve this. He doesn't want anything to do with me anymore, and it's my fault.

I peer around at my friends, and all of the happy memories wash over me, broken and fractured, torn in two by what I've done. No one looks at me. No one says anything more, and as I turn my back to them, I walk away knowing that the grief in that room is something I'll never repair.

8

I'M SITTING ON TOP OF A DINING ROOM TABLE, LAUGHING and leaning against Keith's shoulder. The pool game is almost over, but Ben and Candice are still battling it out for the eight ball.

Ben aims a wildly inaccurate shot, skipping the cue along the length of the table. It smacks the border, jumping onto the floor and rolling away. Audrey, dipping low with a wicked smile, flicks it back with her pointer finger. She giggles, and Candice pulls on Ben's arm with an 'I'm going to win' look plastered all over her face.

Darren gives Ben an apologetic pat on the back as he hands the pool stick to Candice. She snatches it up and grins, tossing her dark brown hair over her shoulder. Keith squeezes my hand, and I hold my breath as the cue zooms across the table, knocking the eight ball into the left corner pocket.

Everyone cheers, and I throw my hands up in celebration.

Keith leans over and kisses the top of my head. Candice wiggles her tongue at Ben, and he pulls her into a massive bear hug, nearly tackling her to the floor.

The pool stick smacks the concrete, and the noise reverberates off the walls. I jump.

"Careful," I say, chuckling.

"Why did you do it?" Darren asks. He's staring at me, his dusky eyes unblinking.

"What?" I look up at him, confused. "The pool stick? It just fell—"

"Why did you do it, Hollis?" Candice says, relinquishing her laughter and walking straight up to me. Her pretty face is blank, lips pressed into a thin line. Her blue eyes are unnaturally wide.

Ben joins her side. "Look what you've done."

Keith's hand slides out of mine, and he joins them as his features transform. Blank. Unfeeling. Dead. "How could you, Hollis?"

"No . . . wait," I murmur, skidding off the table and moving away from them. A fresh dose of fear spikes through my chest.

"I'm hurt, Hollis."

I gasp, stumbling backward. Audrey's skin hangs in folds off of her face and arms, and her leg is drenched in blood. It dribbles down at an alarming rate.

"You hurt me."

The group begins to advance, creeping forward as a connected unit, all of their faces pressed in and mutated—staring at me with blackened pupils.

"I'm sorry! Wait, please!" I screech, my pulse pounding. I hold my hand up to ward them off as I feel the edge of another table at my waist. I'm cornered.

"You hurt us," the group says in unison, prowling up to me.

"I'm s-sorry, I—"

My back slams into solid concrete, and I gulp, my chest tightening. I can't breathe. I'm lying on the floor, dazed, and the face that's staring back into mine prickles my skin.

Tiffany is standing over me, bearing down on me with an eerie stillness I've never encountered. The whites of her eyes are murky, and as her face inches near mine, her stringy, wet, black hair sticks to my cheeks with the smell of rotting flesh.

The urge to scream is overpowering, but my voice has been stolen from me. Tiffany clutches the remains of the smashed tracker in her bloody hands, dangling it an inch from my face.

She cocks her head to the side, hovering over me, eyes never wavering from mine. "Why did you do this to me?"

I'm gagged, suffocated by her presence, unable to move and unable to breathe. A hot, putrid smell emanates from her decaying body, and drops of blood trickle into my open mouth.

Her thick voice comes out in a singsong. "I thought we were friends." She tilts her head even further until the angle becomes unnatural. Her cracked lips lower to my ear, and her singsong turns into a deep, guttural growl. "You betrayed us, you wicked girl! Look what you've done!"

Pain.

"You selfish girl."

I'm writhing. Burning.

"You hateful girl!"

Tiffany's knee is to my chest, slowly crushing me, squeezing the air from me. My rib cage is heaving.

"You horrid creature!"

My friends have surrounded me—closing in on all sides—laying themselves on top of me one by one. My brain begs for oxygen. I'm going to die. I'm sorry. I'm sorry. I'm so sorry . . .

■　■　■

I wake, bolting upright, covered in sweat. It drenches my hairline and armpits, sending chills down to my spine—and the forest breeze isn't helping.

I throw the blanket from me and swing my legs around, scraping my boots against the earth. Snatching the cup of water sitting by the peg of my cot, I down it in one go. It only temporarily soothes the cotton feeling in my mouth and throat.

"Just a dream . . ." I murmur, trying to shake myself out of it.

I close my eyes and cross my arms, shivering, but Tiffany's rotting face singes the inside of my retinas. I stand to my feet.

"Just a dream."

But it's not. My wretched thoughts are back to torture me. It's not a dream. Just look around. It's reality. Tiffany is dead, and it's my fault.

I pace back and forth as my sight shifts in and out of focus. Bracing myself against the nearest wooden bar, I lean my forehead to it, trying to concentrate my breathing. I can't do this. I'm going to faint. The ground below me turns to black near the edges, but after a few moments, the darkness fades back into sight.

Twelve bars. I count twelve bars. I grab each one, centering myself on the feel of the smoothed wood. Its scent is fresh, mixing with the pine needles and cold air.

"Jonah?" I crane my head around, but as I gaze into the deserted dome of twisted trees, no one answers. It's early, and everyone is still asleep.

I release my grip on the bars, pacing once more. I'm nervous, but not from the dream. Today I'll be assigned the tasks required of me for the next thirty days. My probationary period is set to begin, and if I fail, execution awaits.

I shudder. I don't know what to expect, but there's one thing I know for sure: Jonah must accompany me everywhere I go. I hate that I'm a burden to this kind man.

The forest air tosses a few of my blonde strays across my nose. I brush them out of the way and square my shoulders. I can't even think about going back to sleep. Who knows what fresh horrors await me in my dreams.

"I'll wait for Jonah," I say, and the simple utterance of this plan calms me.

I return to my cot, seizing the thin blanket and wrapping it around my shoulders. I pull it snug, trying to beat the creeping cold, but the attempt feels vain. I'm numb, and as I sit crisscrossed and jittering, my mind wanders through a thousand agitated thoughts . . .

"Hollis, time to get up."

I give a little start, coming out of my restless haze. "Jonah."

Springing to my feet, I throw the blanket down as if it had scorched me. Jonah tilts his head with a curious look.

"Couldn't sleep," I mutter. "I'm ready."

"Very well then, let's get started. We'll be working outside the dome."

"Yes, sir."

The enchanted branches slink back at Jonah's touch, and I join his side. "Follow me."

I obey, keeping my eyes down. I still can't bear to look at anyone. We trek through the enclosure, twigs snapping underfoot as we move toward the other end. I remain in Jonah's wake, keen to keep as close to him as possible. Everyone is staring at me. I can feel their burrowing eyes. It makes my skin crawl.

"Just over here," Jonah says, pointing to the last of several openings in the side of the compound. I nod, hooking a left and following my teacher as he exits the dome.

We emerge into the forest beyond, and the sound of rushing water pulls my attention away from Jonah's heels. It rumbles in the distance, churning froth that catches on the staggered rocks.

"This way."

The crisp air brushes my face, its sweet scent poignant. To my left, a warbler chirps, landing on a low hanging branch a few yards off. It pecks at the bark, darting its yellow head back and forth.

"Beautiful, isn't he?" Jonah asks, nodding to the bird.

I can't help but feel that Jonah is trying to lighten the mood, but the knots in my stomach refuse relief. I'm going to be sick, but I oblige him by saying, "Yes, sir."

We continue through the thick of trees for several minutes until we come upon a clearing. A massive pile of stumps sits at its center, and the glint of an axe catches the sunlight.

Jonah approaches the pile, selects the largest log, and drags it off the side with a great amount of effort. I stand there awkwardly, wondering if I should offer to help. Before I can make up my mind, he dusts off his hands, grabs the axe, and sits on the face of a large boulder near the tree line. He waves me to his side.

I trudge over to him, looking warily at the pile. "How did this get here?"

"Libbie Lizette," he says. "She was kind enough to use her ability to provide work for you."

"Oh. Right." I grimace. I can't help it. The fact that Libbie had to go out of her way to arrange this for me demonstrates how utterly useless I am. I bite my lower lip, trying my best to gain perspective. I know I'm not needed here. Libbie could easily supply firewood to the camp without even breaking a sweat, but the Council chose to offer me a job, and I should be grateful for it. I *am* grateful for it. "Can you thank her for me?"

"Of course."

I nod, raising my hand to block the sun. I glance over my shoulder at the formidable stack of wood.

"I trust that you've figured out your task for the next thirty days."

"Yes, sir."

"Then let's get started." Jonah slides down from the rock and heads over to the pile, grabbing a second log. It's much smaller than the first one. He props the smaller log up against the larger one, forming a 'T,' and then turns to me. "Have you ever cut firewood before?"

"No, but aren't you supposed to set the piece up on its end?" I ask.

Jonah chuckles, lining up the axe at the crux of the 'T.' "Is that what you've seen before?"

I shrug. "I guess so."

"I'm going to teach you a much easier way to do it," Jonah says. "And a much safer way."

"Okay."

In one fluid motion, Jonah raises the axe and swings straight down, hitting the smaller log at its intersection with the larger one. It splits clean in two.

"Woah." I bite my lower lip. How on earth am I going to do this?

"Cutting the log this way prevents you from swinging into your legs," he explains. "The larger log will catch the axe if you miss. It acts as a brace."

"I see."

Jonah takes the wood and places the two flats against the brace. He repeats his swing two more times, splitting the halves into fourths and tossing the pieces to his right.

"That's all there is to it. Now I'd like you to try," he says, handing me the axe. He walks back to the heap and grabs another log, propping it up to form the 'T.'

"Right," I say, swallowing the knot that's formed in my esophagus.

"Hold the axe with both hands," Jonah instructs. "Position it. Then lift it straight up and straight down. And remember, keep a firm grip on that handle."

I set the sharp edge against the crux of the 'T,' aim it for way longer than I need to, and swing with hardly any power. The axe sinks into the log, sticking out at an odd angle. I pull on it, but it doesn't budge. I shake it in every direction, practically lifting the log in my attempt to free the blade, but nothing happens.

"Come on!" I say, now jiggling it wildly about.

Jonah grins. "You've got the right idea."

I give him an exasperated look. He's clearly amused by me. "Jonah."

"Alright. Let me help you."

He puts his foot down to anchor the log in place and yanks the handle up. "Try again. This time swing a little harder."

"Yes, yes."

I squint, determination filling me. Repositioning the log, I lift the blade and slam it down, splitting it in two. Perfect.

"There you go. Now into fourths—and take your time. I don't want you to hurt yourself."

"I won't." I take the halves, and before Jonah can say another word, I finish, tossing them to the right. "Like that?"

"You're a quick study," Jonah says, giving me a nod.

I smile. "Well, I was the top student in my . . ."

I trail off, regret hitting me with the force of a sledge-hammer. This feels all too familiar, and memories of the underground compound attack me. The training mat. Tiffany's laugh. Jonah's encouraging words: "I've also found that type twos learn to command their ability faster than type ones, and from what I've seen, you seem to be a quick study . . ."

My thoughts turn into a torrent, rushing like the river just beyond the clearing. I bow my head, stooping to touch the dirt with both of my palms. I need to ground myself to something real or I'll pass out.

"Hollis?" Jonah kneels in front of me. "Are you alright?"

I'm panting as a stabbing sensation pulses between two of my ribs. Panic is suffocating me, so I close my eyes and focus on the feel of the forest beneath my fingertips: soft, damp, and cool. But Tiffany's dead face screeches at me, and my eyes fly open again. I sit back into the dust, overwhelmed.

Jonah remains in front of me, leaning his head to the side and studying me. We stay opposite each other for quite some time, the sound of birds and the river slipping in and out of my hearing.

"Jonah?" My voice is barely above a whisper.

"Yes?"

An intense wave of grief closes my throat, so I cough to try and clear it. I'm on the brink of another breakdown. This is stupid. I don't want to cry. I have work to do. I swallow, pushing back the angry tears. I hug myself and look into the face of my only advocate.

"Thank you for speaking for me," I say. "I don't deserve

this . . . Thank you. I don't know how I can ever repay you."

For a moment, Jonah doesn't speak, and my heart falls. I look down at my feet, but his soft voice picks my head up. "You don't need to repay me, Hollis." He smiles, but there is sorrow beneath it. Folding his arms across his chest, he nods back to the pile of wood. "You have a lot of work to do. Are you okay?"

"Yes, sir."

I stand, head spinning, and grab the handle of the axe. For the next few hours, I work my hands raw, never stopping to rest. I've hit a cruel rhythm, as if I were punishing myself instead of working for the good of the camp. Every swing tears my muscles. Every grip reset turns my skin to fire. It's the hardest I've worked in my life, but I need this. It's making me too exhausted to grieve.

I'm determined. My mind is made up. I'll prove my worth to the Council, however small. I'll be the best worker I can be. But cutting firewood is more brutal a task than I anticipated, and soon, the fresh blisters on my palms and the weakened muscles in my arms ache for relief.

"Let me show you where to put the wood," Jonah says, interrupting my trance-like state.

I drop the axe, keen for a break, and the butt of it lands on my foot. "Ouch!"

"Careful," Jonah chortles.

"Yeah, thanks," I say, throwing him an irritated look, but I let the smallest grin slide onto my face. "Where are we going?"

"There's an alcove inside the dome," he says. "This way."

Jonah stoops to collect a stack of chopped wood, and I do

the same. After a few minutes of walking back through the forest, we enter the compound. The hustle and bustle of the camp is electric, and out of habit, I turn my eyes down to my teacher's feet. The best thing I can do is keep to myself and do my work. I don't need anything to distract me, but the further into the dome we move, the worse the staring gets.

"Just here," Jonah says, and he lays his wood by the side of the largest alcove on the right. It's a curved, wooden, half-sphere structure three times my height, and the side wall is broad with plenty of space. "You need to make a stack against this wall. Keep it organized and full. It's cold here in the forest, so we'll be using this up quickly."

"Okay," I say, unloading my armful. I stack it as instructed.

"Good."

The rest of my workday passes in a blur, and as dusk falls, Jonah escorts me back to my cell. I flop onto my cot, exhausted beyond belief. Every muscle burns, both of my arms feel like noodles, and my hands are raw and searing. I've never been so spent.

"Get some rest," Jonah says. "We'll begin again tomorrow morning."

He stops at the door, turning back over his shoulder, mouth open, as if he were going to say something—something important. But his brow furrows, and sorrow overcomes his face. He shakes his head.

"Jonah? What's wrong?"

The door shuts and the branches twist back into place.

"Get some rest, Hollis."

I watch him walk away, and a single tear slides down my cheek. I caused this . . . I close my eyes, and sleep claims me. I don't even dream.

9

I'M SORE—SO SORE I CAN BARELY MOVE. EVERYTHING IN my body is screaming at me to stop working, but I continue to swing the axe over and over again. Jonah and I are back in the clearing, and as the sun beats down on us, my mind keeps wandering over to the stream. My tongue dries up at the thought. How good would it be to jump into that cold water?

But I can't quit. I have to keep going.

The axe shakes in my hands as I grab another log and chop it into fourths. The repetitive movement is excruciating because my muscles are torn to shreds from the previous day. I don't say a word. I just work—and if I'm being honest with myself, since yesterday, I haven't had much time to dwell on the heartache of my circumstances. This has proved to be an excellent distraction—so much so that I'm more determined than ever to produce a remarkable amount of firewood.

I've stacked the alcove three feet high, a feat Jonah's

deemed impressive considering I haven't built up much stamina. It's strange. I'm finding a sense of joy in this, small though it may be. I cling to the feeling because I don't have much else.

Another swing in and my grip on the handle slips. The axe catches on the larger log and I stumble, my legs giving out. I sink to my knees.

"Hollis, are you alright?" Jonah asks, running over to me.

"Yes." I brush my hair out of my eyes with the back of my arm. Sweat is pouring from my brow in waves. "I'm just... sore."

Jonah nods. "You'll grow strong from this. It won't always be hard. I promise."

I put my foot down on the larger log and pull the blade up. I go to select another piece, but Jonah stops me.

"Hollis, let's take a break for a minute. I have something I need to tell you."

A pit forms in my stomach. His tone doesn't command confidence. "Okay." I drop the axe next to the pile and join him.

We walk over to the large boulder near the tree line and sit on its smooth surface. Jonah shifts over to make room for me, tucking one leg up. He stares out across the clearing toward the river.

"We aren't going to work tomorrow," he says.

I look at him, brow furrowing. "Why?"

"There's going to be a memorial service for everyone who didn't make it." His voice is heavy, and he pauses, appearing to take a moment to himself. "And the Council and I have agreed that you are to remain in your cell for the duration of the day."

My heart feels like it's been weighed down by a bag of rocks. Cold spreads into my fingertips and face.

Tiffany. I'm overcome with the desire to protest, but I know that wouldn't be right. I understand why I can't come together with the others to pay tribute to her and celebrate her life. I'm the reason she's dead. I'm still grieving, and I need to say goodbye, but I must do it on my own. It's my burden to bear alone. I bow my head, keeping my ragged breathing as controlled as possible.

"Your presence would be inappropriate," Jonah continues. "This is a sensitive time for everyone."

My chest is heaving, and my eyes collect with tears. All I can manage to say is, "I understand."

These words choke me, swallowing me whole and plunging me into a dark depression.

"I'm sorry, Hollis."

My brain is fuzzy and there's nothing left to say, so I repeat myself. "I understand."

For several minutes, we don't speak. The sound of the river babbles about, mixing with the scuffling birds. The forest is alive—almost cheerful. Nature is moving, blissfully ignorant of worry. I wish I could be a part of it.

"Things will get better," Jonah says. "Grief will play its part, but time can heal many wounds, and it has a way of making forgiveness a dear friend. It won't be like this forever, Hollis. Remember that."

I nod, sniffling and wiping my nose. I'm still attempting to gain back my composure. Tiffany is pervading my thoughts. I don't know how I'm going to do this. She saved me, and I won't be there to honor her or thank her. It feels unjust, but I know it's not. No one wants their loved one's murderer at their funeral.

"I need to get back to work," I say, leaping off the rock and returning to the pile. My tone is casual, but my heart is throbbing. If I talk anymore, I'll start crying, and I can't do that. Not now.

I grab an armful of chopped wood and start the trek back to the dome. To my surprise, Jonah doesn't follow me. He's giving me space, and I'm grateful for it. Maybe if I work myself numb I'll be able to sleep through most of tomorrow.

As I enter through the twisted trees, I move quickly, keeping my head down. Avoiding all contact with others seems to be the best approach to my new work routine. The splintered wood bites into my forearm, rubbing it raw, but I'm almost to the alcove. If I can stack it four feet high today, then maybe—

I collide with someone and the wood tumbles out of my grasp, scattering in every direction. I trip over the nearest piece and land sprawled onto the ground.

"Ow!" I say.

"Oh! I'm so sorry. Are you okay?"

I'm face to face with Keith, and my cheeks turn hot. It appears that he's just noticed who he's run over, because an uncomfortable silence ensues.

"I should have been watching where I was going," I mumble, holding my knee and wincing. A fresh scrape is beading with blood.

"It's alright. I wasn't watching either." Keith's handsome features are flushed. "Here, let me help you up."

He holds out his hand, but I don't register what he's said.

"Hollis?"

"Right," I say, shaking my head.

I take his hand, feeling a jolt as my skin touches his. He relinquishes his grip the moment I'm to my feet. Neither of us says a word. He peers at me with curious eyes, and after what feels like an eternity he says, "Well, I . . . are you okay?"

"Fine, yes. Thank you. Sorry, I . . . I have to—"

I want to melt into the forest. This is worse than when I first met him. Back then, I was just awkward, but now I'm downright inept—and a horrible person too. I wouldn't blame him if he never wanted to mend things, and part of me understands that this may be the case. The awkwardness between us is palpable, creating an unpleasant thickness in the air.

I gather the fallen pieces, propping them against my hip and doing my best to avoid his deep blue eyes.

"I should go," he says. "Sorry again."

"Okay."

And without another word, he turns and walks away. My eyes linger on the back of his neck, but only for a second. I can't go there. I can't start the spiral of thought concerning our relationship—or if we even have one anymore. I'm too spent to contemplate it.

I continue toward my destination, keen to stack the wood and get back to the clearing. This is my first venture without Jonah by my side, and I don't want any of the Council members catching me alone. That wouldn't bode well.

I round the corner of the alcove and gasp aloud. The wood I'd been collecting over the past two days lies scattered across the ground—my meticulous stack destroyed—splinters and shrapnel everywhere.

"I thought you were supposed to keep this area clean and organized," a snide voice says.

I whirl around to find Ashton a few yards from me, a wicked grin smeared on his haughty features. He takes a step toward me and then pauses, staring at me with watery grey eyes.

I tense out of instinct. "You."

"What would the Council think?" he says, holding his arms open in a grand gesture. "Poor, sloppy Hollis. Can't even keep the firewood stacked and ready to go."

I glare at him. "I *have* kept the firewood stacked."

"Oh, clearly," he says, his voice slippery. "Because everyone will believe you over me."

He takes another step toward me, cocking his head to the side. His eyes never leave mine. I flex my free hand, and this small act seems to hold Ashton at bay. Does he think I still have my ability? I back away, feeling the sharp edge of an uneven stack at my ankles. I anchor myself to keep from falling over.

"You did this on purpose," I say, gritting my teeth. "This

isn't my fault." I make to move past him, still clutching the armful of wood, but he blocks me, knocking the pieces to the ground with a powerful sideways blow.

I gasp, my fear spiking. Creeping cold moves its way to my spine. I can't panic. I have to pretend like I still have my power. It may be the only way to get out of this. We're alone, and the broad side of the alcove blocks the rest of the dome from view.

"Don't make me hurt you again," I threaten, trying to keep my tone confident, but I'm wavering. I clench my hands into fists. "What do you want from me?"

Ashton speaks slowly, each word laden in an eerie singsong. "I want you to tell me what you did to me."

"I don't know."

"Not good enough."

Ashton moves closer to me, his stale breath trailing into my nose. I feel the wall of the forested compound at my back. I can't retreat anymore.

"You took my power away," he snarls, his face careening over mine. "How did you do it?"

"I don't know," I say, keeping my attitude defiant. I push past him, but he catches my upper arm, swinging me around to face him. He pins me against the pile of dislodged wood.

He coos. "Where do you think you're going?"

"Let go of me!" I cry, struggling against him. This form of touch is terrifying. Flashes from the Testing Center arise—the military men grabbing me and strapping me down to the metal throne. I don't like this. I want him to stop. "Let go!"

"No," he says, tightening his hold. Pain shoots up my arm

and into my shoulder. He pushes me against the wood. "I want my power back. Tell me what you did."

"You're hurting me!" I say, twisting in his grip.

"Good," he says, getting closer, his mouth an inch from my face. "Little payback. You know? Because what happened, you see," his free hand moves to my neck, and his lips brush my ear, "I was burning. It was like I was on fire. And *you*—you did that. So let me ask you one more time—and my patience is running out, Timewire. What did you do to my power?"

My hand moves to the one at my throat, but my clammy fingertips can't pry it away. I'm pinned to the wall, unable to move, and I'm panicking. "I don't know!"

"Liar!" he shrieks, striking me across the face with the flat of his palm. "You attacked me! You know!"

The sting of the blow feels like a thousand pinpricks. I'm stunned. "Please, Ashton! I don't know. I don't know how I did it. Please, you're hurting me!" I'm twisting back and forth to free myself, but to no avail.

"Oh come on," Ashton taunts, his hand closing around my throat. "You're not even trying to get away from me. Aren't you going to freeze me again? Go crazy on me, Timewire. Freeze me."

He doesn't know I've lost my power. My heartbeat pounds up into my head. "No."

"Go ahead. I give you permission this time." His hands stiffen, and stars begin to swim into view. "Freeze me."

"No."

Blackness creeps around the edges of my sight.

"Come on! Get away from me, Timewire."

"Ashton . . ." I scrape at his wrist, still struggling. "I can't breathe. Please stop, I . . ."

His fingers tighten. An icy sensation enters my legs, and the darkness grows, prowling up to me, threatening to overcome me.

"Freeze me!" he screeches, spitting into my face.

Spots of light splotch across Ashton's face—deep purples and blues. I'm writhing, unable to breathe, unable to think, clawing at his hands. I'm going to die. I can't stop him . . .

"Ashton!" A deep voice roars from beyond my view, and the pressure on my neck vanishes, wrenched away with an incredible amount of force. The second I'm free, I collapse on all fours, coughing and sputtering. Jonah is here, standing between me and Ashton.

"How dare you touch her," he says, his tone running dangerously close to a growl. I catch a glimpse of his face between the mesh of colored stars still hanging in my vision, and for a moment, I'm terrified. I've never seen Jonah so enraged. "If you have a problem, you will take it up with me."

Ashton's arrogant features fall back under the intensity of Jonah's gaze.

"But my ability—"

"Enough!" Jonah seizes Ashton, gripping him by the collar of his shirt and pushing him back several feet. "Let me make something perfectly clear to you, young man. From now on, you will not interact with Hollis. You will not speak to Hollis. You will not go anywhere near Hollis. And if I catch you disrupting any of her work again, I will leave you to the mercy of the Council's discipline, and you will be stripped of all privileges in this camp. Consider this your one and *only* warning. Do you understand me?"

Ashton appears dumbfounded, the slightest look of genuine fear flickering across his face, but it vanishes. He tries to shove Jonah away, but this only cements Jonah's hold on him.

"I said, do you understand me?"

He nods slowly and speaks with a honeyed, mocking tone. "Yes, sir."

Jonah relinquishes his grasp. "Now leave."

Ashton backs away, shooting me a horrible smile, and then disappears into the midst of the dome.

Jonah turns to me, crouching on the ground by my side. "Are you alright?"

I'm shaking, staring around at the pile of destroyed wood. "What . . . w-what will the Council think? How am I g-going to fix all of this before tomorrow?"

I'm tearing up. Adrenaline is overdosing my system to the point where I can't coordinate myself. I begin to collect the firewood, still kneeling in the dirt, but Jonah stops me, placing a hand on my shoulder.

"It's alright," he says. "I'll take care of it. You don't need to worry about the Council. Let's go back to your cell. You've done enough work for today."

"No, I can fix it," I say, pushing his hand away. I'm crying, almost sobbing. "I'll p-put the wood back. I'll c-clean it."

"Hollis, you don't need to. It's okay. I will fix it."

His tone is gentle, and his demeanor is kind. The old Jonah is back, and his frightening anger is gone. Hot tears spill down my cheeks and I wipe them away.

"I'm s-sorry. I-I'm—"

"Hollis, you don't need to be sorry," Jonah says. "Come on, let's go." He takes my arm and places it over his shoulder, helping me to my feet. "There we go."

My legs wobble, muscles spent with exhaustion. I look up into the face of my mentor—my only support—and gratitude fills my heart to the brim.

"Thank y-you."

It's all I can manage to say before pain cuts deep to my bones—because tomorrow is the day I'm not allowed to say goodbye.

10

THE MEMORIAL SERVICE LASTS ALL AFTERNOON AND WELL into the evening. I only see Jonah long enough for him to bring me food, and he doesn't say a word. I can't imagine the loss he's suffering—students, friends, maybe even family—but I dare not ask him. Not today. I'm alone for a reason, and although I'm stuck in my cell, my heart mourns for Tiffany.

She was a true friend, and I wish I could have spoken to her. I wish I could have told her that I was wrong, that I should have trusted her. I can only guess at how frightened she must have been, rigid and voiceless, bound under my power. And I made her come. I made her watch as my hideous betrayal destroyed everything. And yet... she came back for me. She came back for me, and I can't explain it.

"I'm sorry," I whisper into the falling shadows of the dome. "Tiffany, I'm sorry."

I reach into my pocket, pulling out the smoothed pebble

I'd been working on earlier. On its surface, I'd carved 'Tiffany.' It's not much, but it's the best tribute I could think of.

Jacob Ganiston's words haunt me: "I beg you. Start over here. Forget what you knew on the outside . . . . Fall in love. Live a meaningful life. Find joy in the ability that makes you who you are, because what's in here, with these people, that's what true life is about."

How I wish I had heeded him . . .

Late last night, per my request, Jonah allowed me to look through the names of the departed. Jacob Ganiston was among them—lost in the depths of the collapsed compound with one hundred and six others.

Night creeps into my room, and with it, the chill of the black forest. I hug my blanket around me, but I'm finding it impossible to stay warm. The camp is silent now. Everyone is tucked away, falling into a troubled sleep. But not me—I don't want to go there. The rotting corpses of the departed meet me in my dreams, ready to torture me. I must stay awake.

As time stretches on, however, my eyes grow heavy and my body aches. The skin on my neck is irritated, and bruising has cropped up on my arm. Ashton's attack left me perturbed and on edge. I don't know what would've happened if Jonah hadn't come.

I wince, tucking myself into a ball and wishing for relief. If I could just have an evening of oblivion—sleep without thought, rest without imagining. But the longer I fight it, the more sleep invites me in, until it takes me captive once more.

■　　■　　■

The Chief Overseer of the Area 19 Testing Center stands by my side. Tiffany, frozen under my control, stares at me with wild eyes, her voice shaking.

"You can still fix this. Come back with me, please. Jonah can help you."

"Tiffany, I can't . . ."

"What about Keith?" she says, and my power slackens. She's fighting me. "Is he murderous? What about Jonah? Would he kill? What about me? We're not dangerous."

"Even if you're right—"

"Please come back. It's not too late. We can help you. We're your family."

"Tiffany." I choke on the tears smeared down my face. "Even if you're not dangerous . . . I am . . . and that's why I can't go back. I have to do this. I have to get rid of it. I can't let it hurt anyone else. I'm sorry . . . Thank you for showing me your world. It was wonderful . . . but it's not my home."

"No, Hollis, please—"

With one swift movement, I close her mouth, and intense control washes over me once more. She stops shaking. I turn away from her, and back to the Chief Overseer.

"I don't want this anymore. I don't want my power. I just want to go home."

She gives me an understanding look. "My dear Hollis, you've made a wonderful choice."

In a snap, Tiffany is gone and I'm kneeling in front of the little boy. His blond curls dance around baby blue eyes, and a sweet smile lights up his face. He peers up at me with charming innocence.

"Hi."

"Hi."

"Are you the girl?"

"I'm the girl."

"Okay."

And now, my power is draining from me, and golden light is arching between us. Its intensity reverberates around the room, and the warmth leaves my body, sapping me of all energy.

"Wait!" I say, shaking my head. I hold my hand out. "No. I don't want this anymore!"

I try to move, but I'm rooted to the spot, and the golden light pulses, pulling my ability from me. It flows into the boy's hands at an alarming rate.

"No!" I cry. "I change my mind. Don't take it, please!"

The boy stares at me, wide-eyed and trembling. His arms are vibrating with the strength of his power. He's crying, shaking his head back and forth, as if he were trying to stop, but the flow of his power only gains strength.

"No!" I scream. "I'm begging you! Please don't take it!"

Pain sears across my entire body, hot and dreadful. But something new is draining my energy now, and the little boy vanishes. Ashton Teel is standing over me, extending his hand out in a terrifying grip of ability. I'm bound in place, unable to move. I'm yelling, but no one can hear me. Blood pours from my nose and ears as the torrent continues. Ashton is laughing—horrid, rasping laughter.

Stop. Please. Just make it stop. I don't want this anymore. Please, just make it—

■ ■ ■

I inhale forest air, screaming and coming out of the nightmare as if surfacing from the depths of the ocean. I'm soaked in clammy sweat, trembling so badly that I'm temporarily paralyzed. My fingertips grasp for the cup by my feet, and I down the water, feeling the cold slide past my throat and into my stomach.

The little boy—he was so real. I touch my forehead right where his hand had been moments ago, and a single tear slips down my face. He was scared. He was trying to stop. It was like he could see me . . .

Scraping noises echo from my right, and I clap a hand to my chest, dropping the cup. Jonah is at my door, looking bleary-eyed, his dark hair disheveled.

"Hollis, are you alright? I heard screaming."

I hold my hands to my face and bury my head. "I'm fine. I—it was just a dream. Nothing happened. I'm fine."

"Okay," Jonah says, surveying me. He looks back over his shoulder at the rising sun. Its rays are breaking through the base of the pines. "Well, it's dawn. Would you like to get started?"

"Yes, please."

He nods. "Right. Then let's go."

It's as if he knows that work will calm me. I throw the blanket from my lap, shoving my feet into my boots and hurrying to the door. Work is all I want to do right now—anything to forget that dream.

I follow Jonah back to the clearing, breathing the sweet morning air and taking in the sounds of the babbling brook. The forest is soothing, each noise blending into the melody of nature, all singing together in perfect harmony—bugs and birds alike. By the time we arrive, I'm peaceful. The walk grounded me and focused my feelings. I'm safe. Nothing is going to hurt me.

I stoop to pick up the axe and grimace, staring at the angry red blisters on my palms.

"You'll get calluses soon," Jonah says, propping himself up on the boulder.

"I hope so." I select the nearest piece and set it up on the 'T,' chopping it into fourths and starting a new pile.

I work in silence, hitting the rhythm I've been craving. This is when my mind goes blank and the inundation of thoughts stops. It's a strange suspension between dreams and reality. Working keeps my mind structured, giving me time to center myself. I've never had to deal with emotions this deep. How do people come out of this? How do they handle it?

"What do you like to do for fun?" Jonah asks, tossing a stone at a knot on a pine trunk a few yards away. It hits just to its left.

"What?" I say, thinking I may have misheard him.

"Before you came to live with us, what did you like to do for fun?"

"For fun?" I repeat, puzzled.

"Yes. *Fun.* It can also be called enjoyment, amusement, or lighthearted entertainment," Jonah clarifies, raising an eyebrow and grinning. He tosses another rock at the knot, but it misses.

"I know what fun is!" I retort, squinting at him, but I crack the smallest fraction of a smile.

"Well?"

"Okay," I say, setting down the axe and looking up into the sky. "Well, I didn't really have much time for fun. I just did school. I studied a lot and... that's it." I finish feeling incredibly lame and shrug at Jonah's smile. "Well, I don't know!"

"What about when you were younger?" he asks.

I bite my lower lip, grabbing my left arm with my right. "Well, there was this little pond near the edge of the city, and my mother... she would take me on these long walks, and when we would get to the outer limit, she would put her finger to her lips and say, 'Shh, we're not supposed to be here, but anything for you, darling.' And by the pond, there were these stones, and just for a little while... we would skip rocks—just me and her. It was nice."

I swallow the tightening sensation working its way up my throat. My mother. Despite everything, I still miss her. It doesn't make sense to me. My parents turned me in, but I still care about them. Am I allowed to feel like this?

"It was fun." I pick at my fingernails, staring out at the

river. My friends surface in the back of my mind. "It's funny because I'm terrible at games, but I was good at skipping rocks."

"That sounds nice."

"It was." I brush my face with the back of my hand. "What do you do for fun?"

Jonah shakes his head. "I don't have much time for fun these days."

"Well, these days you're stuck with me," I say. "But before? Back at the compound? What did you do for fun? Or rather, 'enjoyment, amusement, or lighthearted entertainment.'"

Jonah chuckles. "Still talking back, I see. It's good to know your fiery spirit is still in there somewhere."

My face flushes.

"Well, let's see," he says. "I enjoy training. I like exploring power. People don't realize that there's so much more to an ability than its apparent function. Each ability is alive—living, breathing, and growing with the individual. A kind of symbiosis, if you will. It's fascinating."

My ears perk up as a thought occurs to me. "You mean the voice? The one I heard inside my head? Do other people have that too?"

Jonah's countenance sobers, and he shakes his head. "No, I'm afraid that aspect of your power was new to me."

"Oh." I look down, disappointed. "So this symbiosis, was it somehow . . . stronger with me? Is that why I could hear it speak?"

"Your ability was incredibly vast," Jonah says. "I will say this, ordinarily I can gain a pretty good sense of someone's power within the first few days of training. But your ability, in all our time together . . . I hadn't even scratched the surface."

My stomach twists in on itself.

"You fascinated me," Jonah admits, fiddling with another rock. "And I got carried away studying you. I wanted to know more about you. I wanted to understand how an ability of this magnitude could have appeared in someone whose parents never carried the biomarker. It's incredibly rare."

Jonah turns the stone over and over in his palm.

"You stumped me, Hollis, and that was something I couldn't put to rest. Your ability stretched me beyond my experience, and I let curiosity get the best of me."

His brow furrows, and sadness falls onto his face.

"I was a fool, and I turned a blind eye to the person behind that ability . . . So to answer your question, I don't know. You were the mystery I couldn't figure out."

My pulse picks up in my ears. Do I dare ask this? But I so fervently want to know that I throw out my reservations. "What's your best guess? I know you have one."

Jonah stops turning the stone, looking up at me with an expression I can't quite pin down. "Your ability had a voice—a voice no one else has. My best guess is that somehow, you were more in tune with your own ability than anyone's ever been. Perhaps that will be the direction of this biomarker's mutation— an extrapolation of the relationship already present. Power and person as two separate entities in one. I'd never encountered anything like it."

My lower lip trembles, and my hands fidget with one

another. Part of me knows that this doesn't concern me anymore. My ability is gone, and there's nothing I can do about that, but the other half of me mourns the high cost of my decision. I am no longer like them. I'm not a Diseased One anymore, and I never thought that it would make me feel so sad.

I catch sight of Jonah's complexion. His brown eyes look worn, his wrinkles appear more defined, and the smallest hint of grey has cropped up in his beard. This is getting to him, and my heart breaks.

"Jonah, this isn't your fault," I say, approaching the boulder. "You shouldn't blame yourself for what I did. You can't think like that. Please."

He gives me a tired smile, folding his hands up and resting his elbows on his knees. He peers off across the clearing. "Other than that, I do enjoy a good book."

I'm taken aback by his calm and defeated look. "For fun?" I ask.

"Yes."

"Me too. I like books." I give him the most encouraging look I can muster. "Jonah?"

"Yes?"

"It won't be like this forever. Remember that."

He smiles. "Wise words indeed."

II

IT'S TEN DAYS INTO MY PROBATIONARY PERIOD, AND I CAN already feel a difference in my body. My muscles are beginning to tone, my hands have developed thin calluses, and my stamina has increased. I feel strong, and this gives me a sense of accomplishment.

I'm good at what I do, and though the end of the day brings fatigue, I'm not nearly as exhausted as I was when I started. I'm proud of my work. I'm filling the required quota and finding a new normal—a purpose and place within this group.

Jonah wasn't kidding. It's cold here in the forest and getting colder every day. Winter is coming, and even with the firepits staggered throughout the dome, it's freezing. My woodpile goes fast, but that's the incentive I need. The stack by the alcove is the only thing I have to show for myself, and I'm determined to continue to prove my usefulness, small though it may be.

Back in the clearing, I hoist another armful of chopped wood onto my hip and start the trek back to the dome. The rush of the river sings with an ever-present tune, its crystal waters slipping over rocks and reflecting the sunlight in bursts. I breathe it in. I've come to love the nature around me. It doesn't carry any burdens.

I duck through the entrance, keeping to myself amidst the bustle of the compound. Everyone appears busy—a group to my right preparing bread, a trio to my left digging another firepit, two children playing make-believe in the dirt. It almost feels . . . normal.

I know it's not. Jonah expressed to me how difficult it's been to maintain the food supply. Two of the three fields offsite from the old compound were destroyed in the government's raid, and the dried meat and nuts from the ready packs are almost gone. As a supplement, several of the camp's more adept huntsmen have turned to fishing from the river or setting snares to catch small game like squirrels and rabbits.

I've pondered offering to help. I'd like to learn how to snare and fish, but I'm not sure if I could keep up my quota. Firewood is my main concern.

I weave around a group of spirited women, all chattering away about something I can't be bothered with. I skitter to my usual spot behind the alcove, placing the wood on top of the growing stack. I turn to make my way back through the compound when a familiar voice stops me in my tracks.

"Hey Vianne, want to play?"

It's Candice. I hang back behind the wall of the alcove, just out of sight.

"What are you guys playing?" she asks.

"Shuffleboard!" Ben's voice exclaims. "But with rocks."

Candice snorts.

"With rocks?" Vianne repeats, and I can hear the playful skepticism in her tone.

"Well, it's not really shuffleboard. We're just throwing rocks into some rings we've drawn in the dirt," Ben says. "It's actually a lot harder than it looks."

"There's four of you," Vianne chimes, and my stomach turns over. Who else is there? But I don't peek my head out. They're so close to the wood stack that they would see me. "If I joined, the teams wouldn't be even."

"No teams," Candice says.

"Every man for himself," Ben says, his enthusiasm bursting forth. "And every lady, I suppose."

Another voice joins in, and I freeze. It's Keith. "We're just asking around to see who wants to play. It's fun when it's a large group."

Remorse hits me all over again. A few short weeks ago, I'd have been asked to play, but now I'm standing behind a wall, afraid to be seen by the people I call my friends.

"Maybe Rosalie wants to join?" Darren has entered the conversation now. "It might take her mind off things."

"Sure. Alright, I'll play," Vianne says. "Let me go find Rosalie. You're right. This will be good for her. She's been off lately."

"I think we've all been off lately," Darren adds.

"Excellent, and just so you know, I'm a formidable opponent," Ben says. "Best of luck to you all, but don't worry, I'll go—"

"Oh formidable as ever," Candice interjects, giggling, and I can practically see her rolling her eyes.

Ben clears his throat. "I'll go easy on you guys."

"Oh right! 'Going easy.' I forgot that's what you call terrible aim."

The group snickers, and there's a great scuffle. Candice yelps as a result of what I can only imagine is a huge bear hug from Ben.

"Hey! Cut it out."

I slink against the firewood. I need to get out of here. I'm sure Jonah is wondering where I am by now. I've been gone for too long, but the only way to return to the clearing is walking out in plain view, and I don't want to do that. Maybe I can slip behind the alcove?

I turn to scope out my options, but my foot catches on the base of the stack. I try to rescue my balance by swinging my leg in the opposite direction, but I trip out from behind the wall and fall, to my horror, directly into their midst. I stare up at them, unnerved.

"So you're spying on us now?" Darren's tone is as icy as his glare. He folds his arms across his chest, and apprehension temporarily closes my throat. "Well?"

"N-no. Not spying," is all I can manage.

Darren scoffs. "I'll see you guys in a minute. Let me know

when you've taken out the trash." He stalks off without a second glance.

I find my footing and brush myself off. "Sorry, I was just stacking the wood. I tripped." I can feel the color rise in my cheeks. "I wasn't spying."

No one says anything to this, and my heartbeat picks up. I catch sight of Vianne's hair as it flitters from deep teal to light pink. I should just walk away, but the desire to act normal overpowers my urge to run. I survey them for a fraction of a second longer before asking, "How's Audrey? Is she okay?"

Ben and Candice exchange looks, but it's Keith who responds. "She has a pretty nasty infection. But her fever broke this morning, so that's good."

"Oh," I say. My hands turn clammy. "That's . . . that's good." The squirming sensation in my gut is making me dizzy. Again, no one says anything, and it makes me want to disappear. "Well, I better go. I need to get back to work."

I walk past them, making my way to the dome's exit. I don't look back. I can feel them staring at me, but I can't give them the satisfaction. I've almost gotten used to it, but it's still horrible. I hate the fact that everyone always stares.

Once I'm free of the dome, I make a beeline for the clearing, jumping over roots and rocks. At least with Jonah I don't feel judged. It's the only safe space I have.

When I arrive, I find the clearing deserted. I run to the pile of logs, panning around. "Jonah? Where are you?" But to my relief, I find him standing on the bank of the river several yards off. I walk over to him.

He's gazing across the water. The muddy bank on the other side, littered with pebbles, reflects the midday sun, and I hold my hand up, shielding my eyes from its brightness. The river is nearly forty feet wide, and as I join him, I take in its soothing sound. The water is tranquil here but turns treacherous half a mile down. The rumbling churns in the distance, adding to the ambiance.

"What are you looking at?" I ask.

"The forest," Jonah says. "It's peaceful here."

"It is," I say.

"Quite."

The water laps at the bank, moving up and down in an even flow. "Audrey is okay," I say, more to myself than to Jonah.

"Yes, she is okay."

"Keith told me."

Jonah nods. "Your friends are talking to you. That's good."

"Well . . . not really. I sort of ran into them by accident just now. Darren left when he saw me."

"But Keith spoke to you?" Jonah shifts his stance on the rocky shore.

"Yes, but only to say that Audrey is fine."

Jonah nods. "Give them time."

I bite my lower lips, twisting my boot in an 'S' pattern through the mud. I don't think time is going to fix this, so I say, "I know."

"Give *him* time," Jonah adds. "He's hurting, but he cares for you."

I watch the water slip by carrying a clump of twigs. I carve the 'S' deeper into the silt. "He does?"

"He does."

I bite the inside of my cheek. Keith did care about me, and for a moment, we had something. And it was wonderful—more real than anything I've had before. But it's gone now, and I don't know if it will ever come back.

"What do we do now?" I ask, changing the subject. I don't want to dwell on Keith. It's just upsetting.

Jonah turns to face me. "What do you mean?"

"I mean . . . there's only a few hundred of us left. That's it. Where do we go from here? What do we do? We don't have a home anymore, and we're in hiding. What happens now?"

He stares out across the river once more. "I suppose that we'll continue to do what we've always done."

"And what's that?"

"We'll find others with abilities and give them a home," he says. "No one should be without a home—not in this world."

I nod, experiencing an overwhelming sense of acceptance. That's all these people ever did. They accepted me without question, and I was so blinded by my past that I couldn't see it. I'm ashamed, but I've been working through it. When we first arrived in the forest, the pit of despair seemed bottomless, but my work has given me comfort, and my teacher, encouragement. And despite my treachery, things don't seem as bleak as they once did.

"Thank you," I murmur.

"For what?"

"For giving me a home."

The water trickles up the bank, its blues and greens deepening with the sun's movement. It's beautiful here. I can see why Jonah left the clearing for a bit. I look to my left, back against the current, taking in the view, when something odd bobs up through the water. I squint, careening forward to get a better look.

"Jonah, what is that?" I ask, pointing upstream.

He holds his palm up against the sun. "It looks like—"

An eruption of screaming causes me to slip. I catch myself just in time, skidding on the mud until the tips of my boots are in the water.

"Jamie!" a woman shrieks. "Somebody help! My son!"

A small boy who looks to be about five years old is flailing in the depths of the river, carried along by its powerful current and moving toward the place where Jonah and I stand.

Without thought, I plunge into the icy flow, gasping as the cold attacks my skin. I strike out into the current, every nerve in my body screaming.

"Hollis!" Jonah shouts.

The boy is several yards from me, approaching fast, but to my horror, his copper-haired head dips below the surface, and his little hand slides out of sight. With a huge breath, I dive under the water, and the cold disorients me, stabbing my flesh with a thousand pinpricks. I force my eyes open just in time to collide with him. He thuds against me, nearly knocking the breath from me, but I manage to wrap my arms around his tiny waist.

I hit the rocky bottom with my boots and push up to the

surface. As we emerge, I kick out, trying to keep both of our heads above the churning flow.

Intermingled shouts echo from somewhere beyond my view. I'm treading water, propping the boy up on my chest to keep him afloat. I have to get to shore. With my free arm, I pull large strokes and kick, my muscles straining as my feet scrape the bottom. But every time I almost gain purchase, my grip slides, and we fall further in.

I'm beginning to panic. We've moved downstream quite a ways, and the water is becoming perilous. We have a minute, maybe less, before we're both sucked into the start of the rapids. I have to get us to the bank. Now.

I take in gulps of air, keeping a firm grasp around the boy's waist. Jonah and the woman are running along the shoreline, but Jonah is charging ahead, darting through the trees to a spot beyond where I'm swimming.

I push us closer, edging my way toward safety, but it's still out of reach. My boots grind against the sediment as I fight to stay upright. I'm slipping, losing against the torrent. Whitewater breaks a hundred yards from us . . .

Jonah plunges into the current directly in front of me, catching my outstretched arm. My fingers find his and he pulls us into the shallows. I'm panting, struggling to maintain my hold on the child as we trudge onto the dirt. In one fluid movement, Jonah lifts the boy from my arms and lays him flat on his back. He's not moving.

"Jamie!"

The woman is beside herself as she drops down on all fours

next to her son. She's sobbing, holding a hand over her mouth and rocking herself over his still frame.

"Chrissie, move," Jonah says, his hand on her shoulder.

The woman obeys, slinking back with untamed eyes. She's whimpering.

Jonah begins to pump on the boy's chest for several beats and then tips his head back to breathe into his mouth. He does this for a minute, and the longer it goes, the heavier the atmosphere gets.

"Come on," I whisper, unable to take my eyes away. My hands are folded together under my chin. "Please. Come on. Please don't be dead. Please."

Chrissie weeps into her arms and paces back and forth, running her hands through her sleek copper hair as Jonah continues the cycle of resuscitation.

"Come on . . ."

After two more rounds of pumping and breathing, the boy coughs, and water trails from his mouth.

"There we go," Jonah says, relief in his tone. "Atta boy."

"Jamie!" the woman cries, dropping down to grab him.

I stand there, sopping wet and quivering, watching the reunion as Chrissie embraces her son. The little boy sputters, clearly disoriented. She rocks him back and forth, her arms vice-like around him.

"It's alright, Chrissie." Jonah pats her on the back as Jamie's teeth begin to chatter. "He's alright."

"He was playing in the mud." She sobs, clinging to him like a lifeline. "He was just playing, and I turned my back for a moment—just a moment! And he was gone."

"Everything is okay," Jonah says, giving her a reassuring nod. "Jamie is fine. Chrissie, listen to me. We need to get him into some dry clothes and by the fire. Hypothermia can set in quickly."

"Yes," she says. "Of course."

"You too, Hollis."

I nod, shivering and hugging myself. My jaw is tight from the cold, and the breeze whistling through the pines is agony against my skin.

The woman stands to her feet. Her light brown eyes find mine, and her weepy appearance changes to shellshock. She recognizes me. I can see it in her face. For several seconds she doesn't say a word, and I look down, resigning myself to the worst. I shouldn't expect anything different because what I did to these people is inexcusable.

"Thank you." She rushes me, embracing me with gentle arms. I'm completely taken aback, and I almost lose my footing. I catch myself on a gnarled root. "Thank you for saving my little boy."

"You're welcome," I say, too stunned to think of anything else.

She releases me, propping Jamie up on her hip and wiping her face with the sleeve of her sweater. "To the firepits, and to dry clothes," she announces.

"Yes, let's get moving."

"You need dry clothes too, Jonah," I say, pointing to his soaked trousers.

"I do."

I catch his arm as he turns back toward the clearing. "Thank you."

Jonah smiles and shakes his head. "You never cease to surprise me, Miss Timewire."

I laugh. "Well, you know me."

"You saved that boy's life."

"I thought for a second that we were going to get sucked into the rapids, b-but—" My muscles begin to spasm, and I bite down to stop from chattering. The bitter cold is seeping through my skin, chilling me to the bone.

"Let's get you to the fire."

"Y-yes, sir."

As the four of us move away from the riverbank, a strange sort of joy surges through me—the kind of energy that fuels the soul. I'm elated. Chrissie hugged me. She actually touched me, and she didn't look at me with disgust. She thanked me. Maybe things are starting to look up after all.

12

THE NEXT MORNING I WAKE WITH AN IDEA. IT BLOSSOMED in my dreams, rekindling my determination. Rescuing Jamie inspired me. I can't believe this never crossed my mind, and I only hope Jonah will hear me out. But all things considered, I doubt it.

"Jonah?" I set the axe down and approach the boulder, tucking a strand of hair behind my ear. "Can I talk to you about something?"

He looks up. "Sure. What is it?"

I pause, pulling at my fingers. How am I going to say this? It sounds crazy in my head. "I've been thinking . . ."

"Yes?"

"The boy at the Testing Center," I begin, keeping my eyes averted from his. "The one who took away my power. He's still there."

Jonah doesn't reply, so I forge ahead.

"He's been there for a hundred years—maybe longer. The

government keeps him cryogenically frozen and they only bring him out to take away a person's ability," I say. "He's a prisoner. A weapon."

An intense surge of resentment wells up in me, and I clench my hands into fists.

"And he's just a kid. He's so little."

Again, Jonah doesn't speak, but I'm grateful for this because I'm not done. Fury is spurring me onward.

"And he's one of us." I begin to pace back and forth. "Yesterday you said that no one should be without a home, and you also said that our purpose is to find others with abilities and offer them safety."

My shoes trace a path through the pine needles.

"Well, we know where someone with an ability is, don't we? It's that little boy, and he's at the Area 19 Testing Center right now. He doesn't deserve a life like that, and," I grit my teeth, "and I think we should rescue him."

The moment I say it, I hear how absurd it sounds. I stand there, breathless. My heart aches on behalf of this boy, but most of all, it longs for justice. I'm angry at the government—the one who bred me to believe the lies that ruined everything. And I don't blame society for what I did—that's on me. But I can't stand the idea of doing nothing while the lies fester on. I won't be that person. Not anymore.

I look to Jonah, expecting him to protest—to say that it's too dangerous or too risky, but his words lift my heart.

"You're right."

I'm temporarily speechless. He slides off the boulder to join me.

"Wait, what?" I blink, swiping another strand of hair from my face. "Are you serious?"

I watch Jonah's face, looking for the joke, but he's never appeared more genuine. He seems to be considering something, and walks past me.

"Jonah?"

"Do you know where the boy is?" he asks, turning back to me. "Where in the Testing Center, I mean?"

"No," I say, deflating a bit. "They brought him to me. I was on the top floor of the facility in a large, white room. The Testing Center has a lot of halls and—oh, I wish I could just show you. It would be so much easier if—"

I stop in the middle of my sentence, and my mouth falls open. "Oh my goodness . . ."

"Hollis, what is it?"

I whack Jonah's arm in excitement. "Rosalie! Rosalie can show you! You can see the Testing Center from my memories."

I'm bouncing up and down, fueled by a strange kind of exhilaration. If we can figure out where they're holding the boy, then this crazy idea might just work.

"Alright," Jonah says. "I will speak to Rosalie, and if she agrees, you can show me. Go back to your cell and I'll meet you there."

"Yes, sir."

I skip off, jogging through the trees back to the dome. My mind soars at the thought of helping this boy. I can play a part in what these people have been doing for a hundred years. I can serve a purpose—a real purpose—and in some small way, it feels like I'm beginning to undo what I've done. I know that's not possible, but Jonah's words are ringing true: it's the choices I make now that define who I'll become.

I sprint the last stretch after entering the compound, and take hold of my cell door, swinging it wide. It scrapes across the ground, and I pull it in behind me. I'm too excited to sit, so I pace back and forth across the six feet of space.

This is wild. I can't believe Jonah is actually considering this. I haven't thought about the logistics, or how we could possibly pull something like this off, but he didn't say no.

"Freeze me," a chilling voice says.

I jump a foot in the air, spinning around to find Ashton standing at the bars of my cell. I tense, steadying myself in place. Out of the corner of my eye, the door stands open just a sliver, but I don't look at it. Instead, I scowl at Ashton, putting up my best front.

"You shouldn't be here. You heard what Jonah said. If he finds you—"

"I'm not scared of Jonah," Ashton snaps. He runs a hand through his coarse, blond hair.

"Leave." I draw myself up to my full height, refusing to show him any fear.

"No."

I swallow the desire to raise an alarm. People are milling about in the belly of the dome, but no one seems to notice us. We're tucked away at the end of the compound, and almost out of sight.

I give him a nasty look. "Leave!" I say, this time more forcefully.

"Are you going to make me leave?" he asks, cracking a sinful smirk. He tilts his head to the side and stares at me, unblinking, his face an inch from the bars. "Come on, Timewire. Do it. I dare you."

Anxiety pumps through me, but I do my best to remain unphased. I don't break the facade.

"Get out of my face, Ashton."

"I know your little secret," he says.

"Secret?" I repeat, crossing my arms.

"See, I couldn't work it out." He grabs the bars, and it takes everything in me to stand my ground. "Something didn't add up. Why would *you* need big, strong Jonah to come and save the day?"

I glare at him, but my unease is making it hard to play dumb. "What are you talking about?"

Ashton scoffs. "You know exactly what I'm talking about."

The muscles around my jawline tighten. I have to stall. It's my only option. "Jonah will be here any minute, and if you don't—"

"So you know what I did, Timewire?" Ashton's upper lip curls to expose his teeth. "I started asking around, and you know what I discovered?"

"Get out!" My voice wavers, cracking a bit.

Ashton smiles, staring me straight in the face. He says the next two words with venom: "Make me."

I falter, my mouth trembling. I don't know what to say to this.

"You can't, can you?" His head leans to the other side, methodically studying me as a predator does prey. "Little birdie told me that you don't have your power anymore."

My stomach drops, and my hands begin to shake, so I ball them into fists.

"No ability. Nothing." He presses his face in between the bars, sneering. "You're powerless, just like me. Only difference is, you don't belong here." He puts a finger up to his lips and whispers. "Shh. It'll be our little secret."

He licks his lower lip, and then backs away, winking at me. And just as quick as he had come, he disappears into the dome.

I stand there, fighting the urge to yell out to someone. Running over to the door, I pull it shut. My hands are quivering, and I take a seat on the cot, shaking them out as if I had just dunked them under water.

"You're fine," I whisper to myself. "It's fine. Nothing happened."

I toss my head left and right, rolling my shoulders out. I can't let Ashton get to me. I'm safe. But he's becoming my waking nightmare.

I peer out across the dome. The smoke from the firepits rises through the twisted trees, snaking and dissipating as it moves. I wish Jonah would hurry up, but I don't have to wait long. He traipses over after another five minutes.

"Hollis, Rosalie is waiting in the clearing. Let's go."

"Yes, sir."

I don't mention Ashton's surprise visit. Jonah would likely pause this venture to go and deal with him, and he's not worth it. Besides, he's the least of my problems. I'm going to talk to Rosalie for the first time since the bombing, and I don't know what to expect. Darren's words play in the back of my mind: "Maybe Rosalie wants to join. It might take her mind off things."

A few minutes later, we arrive. Rosalie is waiting by the large pile of wood, and when our eyes meet, her heavily freckled face turns pink. She tucks her red hair behind her shoulder, and my stomach turns over. Tiffany was Rosalie's best friend . . .

"Hi," I say.

"Hey."

I walk up to her, battling the urge to tear up. She wasn't in the alcove the night I spoke with the rest of my friends.

"I want you to know how sorry I am," I say, feeling completely inadequate. "For Tiffany and for you."

She twirls a lock of her hair, looking down at my feet for a few seconds. "I know."

"I . . . you what?"

She picks her head up again. "Tiffany was your friend too, right?" Her tone is conversational, almost cathartic.

"Yes. She was."

"I'm sorry that she died."

"Me too."

Her green eyes are sparkling, but she adjusts her footing, appearing to shrug it off. She clears her throat.

"My memories will show Tiffany," I say. It's only fair to warn her.

"I know."

Her calm demeanor is unnerving, but I brush past it. I can only imagine what's going on in her head. But I know one thing for certain: for her to use her ability on a memory like this displays nothing short of bravery.

"Thank you," I say.

"For the little boy."

I nod. "For the little boy."

The rustling of the forest chimes up around us, and the water churns past the rapids in the distance. Birds bustle about, bursting into song and zipping above the trees. A breeze catches my blonde strays, and they tickle my forehead.

"You can stop at any point," I say. "Okay?"

"Okay." She takes several deep breaths, closing her eyes and positioning her palms upward toward the sky. "Where do you want me to start?"

"Right when I teleported us," I say. "Tiffany and I should be standing outside of the Testing Center."

"Okay."

After a minute, Rosalie approaches me, gazing into my face, and I stand still in anticipation. Her power will display a perfect record of what happened—not simply my perception of it. I'm about to show Jonah everything, and the idea of it makes me sick. I already told him what occurred at the Testing Center, but for him to see it played out in detail . . . What if he doesn't look at me the same way? He's my only advocate. I fear my memories will change that. But it's the only way for him to see the layout of the facility.

Rosalie throws her hands forward, spreading her fingertips wide. A grey substance spills from her and scatters around us in a thick mist. It coalesces into the outside of the Area 19

Testing Center, and Tiffany and I materialize in the middle of the clearing.

A jolt of nerves turns my blood cold. Tiffany's silvery face is streaked with tears, her mouth pressed shut under my power. I'm wearing a determined look, cold and calculating—ignorant of what the future holds.

The Testing Center looms over the trees. Transparent columns of richly decorated craftsmanship tower high against dozens of glistening steps. It appears to float there, the forest visible through its silver hue.

My doppelganger flicks her fingers at Tiffany. "Follow me."

Tiffany falls in step behind me as the memory moves, transitioning to the curved reception desk inside.

"Jonah, this is the lobby," I say, walking around the perimeter of the room and taking in its grandeur. It's just as I remember it: marble walls, smooth stainless steel lifts, and glittering glass windows.

At the desk, the chestnut-haired receptionist looks up from her papers, her poise slipping. "Oh my. My dears, what are you . . . ?"

My translucent hand launches from me, silencing her. "Take me to the Chief Overseer of this facility. And don't even think about signaling anyone for help."

Her eyes bulge and she jerks up, taking several mechanical steps. She moves out from behind her desk and joins Tiffany's side.

This is horrible. I'm watching myself make the biggest mistake of my life, and I haven't even shown Jonah the worst of it.

"I don't want to run into any crowds," my misty figure says. "So don't lead us to the lift."

I wave Jonah to my side, moving through the midst of the memory. "This is the staircase," I say, pointing to the right as our trio moves away from the lobby. "There's also another one mirroring this on the left."

Jonah studies the memory intently as it shifts up the spiraling staircase to the top floor. The receptionist places her hand against a misty panel and it flashes, opening up to reveal a long, white hallway.

"The building is full of these kinds of halls," I say. "It's like a maze, and there's a lot of doors."

Another figure materializes in the forest—a facility worker strolling down the hall toward our group. He stops and addresses the receptionist, his face perfectly collected.

"What are you doing up here?" he asks.

I grimace as I watch myself pull the man in line with the others. I wish I could reach into the memory and stop this. I'd grab myself and say, 'You're making a mistake. You can go back. You don't have to do this!' But the scene trudges on.

"Take me to the Chief Overseer."

"We're almost to the room," I say, glancing at Jonah. My palms are getting sweaty.

The ornately decorated golden door forms from the scattered mist, and my peppered hand pulls at the handle to reveal the white office. The arcing desk sits at the end, and wall screens line the sides.

Rosalie's hands shudder, and she staggers forward as a

dozen military men spill forth like ink from a bottle. The temperature of the forest drops. The memory is affecting its surroundings just like it did the time Rosalie showed me Jacob Ganiston's history. I brace myself, keen to keep my composure. The wolf-like woman appears, chic and terrible. Guns raise at my counterpart's arrival, and my transparent hands fly from me in a torrent of power.

"Put your guns on the floor."

"Rosalie, can you move ahead?" I ask, stepping closer to her.

"Yes," she says. "Where?"

"Past the videos," I say. "Tiffany should be gone. I made her . . . leave." I chew on my lower lip. I can't get emotional right now.

Rosalie repositions her hands. "Okay. Tell me when to stop."

She flicks her fingertips and the memory speeds into action, blurring around us as everything unfolds on fast-forward.

I squint, waiting for the moment. "Just here," I say, waving. "Stop."

Rosalie pulls her hands back, halting the memory in its tracks, and turning to me. "Here?"

"Yes."

With a snap, it resumes.

"You've done the right thing, Hollis," the Chief Overseer says, peering down at me with tenderness. "I can see the pain you carry, but you don't need to suffer anymore. Two of my men have gone to get the boy, and then this nightmare will be over."

"Okay."

"It will be quick and painless. Easier than falling asleep. I promise."

I shift my stance, painfully aware that this was the moment I cost everyone their safety. I run my hands through my hair, unable to look away. The military men part, and the little boy walks in accompanied by his nurse.

"There he is!" I say, holding my breath.

"Here we are sweetheart," the nurse says. "Go on."

The little boy approaches my shimmering figure, and his sweet voice carries through the trees, chilling me to the core.

"Hi."

"Hi."

"Are you the girl?"

I see myself nod. "I'm the girl."

"Okay."

He looks back to his nurse, and she says, "Go ahead, sweetheart."

At this, he places his hand to my forehead, and the memory erupts with color as the golden light arches high above the clearing. It persists for several seconds and then folds itself up into the boy's palms.

"Alright sweetheart. It's time to go."

I step over the twig-littered ground and say, "Okay. That's it. If we could somehow figure out where they're keeping him, then maybe we could—"

But the scene continues.

The wolf-like woman points to the military men and gives

them a curt nod. "You know what to do. As quick as you can."

"Now I can go home," I hear myself whisper.

"Rosalie, that's it," I say, walking up to her. "Stop."

Rosalie stands statuesque, her hands out in front of her chest, as if in a trance. Her lips are parted, and her green eyes are wide. I wave my hand in front of her face, but she ignores it.

"Hollis, I want to thank you," the woman continues.

"Thank me? For what?"

"Before tonight, we were unaware that more Diseased Ones were infesting our world."

Alarm enters my voice. "Rosalie, stop." I tap her on the shoulder, but she doesn't move. She's transfixed—consumed by the memory. Jonah runs over to her, grabbing her shoulders and looking her up and down.

"Rosalie?" He puts his hands on either side of her face, but she looks right past him.

"Jonah, what's wrong with her? Why won't she respond?"

Rosalie's arms begin to tremble, her skin turns white, and the memory expands, breathing like a creature. I stumble, tripping over a root as the mist pushes us back to the tree line.

"And now you have led us right to them," the women leers.

"No."

"Your friend," she says, her teeth bared. "I placed a tracking device on her clothing. We will have thousands of our military there within the hour. You have made me a very rich woman, Hollis Timewire."

"No!" my twin cries out. "No! You can't!"

"Rosalie, stop!"

I'm horrified, watching the worst day of my life develop in real time once more. The power of the scene throws me and Jonah to our knees, but Rosalie remains upright, unable to break the haze pouring from her palms. The memory expands again, filling the entire clearing.

"You wonderful, foolish, idiot girl." The woman's voice booms over the trees, drowning out the sound of the river. "You and your kind have soured us."

I'm helpless to stop the onslaught of mist as the woman lifts me from my feet, towering high.

"Society must rid itself from the infection that threatens to kill. The Diseased Ones must be wiped from the face of the earth, and you have helped us accomplish this."

She throws me from herself.

"No, you can't! You can't!" My own voice tears at my ears, shrill and almost inhuman. "You can't kill them! Please! Don't do this! I beg you, please!"

The gun hovers in place, the woman bears down on me, and Tiffany appears in the midst of the forest. She grabs me, and the scene freezes in place, but only for a flash.

The gun fires, and the memory explodes into a thousand inky pieces of misted black . . .

13

"I'M SORRY!" ROSALIE GASPS.

She comes out of her trance trembling from head to foot and stumbles forward, sinking to her knees in the dissipating mist. Jonah and I spring to our feet, running over to her. We kneel in the dirt by her side.

"I didn't mean to do that!" Tears trace her cheeks, and her hands are on her face. "I wanted to stop. I'm sorry. I tried, but I couldn't break the memory."

Jonah's alarm increases. "What do you mean?"

"I couldn't make it stop," she says, still shaking. She looks past us, as if the scene were still present. "The memory was so powerful. It wouldn't let me stop."

"The *memory* wouldn't let you stop?" he repeats.

Rosalie's breathing turns shallow. "It was holding me. I couldn't move, and every time I tried to pull it back into my hands, it kept pouring out, stronger and stronger."

"What?" I clasp my fingertips together, wringing them out in anticipation. "But how could it do that?"

"When a memory is strong," she says. She balls her hands up, still staring into the middle of the clearing. Her pale face is clammy with sweat.

"Rosalie." The urgency in Jonah's tone is frightening. "At what point did the memory hold you?"

"When the little boy came in," she says, without missing a beat. "I couldn't control it anymore. The memory just grabbed me. It was like . . . it was like he could see me, and I could see him. He felt so real—like he was actually standing there."

I gawk at her, my body dousing itself in cold. My mind moves back to the last nightmare I had—the one where the boy took my power and I was screaming at him to stop. "What did you just say?"

"He was so real."

"No, no." I wave my hands, shaking my head. "You said it was like he could see you?"

She nods, still transfixed on the spot where his memory stood. "Yes."

I look to Jonah, bewildered. "But how is that possible? It's just a memory. He's not actually here with us."

Rosalie shakes her head. "No, it wasn't like that. He didn't actually look at me, but I could sense his power—like this overwhelming instinct. It was like I could feel what he was feeling. He was . . . sad." She turns to Jonah, and her concern mirrors his. "What just happened to me?"

Jonah sits on the ground, still gazing intently at her. "A connection point."

"A what?"

"Abilities can become connected, and the energy from one person can join with the energy of the other. I don't know much about this boy's power yet, but it's clear that his ability linked with yours for a moment, and because this memory was a potent one, that link carried force."

"A connection point? Jonah, what are you talking about?" I ask.

"I can do it when I take on another person's power," he says. "When I use someone's ability, they can still use it themselves, but the force of it combines with mine—doubles, if you will. I'm like a mirror. I can reflect whatever ability I come into contact with." He looks into Rosalie's wide eyes once more, searching her face. "But I've never seen it happen with anyone else."

"So that's why I couldn't break it? I was connected with him?" Rosalie asks.

"Yes, it appears so."

I fiddle with the edge of my sleeve, troubled. "But it's just a memory."

"Hollis," Jonah says, his voice gentle. "The government kidnapped this boy because his ability is incredibly powerful—and he's young. The biomarker usually matures at sixteen. I don't know what he's capable of, but just as you were once a gifted type two, so is he. He hasn't explored the extent of his ability yet."

"Powerful type two," I say, thinking back to my first training session. Jonah's words crop up in my mind: "Type one abilities don't require other people to work, but type two abilities do. I know that your ability is rare because you're a type two."

"I agree. Incredibly powerful," he says. "Rosalie, are you alright?"

"Yes. I'm okay."

"Can you stand?"

"Yes."

She grabs Jonah's outstretched arm, and he helps her to her feet. The river rushes in the distance, its low hum rumbling through the trees. The three of us stare at one another, and as the tension passes, the sounds of nature return with their soothing notes.

"I'm sorry, Rosalie," Jonah says. "I didn't anticipate that. If we need to access Hollis's memories again, I'll do it. You just need to be present."

She hugs herself. "Okay."

"That's enough for today." He scratches his beard. "Are you sure you're alright?"

"I think I'm just shaken up. I didn't expect to see Tiffany get . . ." she stops herself, and my stomach churns. "But I'm okay—really," she adds at Jonah's surveying look.

"Try and get some rest, then. You're dismissed. Thank you for your help."

"Yes, sir."

Rosalie skitters off, her red hair dancing around her shoulders. She winds her way through the trunks of the tall pines until she disappears from sight. I turn back to Jonah, who at the moment seems to be lost in thought. I keep quiet, knowing better than to interrupt him when he's like this.

After a few minutes, I make my way to the pile of wood and grab the axe, but before I can begin, Jonah stops me.

"Hollis, I'd like a word."

I relinquish my grasp on the handle and jog over to him, budding with anticipation. "Well? What do you think? You saw the Testing Center. Is a rescue even possible? I mean, if we can find where they're keeping him, that is."

"You are right in several regards," he says. "This boy is one of us, the government is keeping him prisoner, and they are still using him as a weapon. A rescue, however, would be an extremely dangerous undertaking."

My heart falls, and I twist the sole of my boot in the dirt. I knew this was too good to be true. I'm about to protest, but Jonah holds his hand up, and I fall silent.

"Nevertheless," he says. "I think this idea is worth the Council's attention because, as you so eloquently put it, no one deserves a life like that, and our purpose is to find others like us." He folds his arms across his chest. "Honestly Hollis, I don't believe the Council will take fondly to a rescue mission. They will likely say that it's too risky—and they will object to more exposure."

"What are you going to say to them?"

He smiles. "I'm not going to say anything."

"What? Why not?"

"Because *you* are the one who will propose this."

I laugh out loud. "Me?"

"Yes, you."

My knees are weak, and my body is tingling. I gape at Jonah, half expecting him to break his composure and tell me that he's joking, but nothing happens. He just stares at me with a calm 'I-know-all-things' demeanor.

"Are you crazy?"

Jonah chuckles. "I don't think I am."

"But why me?" I ask. My only thought is that the stress of everything must be getting to him. He can't be serious. "They won't listen to me. I'm a traitor—a prisoner, for all intents and purposes. I'm the one who did this, remember?" I gesture to the surrounding woods. "This is my fault. We're here because of me. You should do it. They'll listen to you. You're on the Council!"

"This was your idea, young lady."

I put my hands on my hips. "So?"

"And do you know what that shows me?"

I shake my head.

"It shows me that you are integrating yourself into the core of our identity. You are actively trying to participate in this community—and not just with your work—with your attitude. Coming up with this idea shows me your determination and leadership, and more importantly, it shows me your character, and I think that's something the Council needs to see."

My heart lifts at Jonah's words. "Really?"

"Really."

I smile, a warm look replacing my incredulous one. Jonah

never ceases to amaze me. How can he believe in me after all this time? It's astounding. But my tortured thoughts turn sinister and defeat returns. There's no way this will work.

"But Jonah, they think I'm worthless. They won't listen to me. I just know it. They think I turned them in. I'm a traitor, okay? And that's never going to change. They think . . ."

I stop speaking and hang my head, overcome by an intense rush of grief. It washes over me, crushing my fleeting joy. I feel a hand on my shoulder, and then one that nudges my chin up. Jonah speaks, and his words ignite my soul, showering me in an explosive wave of purpose.

"Hollis, I don't give a damn about what they think of you."

14

IT'S DAY TWELVE OF MY PROBATIONARY PERIOD, AND I'M hard at work chopping wood in the clearing, but my mind is far away from this task. All I can think about is the boy. I can't believe that I'm going to make a difference—that I can actually help. But the idea of presenting this to the Council and convincing them to sanction a rescue mission is almost laughable.

"Alright, Jonah," I say, splitting a particularly large log in two. "How am I supposed to do this? Just call a meeting, waltz into the Council room, and say, 'Hey everyone, we were thinking about infiltrating the Area 19 Testing Center to steal the government's secret weapon. Sound good to you?'" I swing the axe again, and its crack echoes through the trees. "I don't have a plan. I don't even know where the boy is being held. So how on earth am I supposed to convince them to organize a rescue mission?"

"*We* will organize the rescue mission," Jonah says. "And

come up with a detailed plan. *Then* you will present it to the Council."

"Oh."

Jonah chuckles. "You've got the right spirit, just keep it respectful, young lady."

My face turns hot, and I back off of the sarcasm in my tone. I toss the cut pieces to my right. "Sorry . . . yes, sir."

"It's alright."

"Well, do you have a plan?" I ask tentatively, tucking my left foot behind my right. I run a hand through my hair. "I was up all night thinking about it. Assuming we can figure out where they're holding him, you'll need a team."

"I have something in mind," Jonah says.

"What is it?" I drop the axe and join him at the boulder.

"When you present this, you'll need to be absolutely prepared. You must propose a team and a well-developed plan. We can't afford any mistakes."

"Yes, of course. But you won't be starting from scratch, right? Haven't your teams done this before? A rescue mission?"

Jonah smiles. "A rescue mission? Yes. Breaking into a heavily guarded government facility? No."

"Right," I say, biting my lower lip. I kick at the pine-strewn dirt. "So, what do we do?"

"One thing at a time," he says.

I laugh. "Sometimes you say the most obvious things."

"Sometimes the most obvious things need to be said."

"I suppose you're right."

I climb up the boulder, sitting next to Jonah and peering

out across the clearing. It's a beautiful day. The sun is high in the sky, and the clouds are far away. I adjust my footing to keep from sliding down the rock's surface.

"So, you have an idea?" I ask.

"I do. I have a few people in mind. I'll have to train with them to see if it's feasible."

"Great. I can help!" I say, shifting sideways to face him. "I can help with training." Jonah gives me a surveying look, but I forge ahead. "And before you say anything, I promise I'll keep up my quota for firewood! The team can use their abilities on me—to practice whatever it is you need to practice."

Jonah scratches his chin, appearing to contemplate this. "Normally I like to have people use their abilities on me due to difficulties that can arise while training. Often, when someone is stretching the limits of their power, things can become ... unpredictable."

I can't help but feel that Jonah is commenting on our brief time together back at the old compound. If anyone knows what it's like to have an unpredictable ability, it's me. Being a puppet master was terrifying, but the fact that I'm not one anymore stings. I'm beginning to mourn the loss. The tingling beneath my fingertips that I so desperately wanted to rid myself of is now the only thing I wish with all my heart I'd never given away. I'm different from society, but I'm also different from them. I'm living alongside people with powers when I chose to forsake my own. I allowed the government to remove an integral part of my identity, and I'll forever regret that decision. Mr. Thomas's harsh words linger: "But she doesn't even have her ability anymore. She's not 'one of our own.'"

"Please? Let me help," I say. "I don't mind someone using their power on me. I just want to help."

"Alright," he concedes. "I'll let you help, but only for certain things."

"Yes!" I pump my fist into the air, but then quiet my demeanor, lowering my tone. "Thank you."

"But remember, your primary task is to supply firewood to this camp."

"Yes, sir. I promise."

"Very well then."

My mind is soaring with excitement. I'm actually going to do this. I'm going to be a part of the groundwork of rescuing this little boy, and by extension, striking a major blow in the framework of the government. Stealing the secret weapon of a hundred years ago would be the best possible victory, and I'm ready for it. They labeled me 'the leader of the second Terror War,' and that's exactly who I'm going to be.

"Okay," I say, clapping my hands together. "Who's on this team?"

"Keith Keaton, Vianne Evolet, Pierce Bodegard, and myself," Jonah says. "I know that you've met Vianne, but have you met Pierce?"

"No." A hollow sort of pang seizes me as I remember throwing Vianne into one of the dining room tables back at the old compound. I was in a fitful trance and my ability was telling me to kill Ashton—but still. We aren't exactly on the best of terms, but I shake it off. "I haven't met Pierce yet. What can he do?"

"His ability is suggestion," Jonah says.

"Woah, so like mind control?"

"Not quite. He can place thoughts into someone's mind, and these thoughts, when planted correctly, seem to be original thoughts."

"What do you mean?"

"I mean that if I were to put a thought in your mind, Hollis, then you would think it's your own," he answers.

"Oh. Wow, that's . . ." *creepy.* I finish the last word in my head. The idea of it sounds so invasive, but I can see how it would come in handy, considering that we're planning to break into the Capitol City's Testing Center.

"And Vianne, as I'm sure you know, can partially shape-shift the appearance of herself and others," he continues. "I'm hoping to develop this further."

"I didn't even think of that," I say. "Great idea."

"And Keith—"

"Can fly," I finish. "I know."

My stomach turns over as I think back to our scandalous excursion in the ceiling—the staggering heights, my hand in his, that kiss . . . It all feels like so long ago. I miss that, and I miss him. But I push my thoughts away because dwelling on Keith isn't going to do me any good. It's not like it will change my circumstances.

Jonah fiddles with a pebble, rolling it between his fingertips. "Yes. Keith's ability will provide an easy means of escape, should we need it."

"And you can double on all three," I say, steering the conversation away from Keith. "Your ability is incredible."

"It's definitely interesting. I'll give you that."

"Are you kidding?" I say, amused. "It's amazing."

"Well, thank you."

"This is great. We have a team!"

Jonah tucks his leg up on the face of the boulder, chucking the pebble at the knot in the pine. It misses. "I'll speak with each of them, but assuming they're all willing, then yes. We have a team."

"Right, but there's still a big problem." I know that Jonah is aware of this, but I have to point it out again. "Say that you train an excellent team and find some way to transport them to the Testing Center—let's even say that you manage to break in undetected. Well . . . I still don't know where the boy is. I have no idea. Jonah, what if we can't figure it out? There's no way the team can go in blind. It's impossible."

Jonah stares at me without saying a word. I'm a little taken aback by it, but I wait for him to speak, the usual hum of the forest buzzing in the background.

"Honestly, I think the answer is in your memories, Hollis," he says.

"But how? I never saw him other than the time I've already shown you."

"You don't have any other memory with the boy?"

"No, I only saw him when they brought him to me, and then . . ." I trail off as a thought occurs to me.

"And then?"

I smack a hand to my forehead. "I do have another memory of him! From one of the videos the Chief Overseer showed me. He's there with his twin sister."

"Good," he says. "Now you're thinking. I'll have to speak with Rosalie again."

"Do you really think that my memories can help us find him?"

"Memory is a curious thing." Jonah raises his brow. "Oftentimes, we can pick up details that we are unaware of at the time."

"So you think I may have seen something?"

"It's possible." He tosses another pebble at the knot a few yards from him. It misses again, hitting just to the left. "I'll have to see all of your memories from the Testing Center."

"Of course. Anything to help." I point to the knot and grin, crinkling my nose. "Also, are you ever going to hit that thing? Every day I see you toss stuff at it."

"Don't you have work to get to?"

"Is that your best come back?" I laugh, jumping from the rock and moving back to the massive pile of uncut logs. I grab the nearest piece and set it up on the 'T.' "You got to do better than that, old man."

He shakes his head. "Alright, Miss Timewire, keep up the good work."

"Yes, sir."

The rest of the day speeds by. I'm so excited by the prospect of training that I hardly pay attention to the time. It's as if my ability is back and I have an upcoming session to get to. Life in the forest is starting to gain a sense of normalcy, and I crave it—anything to keep my mind from the darker things.

I brush my hair from my face, sweating in the cool of the evening. Stars hang above me, thousands of them taking their place in the sky. It's night already? I could have sworn that Jonah just left to go get dinner. I wanted to stay to finish up the last few logs, but I guess the sun sets fast in the forest.

Setting the axe down, I grab my last armful of wood for the night and begin the walk back to the dome. The falling dusk casts purples and deep blues against the horizon, and I breathe it in. Every star appears to twinkle, catching the remnant rays of a vanished sun. It's breathtaking.

A crack sounds from behind me, and I drop the wood at my feet, turning over my shoulder to stare back through the cloaked trees. The darkness hums, and my heart hammers in my chest.

"Hello?"

No one replies. The forest continues its chirping song, the bugs now out and about. The river sighs in the distance, but I don't move. I could have sworn that I saw something move behind that trunk. I stare at the spot for another few seconds, but panic is spurring me onward. I can't explain it, but something tells me not to take my eyes off of the trees. Then another thought occurs to me, and this one is more terrifying than my instincts: I'm completely alone . . .

I stoop down and collect the pieces, keeping my gaze up. Taking care to balance over the uneven ground, I back away, and after a minute, I'm at the opening of the compound.

Warm light showers my back, and with a burst of speed, I turn away from the inky forest and dart into the safety of the enclosure.

15

VIANNE AND I ARE STANDING THREE FEET APART IN THE middle of the clearing. The pile of logs is to my right, and Jonah and Rosalie stand to my left. No one speaks. Vianne brushes her teal hair behind her shoulder. It flickers to a shocking white as she raises her delicate hands to my face.

With a flick, she throws her palms forward and I feel my hair shoot back up into my scalp, growing shorter. The sensation is cold and uncomfortable. Out of the corner of my eye, I catch Rosalie's fit of silent laughter and Jonah's half-smirk. Vianne, on the other hand, looks mortified.

"Oh no," she says, dropping her arms.

"Oh no, what?" I demand. My hands fly to my hair. "Oh no, what? What is it?"

"You sure love pink, Vianne," Rosalie chimes.

"My hair is pink?" I grab a lock, attempting to pull it into my view, but it's too short.

"And a bit spiky too," Rosalie adds.

"Jonah," Vianne says, throwing her hand up. "I can't stop turning things pink. I don't even like pink."

"I don't like pink either," I say.

Jonah chuckles. "Alright. Vianne, what do you find more difficult? Color or shape?"

"Well, both are difficult, but I'd have to say shape—which is why I don't understand why my ability seems to default to pink." She scowls, folding her arms up.

I think back to the packed dining room and the whipped cream. Ben's defeated look after his pink hair makeover is something I'll always remember. Now I'm wondering if Vianne intended that color to begin with.

"I have an idea," Jonah says. "Rosalie, can you pull up Hollis's first memory at the Testing Center? I'd like you to pause it on one of the facility workers. Anyone will do."

"Sure."

She squares her shoulders, pulling her hands apart, and a white mist seeps into the clearing. It settles in front of us. Several figures materialize, foggy and half-translucent. I appear as well.

"This is the waiting room," I say. "Before you go in for the Test."

Half a dozen other sixteen-year-olds sit in silence, their faces blank, all waiting to be called. The scene is chilling.

"Rosalie, skip ahead to when they call me," I say.

She nods, and her fingertips dance through the air, speeding the memory forward. One by one, the patients leave the room, until only I remain.

"Right here," I say, and the memory resumes.

"Miss Hollis Timewire, we're ready for you."

Rosalie halts on the nurse. Her look is muted with control, her eyes are glazed over, and her brown hair is weaved into a thick bun. Her white scrubs are pressed flat with crisp seams that fold at sharp corners.

"Good," Jonah says, approaching the woman. "Hollis, is this how all facility workers dress?"

"With the exception of the receptionist and outside employees, yes."

"Perfect." Jonah puts a hand to his chin. "Okay, Vianne, I want you to focus on this woman as a template. Try to copy her look onto Hollis. There's no need to change Hollis into the woman, just change her outfit and hair to match."

"Okay." Vianne holds her hands up again.

Jonah grins. "Try fixing Hollis's pink hair first."

"Yes, please," I say.

"Right." Vianne walks up to me and places my arms by my sides, so I keep still. She scoots back, her eyes darting between me and the nurse. "Let's see then . . ."

Her fingertips flitter through the air, and a tingling sensation spreads from the top of my head. It's as if someone were pulling my hair back into a ponytail. It lengthens and stretches up, twisting itself into a tight bun.

"Good," Jonah says.

"Is my hair back to normal?" I ask, keeping my head in place.

He laughs. "Well, it's not pink anymore, if that's what you mean."

"Fantastic."

"Now, Vianne, can you change Hollis's clothing?"

"I can try."

Her hands strain as she extends them forward. She braces herself against the dirt, widening her stance. The tingling continues, moving down my arms and legs. It's so cold that I have to remind myself to stay still. I ball my hands into fists and squeeze them to give myself something to do.

"Focus on the shape of the scrubs," Jonah says, pointing to the transparent nurse. "And Rosalie, can you zoom the memory in?"

"Yes." She slides her hands apart, and by extension, pulls the woman into sharp focus. She is proportioned now, standing a little taller than me and a few feet away.

Vianne's eyes move back and forth as she appears to ponder something, and nothing happens for a minute. Her hair flickers from the bright white to a deep and pleasant blue, and her fingers move. A different sensation arises. It's like hundreds of feathers tickling me all over my body. I shut my eyes and clench my jaw to keep from squirming.

"Not bad," I hear Jonah say.

I look down to find loosely fitted grey scrubs. They're too big to be convincing and—

"Too dark," Vianne mumbles.

"Remember, shape first." Jonah walks over to the woman, examining her. "See how her scrubs are sewn with cornered seams, and the outline of her clothing is pointed? Hollis's are flat. Sharpen those up."

"Like this?" Vianne twitches her hand and the scrubs snap against me, fitting to my form.

"Perfect."

"Now color," she murmurs. Wringing her hands out, she backs away a few paces, gesturing to the scrubs in the memory. "Hollis, is everything inside the Testing Center this white?"

"Yes."

Vianne splays her fingers and scrunches her nose up in concentration. My scrubs begin to lighten. The white travels up the fabric, seeping the way water moves when it soaks a cloth. The color, like the hairstyle, feels cold.

"Oh! That looks just like the worker," Rosalie exclaims, walking around the memory and looking me up and down.

"It really does," Vianne says. She puts her hands on her hips and cocks her head to the side. "What do you think, Jonah? Pretty good, huh?"

"I'd say you've created a regular society member."

My stomach wriggles, and I turn my nose up in disgust. I'm not a society member—not anymore. Never again. I'm proud to be one of them, even without my ability. But if my transformation is good enough to warrant a comment like that, then this might just work.

The more I think about it, the crazier this idea gets. We're training the team and we don't have a clue where the little boy is. I asked Jonah why he wanted to do this, and he said that if they're going to pull this off, then everyone needs as much training as possible.

"Let me worry about training the team," he had said. "Your

memories are still in there. We'll find him."

I hope so. This all hinges on me. Maybe Jonah's right—maybe I did see something. Only time will tell. We're starting today, and I must admit, combing through every inch of my memory doesn't sound like it's going to be fun.

"Great work, Vianne," Jonah says. "You are dismissed. We'll meet up again tomorrow."

She dips her head down. "Thank you." And with that, she skips off, her hair flickering back to her favorite shade of vibrant teal.

"Rosalie, if you could stick around," Jonah adds.

"Sure," she says, and she pulls the frozen memory back into her hands. The mist scatters and then vanishes. "What's up?"

"I'd like to start reviewing Hollis's memories of the Testing Center."

"Oh." The wavering in her tone doesn't inspire confidence.

Jonah approaches her. "It's alright. I'll use my ability. You just need to be here."

"Okay." Rosalie hugs herself, backing away to give him some space.

"Jonah, do you really think we'll find something?" I ask.

"I'm not sure. We'll see."

Jonah lifts his hands and my memories explode from them, spraying the see-through mist into the clearing once more. The scene collects around us: a white facility van parked by a pristine curb, a boxy housing unit, and a dark cobblestone path. My house.

"The morning of my Test," I say, staring at the memory in a trance.

A man in a white suit exits the government van and approaches my door, knocking three times. The sound echoes through the trees as crisp as if he were actually here. After a minute, the door opens and a woman steps out. I take in her unblemished high cheekbones, thin nose, and placid hazel eyes. Her regal demeanor commands respect. She carries no fear or anticipation.

"Mother . . ." I whisper.

My twin steps through the door, keeping close to my mother's side. My transparent blonde hair is tucked neatly into a bun, and my blouse is pressed flat under the blue blazer. I wear a blank, controlled expression, but a hint of nerves lie underneath.

"Remember Hollis," and the softness of my mother's voice makes my skin crawl. "It's just one day, and after that, you'll never think of it again."

I can still see so much of myself in my mother. I'm her spitting image. But it's not our complexion's likeness that haunts me. Even though I've abandoned my societal beliefs, the ingrained memory of how I must present myself is still there. My mother's voice of correction is woven into the fabric of my childhood. Her words will always stay with me regardless of whether I follow them.

But what breaks my heart more than anything else is that my mother is lost. She doesn't know the truth of the world like I do, and I don't know that she ever will. That deep longing to go back home is not a part of me anymore, but it makes me ache for my parents in a different way. I'm still their blood, but

I recognize that things will never be as they once were.

"Kindly follow me, Miss Timewire," the man in the white suit says.

I obey, stepping in line and following him to the van, but my head turns back to catch the last glimpse of my dwelling.

"We will have you back shortly. There's no need to fear."

The van door clangs shut, and the memory whirls as the vehicle picks up speed. My misty figure sits with an eerie calm, but even though my face is blank, I know what's going through my mind. I had emotion, but it was suppressed and hidden away. I was a broken little girl—a cog in the mesh of the world, completely unaware of the staggering truth behind this evil.

"The path to a perfect society is perfect obedience."

The phrase reverberates off the vehicle's walls. I want to vomit. Who was I back then? I don't even recognize myself anymore.

The van decelerates and stops at the entrance of the Testing Center. Its grandeur is remarkable. Glittering glass doors shine in the light of the morning sun. The man, keeping himself at a distance, allows me to emerge, and the scene moves along as we trudge up the steps.

"Please. To the reception desk," he says.

"Yes, sir."

The lobby materializes with its vast marble craftsmanship, and the man escorts me to the curved desk. Jonah's hands vibrate, buffeted by an invisible force.

"Ah. Miss Hollis Timewire. Big day," the receptionist says,

her eyes serene. "Your parents must be so proud of you. Coming of age is such an honor."

"Yes, ma'am."

"You will make an incredible addition to society, no doubt."

"Thank you."

An incredible addition to society . . . It's hard to watch this. I wrap an arm around my waist, hugging myself.

"And with your father's recent promotion, you'll have no trouble with your career assignment." She eyes me with as close to an endearing look as she's allowed. "I'm sure you'll follow in his footsteps. The commanding officer of Area 19's military elite. Truly inspiring. What a prestigious family."

My head bows ever so slightly. "You're very kind."

"If I can just see your documents?"

"Of course."

I want to vanish into the forest. The receptionist's words cut at me: the commanding officer of Area 19's military elite. My father turned me in. That's all I can think about right now. How could he do that to me? I'm his daughter—his own flesh and blood. But I suppose the government was always his first love.

I wrap my other arm around me as numbing cold spreads to the ends of my fingers. How could I have been so blind? Was I truly that naïve? I'm reliving this all over again, and the guilt of it is eating me alive.

I have to remind myself: Jonah needs to see *every* memory of the Testing Center. That's why we're doing this. The least I can do is grin and bear it.

"Well, all seems to be in order," the receptionist says, thumbing through to the last page. "If I can have you initial here and sign down at the bottom."

The man in the white suit moves ahead of me, patiently waiting for me to finish. The receptionist collects my papers and tucks them into a file folder.

"Right this way, Miss Timewire," he says.

"That's right," I say, stepping up next to Jonah. "We took the lift that day."

The memory moves into the steel elevator as it clinks shut. The soft musical voice issues from the silvery wall above our heads.

"Identification please."

The man places his thumb over the small bioscanner, and it flashes to admit him.

"Identification verified."

I turn to Jonah. "A lot of doors only open at someone's touch," I say. "You'll have to keep that in mind."

I peer back at the scene. The lift's button panel shimmers in the sunlight of the clearing. There are thirteen polished buttons—twelve silver ones for the twelve floors, and one white one. It isn't labeled.

The memory spills out into the hall just beyond the waiting room, and the panel fades away with the lift. And now the scene appears to unfold on fast forward as Jonah pours my timeline into the forest. The Testing Center expands into the clearing, and I stand there, keen to bear it all again—every shred of memory I own—to search for the buried clue that will lead us to the boy.

I take a deep breath and compose myself. This is going to be a long day.

16

WE'RE BACK IN THE CLEARING. SO MUCH OF MY DAY IS spent here that it's starting to become more of a home than the new compound. I stand facing Jonah, ready for what comes next.

"Hollis, this is Pierce Bodegard. We will be training with him today."

Pierce stands tall and broad-shouldered—quite a lot taller than me. His facial features are distinct: a chiseled jawline set against jet black hair, thick eyebrows, tanned skin, and deep-set brown eyes that appear somber. He looks like he's in his late twenties.

"Hi," I say. "Nice to meet you."

He doesn't return the greeting. Instead, his stoic appearance turns to an off-putting scowl. It's clear that he dislikes me as much as the others. He's staring at me, accusing me with his eyes. I know this look. I've received it from nearly everyone here. It's the look that makes me stare at the ground when I stack wood.

"So how does this work?" I ask, turning to Jonah and breaking the awkward eye contact. "When the team goes to the Testing Center, what will this help with?"

"The idea is to suppress any suspicion and keep people out of our way as we move through the building," Jonah says. "Pierce's ability is the complement to Vianne's. Together, I think we will make a rather convincing group of facility workers."

"Right," I say. "Got it."

Oh . . . I should be sitting down. I haven't sat down in a long time and my feet hurt. I glance around, noting the larger log that I use as a brace when I cut wood. That seems like a perfectly good seat. I'll continue helping from there. I move over to the log and sit, resting my elbows on my knees.

"Well done, Pierce," Jonah says. "Hollis, if you could stand back up please."

"What?"

I look between the two of them, confused, but it only takes me a few seconds to realize that Pierce just told me to sit down with his ability. I stand, feeling the color crop up in my cheeks. That was strange. *I* wanted to sit down . . . or at least I thought I did.

"That was you?" I ask.

"Yes." Pierce's deep voice carries through the trees.

I return to Jonah's side. "What kinds of things can he make me do?" I ask, feeling a bit unnerved.

"Well, his ability only works in the context of what is feasible for the individual," he says. "For example, if you were the kind of person who absolutely hated peanut butter, and Pierce told you to eat some with his ability, then most likely, you wouldn't do it—even though eating peanut butter seemed to be your own thought."

A small wave of relief hits me, and I giggle. "I understand, but that's a bad example. Who hates eating peanut butter?"

"*That* is an excellent question."

I'm salivating at the mere mention of it. I never thought I'd miss something so specific. Now I *really* want to sit down. I walk back over to the log and take a seat, leaning back on my palms.

Jonah's soft chuckle turns my head back to them. He says, "Hollis, if you would stand back up. And Pierce, let's try something else."

I jump to my feet, hands on my hips. "Seriously? He did it again?"

Pierce gives me a curt nod, and an odd smile falls across his face. I can't help but feel like he's having a little too much fun with this.

"Alright," Pierce says in a thick and honeyed tone. "What do you suggest?"

Jonah considers me and then says, "Hollis, would you mind walking to the other side of the clearing so that Pierce and I can talk?"

"Sure."

I move to the edge, stopping just shy of the trees. I rub my hands together to warm them. The crisp morning air is getting colder every day. If I'm being honest, Pierce's ability is rather startling. It's subtle, and I'm not sure I like experiencing it, but the fact that he was able to use it on me twice without my knowledge gives me confidence. The team needs his power. It's perfect.

I peer back across the space to see Jonah leaning into Pierce. He's whispering something. Then after a few seconds, they both straighten up and look at me.

"Okay. Hollis, could you come back over here?" Jonah calls. "Just walk through the middle of the clearing and come stand next to us."

"Sure thing," I say, feeling like this request is nearly as odd as Pierce's ability.

I start my trek back through the open expanse, and at the same time, Jonah and Pierce begin walking toward me. Well, that's fine. I guess we'll meet in the middle. I keep up my pace in even steps. I'm almost to them. But wait . . . didn't Jonah ask me to walk all the way across? He did—I'm sure of it. I'll meet them at the end. They're still in front of me. It's only a few more feet . . .

I stop at the edge of the trees, running into a low hanging branch. It wallops me in the stomach, and I grab onto it to keep from falling. But . . . what? They aren't in front of me at all. I whirl around to find them at the other end, standing exactly where I started.

"But you were right in front of me," I say, my head spinning. "How did you . . ."

"Beautifully executed," Jonah says, clapping Pierce on the back. "Hollis, can you come back over here?"

I cross my arms. "Will you be there if I walk over?" There's a definite edge to my tone.

"Yes."

"Alright." I jog over to them, rubbing the spot where the branch jabbed me. "How did that even happen? One second you two were right in front of me, and then the next thing I know, I'm running into a tree."

"I changed your focus," Pierce says. "You were concentrated on walking to Jonah, but I shifted that to the trees. You walked right past us."

I shake my head. "This is just weird. I'm even trying to anticipate what you're going to do and I can't avoid it."

"This is promising," Jonah says. "If we can evade facility workers like you've just demonstrated, then I'd say we have a pretty good chance of breaking in undetected."

"Good."

These slippery thoughts are unsettling. It's so strange—doing something without knowing it. Those were not my thoughts, but they felt so natural. It's frightening. With Pierce, the team will slip right in.

Jonah claps his hands together. "Okay, now I want to try something a little trickier. Hollis, please go back to the tree line."

I return to my place, waiting for Jonah's instructions. I hold my hand up to shield my eyes from the bright sun. I'm not sure what's next, but I'm ready for it. I'm determined to try and beat

Pierce. I know what his power does now, and I'm not going to be fooled this time. Jonah wants to make it trickier? Then let's do it.

"Hollis, I want you to approach us and ask us to identify ourselves," Jonah says. "Pretend that you're the receptionist."

"Got it."

This should be easy. There's no way they're getting past me now. I start across the clearing, keeping Pierce and Jonah in sight. It's not like they can vanish—and they're headed straight for me.

I walk up to them and stop, squinting in the sunlight. But . . . I forget what I was supposed to ask them. Jonah said . . . he said something, but I can't remember it. Well, I have to ask them something. That much is clear.

I fumble over my words. "What . . . what are you doing?"

"We're walking," Pierce says.

"Right. Of course."

My brain is foggy. Why can't I remember? I'm still struggling with what I'm supposed to say, so I continue to walk toward the trees, attempting to clear my head. Before I know it, I'm at the tree line once again. I spin around.

"But I just—you were just—seriously?" I sputter, completely beside myself. "I thought I had you."

"This is great," Jonah says. "Well done."

"But you were right in front of me again," I say, tugging aggressively at a lock of my hair. "And I just let you by. My mind went all fuzzy. I couldn't remember what I wanted to say."

"Precisely," Pierce says.

"This is going to work!" I bound over to them, beaming.

"It would seem so." Jonah turns to Pierce. "I think that will do for today. Great work, and thank you for your time."

"My pleasure." He stalks off without a second glance at me, winding his way through the thick of the forest.

I shake out my hands. Pierce's ability is intimidating but incredible. That training session went exactly the way I was hoping it would. This is turning into something achievable.

Out of the corner of my eye, the massive pile of logs lingers. I still have to fill my quota for today, but first things first. My least favorite part of this whole venture: sifting through my memories. Again.

"Rosalie should be here any minute," Jonah says. "I asked her to come after Pierce."

"Okay," I say half-heartedly.

We've found nothing—not even the slightest hint of the boy's whereabouts, and I'm starting to feel uneasy. Every word, worker, and setting—every piece I own is set before us again and again, but the secret weapon remains a mystery. The only advantage we've gained from this draining exercise is a floor plan detailing the layout of the Testing Center. The map of the facility hangs on the wall below the silver clock in the waiting room, and Jonah's spent a considerable amount of time studying it.

After a few more minutes, Rosalie walks through the trees, and before I know it, we're trudging through my memories once more. They spill from Jonah's fingertips, filling the entire clearing, and I brace myself to bear it all again.

"Jonah?"

He flicks his hand and the memory halts. My misty counterpart is suspended in a run halfway down the hallway leading out of the waiting room. I look terrified. This is the part where I heard that demonic voice for the first time.

"What is it?"

"I don't think we're going to find anything," I say, frustration catching in my throat. "We've watched these nearly a dozen times. I just . . . I don't think I saw anything."

"I wouldn't say that just yet," he says, turning back to the scene and peering at it intently. "It's almost like there's something hidden here. I can feel it."

"You can feel it?" I repeat. "What do you mean?"

"Like there's more to these memories than what we've seen," he says. "I can't explain it yet. Something about watching them over and over again . . . ."

Rosalie joins him, rocking herself up on her tippy toes. "Yes, I can feel it too. There's something here, Hollis."

"It's helping?"

"Well, at the very least, your memories are helping me familiarize myself with the facility," Jonah says. "And if we're going to do this, I need to know the layout like I actually work there."

"I suppose so." My tone falls flat. "It's just that . . . it's hard to watch."

I hug myself, looking down at my feet. Jonah puts a hand on my shoulder and I look up at him. His eyes hold nothing but compassion. "I can only imagine. Thank you for being willing to help us."

I nod. "Of course."

I shouldn't complain. This is the least I can do. I should be happy that my memories are helping them prepare. In all reality, I'm probably the only reason why this mission is possible in the first place.

"We can stop for today if you'd like," he offers.

"No, it's alright," I say. "Really. I'm okay. Continue."

"Very well then."

Jonah faces the memory again, and his hands slide through the air. Everything resumes, and I watch myself sprint away from the waiting room.

I close my eyes, taking a deep breath to center myself. I can do this. I can watch it again. One more time. And who knows? Maybe this time I'll catch something I didn't see before.

17

"HEY CANDY, WHAT'S THAT YOU'VE GOT?"

Ben's energetic tone carries a considerable distance through the dome. I place the last log on the stack and peek out from behind the alcove, taking care to stay hidden.

"What do you mean?" she asks, looking around her person. Her dark brown hair cascades over her shoulders.

"Behind your ear." Ben plucks a pebble from thin air, twirling it between his fingertips. Candice doesn't look amused.

"Will you stop doing that!" she says, exasperated. "You're cute, but seriously. Pull any more pieces of nature out of my ear and I'll fill your pillow with rocks and dump it in the river."

"Ouch. Harsh," Ben says. "But you said I'm cute, so I'll take it."

He pulls Candice into a backward hug and rocks her back and forth.

"Yeah, whatever," she mumbles, rolling her eyes. But she cracks a smile.

"Hey, I have an idea," Ben says, spinning her around to face him. He holds the pebble aloft as a smirk plays across his face.

"No more magic tricks."

He shakes his head. "No, not that. Ever skipped rocks before?"

I lean out a little further, this time making sure I don't trip and fall.

"Well, seeing as I've lived underground my whole life . . . no," Candice replies, peering up at the ceiling of the dome. "Haven't crossed that one off my bucket list yet."

"You know, your sarcasm feeds my inescapable urge to do magic," Ben muses, holding a hand to his chin with a boyish grin. "I'm sure I have another trick up my sleeve. I'll just go get my deck of—"

"No, no!" Candice says, grabbing his arm. "Let's go bounce rocks or whatever."

Ben laughs. "It's called 'skipping rocks.' 'Skipping.' Not 'bouncing.'"

"Yeah okay," she says. "Well whatever it's called, I'm sure I'm better at it than you."

He raises an eyebrow. "Is that a challenge?"

Candice folds her arms across her chest and scrunches up her nose. "Do you even know me?"

"Fair point. Race you to the river?"

"Well . . ."

But in an instant, Candice darts off through the enclosure,

heading for the exit as fast as she can.

"Hey! Not fair!" Ben shouts.

"Life's not fair!" she calls back.

With a whoosh of air, Ben zooms ahead, zipping past her in a blur of speed and stopping just shy of the way out. He gives a fake yawn, tapping the flat of his palm over his open mouth.

"Hey! No powers!" she cries.

"Life's not fair," he says, beaming and taking off again.

I lean back against the side of the alcove, smiling. They look happy. Good. I'm glad. At least they have each other. Their silliness has lightened my mood, and I skip in step, making my way back through the dome. I need to get in some work before training.

Later today, Jonah is meeting with Vianne again, and I'm looking forward to it. It's time for her to try putting a group in disguise instead of just me.

As I emerge into the forest, I pick up the pace. I want to keep my promise to Jonah. It's been difficult to maintain the same amount of firewood since agreeing to help the team, but I haven't failed yet. And I don't plan on starting now.

When I arrive, the clearing is deserted. Jonah isn't at his usual spot on the boulder. I glance around, but the distant sounds of laughter draw my attention to the water. Jonah is standing at the edge of the river with Ben and Candice, and all three of them are lobbing rocks.

I work my way through the trees, hanging back a few yards as this odd trio attempts to skip stones across the shimmering surface.

Ben, as usual, is failing miserably, chucking wild tosses with no form at all. But Candice and Jonah are decent, catching a double skip every now and then. I'm grinning, holding on to a skinny pine, my hair trailing over my shoulder. They're throwing it all wrong.

I stoop down in the dirt, sifting through the slew of pebbles. I select a smooth, oval-shaped one that's a little smaller than the flat of my hand. I canter down the slope a few yards to their left, stopping a foot from the water's edge. They don't see me. They're still engrossed in tossing.

Ben hurls a terrible throw, and the rock plummets with a distinct 'plop,' sending water splashing into a high arc.

Candice giggles. "You're just throwing rocks, Ben. You're not even trying to skip them. Wasn't this your idea?"

"Whatever, Candy."

She sticks her tongue out at him, and he grins.

I position my feet in the mud and think of my mother. It's been a long time since I skipped a rock. I wonder if I'm still good at it. With one powerfully aimed throw, I fling the stone into the river. It darts across the surface and skips eight times before diving into the depths below. I stand there, a little breathless, but positively glowing.

The three of them turn in slow motion, gawking at me. Ben's mouth is stretched comically, and Candice's bright blue eyes are wide, but Jonah is beaming. My two friends don't say a word, and my heart sinks. I've upset their fun. I can see it on their faces. My presence isn't welcomed here, but just as I'm about to turn away...

"Can you teach me how to do that?" Candice asks, taking a tentative step toward me.

My mouth drops open. "I . . . yes, of course."

"Yeah, me too?" Ben adds, looking eager. He slides a sideways glance at his girlfriend that says 'game on.'

Candice pushes Ben out of the way. "Ben's hopeless. You'd be wasting your time trying to teach him."

"Hey now, easy," he huffs, grabbing her hand and pulling her back. "We'll just have to see, missy."

"You actually want me to teach you?" I ask, thinking that this must be some kind of joke. Do they really want to be around me?

"Yeah!" Candice nods. "I have to continue to beat Ben at everything."

I laugh, the biggest smile stretching across my face. They want me to play. They want me to join them. My heart swells at the idea, and all the little moments of fun from the old compound shower me in the best kind of warmth.

I join them, ecstatic. I catch Jonah's eye. He gives me a wink and then starts back toward the clearing, hands in his pockets.

"Ah, come on Jonah," Ben says. "You don't want to learn?"

"Oh, I'm much too old to compete with you young people," he says. "I'd lose terribly."

"Suit yourself."

Jonah gives me a nod of encouragement and then walks away. I select another stone from the riverbed, jittering with excitement.

"Okay," I say. "First of all, you need a smooth stone. And

when you throw it, you have to keep the flat part of the stone level with the surface of the water, but slightly tilted up."

"Tilted up," Candice repeats, an 'oh-its-on' look spurring her clear determination.

"Yes, like this." I position my stone so that the leading edge of it is slightly higher than the trailing edge. "That way the stone doesn't dip under the water right away."

"I see," she says.

"And you have to put a little power behind it, and then . . ." I angle my stone at the water and hurl it across the surface. It bounces all the way to the other side. Nine times. ". . . it will just skip," I finish.

I give a little bow and Candice claps. Ben, on the other hand, holds his hand up.

"Step aside, Candy. Let me do this. Watch the master at work." He tosses his head back and forth, rolling his shoulders out.

"Oh *trust* me. I'm watching," she says.

"So like this?" he asks, holding his stone at a tilt.

"Yes. Exactly," I say.

"Whelp. Here goes nothing."

In a wild swing, Ben lets the stone fly. It ricochets off the surface once and then lands with a plunk, disappearing below.

"I did it!" he exclaims, smacking a hand to his forehead. "I skipped it! Did you see that? Did you see it? Ha! Take *that*." He pumps his fist high into the sky.

Candice smirks. "With pleasure." She steps up to the water's edge with her pebble in hand. She pops a flame onto her pointer finger and then blows it out. "For luck—not that I need any."

Ben shakes his head. "Go on, then."

She sizes up the water, her arm hovering in place for nearly a minute.

Ben scowls. "Would you hurry up? We don't have all day, Candy."

She holds a finger up, keeping her gaze on the stream. "Technically, we do." In a graceful swing, Candice tosses her stone. It skips four times. She turns around with a look of pure joy. Throwing her arms up in victory, she runs around Ben in circles. "And Candice takes the lead and the crowd goes wild! Ahh!"

She makes a whispery cheering noise, cupping her hands around her mouth. Ben catches her around the middle and begins to tickle her.

"Hey!" she yelps. "Cut it out!"

"Nope. Not a chance."

I stand there, feeling incredibly pleased. They're acting normal around me. I'm not being accused with harsh stares and silent lips. Fun is weaving its way back into my life, and slowly but surely, I'm starting to find happiness in the little moments again.

I should leave these two amazing goofballs alone. I slip away, moving back through the trees.

That was fun, and I can't remember the last time I've experienced that. The pleasant memories of skipping rocks with my mother surge to the forefront of my attention. I miss her. But I have a lot of work to do before Vianne comes, and I need to get started.

I begin the climb up the riverbank, kicking a large wood chip as I go. It skitters up the dusty path, coming to rest a few feet from me. I continue kicking the chip each time I reach it— mostly to give myself something to do.

My feet scrape against the littered stones and twigs. Judging from the sun's angle, I only have an hour before training begins. I better get back to—

The sound of a twig snapping underfoot cracks to my right. I slip, mid-kick, falling on my hands and knees with a thud. I look up just in time to catch a hint of movement from between two trunks. My heartbeat thumps against my chest as my adrenaline soars. A person is behind that tree. I'm sure of it.

"Hello?" I call out, getting up from the ground and dusting my hands off. I wince at the fresh scrape beading with blood. "Who's there?"

No one answers.

My pulse quickens. I stand there, unsure of whether to proceed. Just as in the dark of the forest, something inside of me says I shouldn't take my eyes away from the trees.

"I know you're there," I say, trying to sound confident. "I saw you." But my tone falters.

I take a step toward the trunk but stop myself. Should I really be doing this? I glance behind me. In the distance, Ben and Candice are still wrestling with each other. Their laughter is faint but present. If someone attacked me, they'd hear it.

I grit my teeth, plucking up the courage I need. This is

ridiculous. Someone wants to play hide and seek with me? Is this some kind of prank? Enough is enough.

I make a beeline for the trunk, marching up to it with purpose. I lunge around it, ready to catch the trickster, but with a bang, I'm thrown backward. I catch myself on my wrists and yelp as pain shoots up my arm.

A massive blue orb appears out of nothing, pulsing right in front of me—it's breadth nearly thirty feet in diameter. I stare up at it, petrified. Lines of dark blue slither around its shape as it grows. It bobs up and down, enveloping the forest and expanding toward me with electric energy. It creeps up to me like a predator, ravenous and intent upon its catch.

I scramble away, throwing my hands up as a shield. I open my mouth to scream, but with a blinding flash, it vanishes, and all that remains are the purple and blue spots dancing across the dark of my vision.

I sit there, stunned, my arms limp and helpless as my brain struggles to comprehend what just happened. I find my wits a moment later, and launch myself to my feet, sprinting back through the trees with panic-fraught stamina.

I burst into the clearing, wide-eyed, with a massive stitch in my chest. Jonah jumps up from the boulder, running to me and grabbing my shoulders.

"Hollis, what happened?"

His eyes search mine as I fight with my words.

"I—I'm not—I don't know. There was this—this blue . . ." I suck in a huge gulp of air, fighting with my trembling hands. I grab Jonah's wrists to steady myself.

"Are you hurt?" he asks, examining me.

"No." I shake my head, my mind still reeling. "There was this blue light, and it . . ." I trail off as a thought occurs to me. "I think I just got scared by someone's ability."

"What happened?"

"Well, I was walking back to the clearing when I heard a noise. I thought it was someone spying on me, so I went to see what it was, and then this huge blue light expanded in front of me and then vanished." I bit my lower lip, grimacing. "And then I ran away."

Of course it was an ability . . .

I stare down at the ground as heat crops up in my face. I release Jonah's wrists, my panic coming down from its high.

"Someone just used their ability," I say. "It was really bright and it scared me. I think I just didn't realize what was happening."

"It was bright?" Jonah repeats, his brow furrowing.

"Yes. This blue light just came out of nowhere. It caught me off guard. I'm sorry. I shouldn't be this freaked out. It's silly." I rub a hand against the back of my neck.

Jonah peers through the trees behind me. "Strange. I didn't think Rachel was well enough to use her ability yet."

"Rachel?"

"The girl who can produce force fields," he says. "She saved a lot of lives back at the compound by holding up the ceiling as it was collapsing. Is that the blue light you saw?"

The chaos of that day comes back to me: chunks of earth littering the floor, the bombs exploding overhead, military engines roaring in the distance, and the dark-skinned girl standing on top of the table pouring the blue light into the sky. She saved us. She saved *me*.

"Yes. That's what I saw." I run a hand through my tangled hair. "Is Rachel doing okay?"

"Apparently she's doing much better than I thought," Jonah replies, scratching the top of his head. "I'll have to pay her a visit soon."

I smile, trying to push past the gut-wrenching memories of the burning compound.

"Well, no matter. I'll go and see her later," he says. "Are you alright?"

"Yes, I'm fine."

"Okay. Then I'd like to speak with you about something."

"What is it?"

"With a few more training sessions, the team will be ready. It's time for you to start thinking about presenting your idea to the Council."

My stomach drops, and the blood in my head turns cold. "What? But we haven't found the little boy. What's the point?"

"We still have plenty of time to search your memories, Hollis. There's not a hard deadline for this. But it would be a good idea for you to start collecting your thoughts. Okay?"

"Jonah, I know you say you have this feeling about my memories, but I just don't think he's there. I'm sorry, but maybe this whole thing is—"

I stop myself from saying 'a waste of time.' I know it's not.

But I've watched the memories so many times that it's starting to feel hopeless. The same monotony day after day is driving me insane. I don't know how much more I can take.

"Would you prefer to give up?" Jonah's calm demeanor shakes me.

"No. Absolutely not."

"Good. I thought you'd say that."

I smile. "Jonah?"

"Yes."

"I need to get some work done before Vianne arrives."

He steps aside. "By all means."

I grab the axe and select a log, propping it up on the 'T.' But before I hoist the blade, I gaze back through the trees. That blue light scared the senses out of me. Why was Rachel hiding there? What did she want from me? And more importantly, was she the one hiding the night I was alone in the forest?

18

"HOLLIS, YOUR FRIENDS ARE HERE."

The team arrives from across the clearing, and I stop my work, setting the axe down by the pile. I stand behind Jonah as Vianne, Rosalie, Pierce, and Keith stroll through the trees. Keith and I lock eyes, and I'm so glad to see him that I can't help but stare.

"Hi," I say, giving a lame little wave.

"Hi."

But before I can say anything else, Jonah begins, walking into the midst of the group. "Alright, Vianne. Today you'll be working on disguising the whole team at the same time—even Hollis and Rosalie. Because if you can disguise six people confidently, four shouldn't be a problem."

"Okay," she says, and her favorite shade of teal hair turns bright red.

"And you'll need to disguise yourself as well," he adds.

"Make sure your hair doesn't change colors when you use your ability."

"Oh, right," she says sheepishly. "Good point." Her red locks snap to a neutral brown—similar to that of the facility worker Rosalie used as a template during her first training session.

"That's much better."

Vianne poises her hands at us but then lowers them, scratching the side of her cheek. "Rosalie, could you pull up that nurse lady again? I need to visualize."

"Sure thing."

But Jonah holds his hand up and Rosalie stops. "Vianne, can you try doing it without the nurse this time? You'll need to get used to changing us without a cheat sheet."

She clasps her hands together and then scrunches up her nose. "Okay, you're right. I can try."

She lifts her palms again and aims them at Jonah's chest, backing up a few paces. Her eyes bounce between the five of us as she appears to size everyone up. Her thin hair flutters to an off-white, and then to a pleasant shade of lavender.

"Vianne, your hair," Rosalie says.

With a flick of her pointer finger, her hair snaps back to brown. "I'm like a damn chameleon," she mutters, shaking her head. "I don't even know it's happening most of the time."

Rosalie giggles. "At least it wasn't pink."

"Keep that in mind," Jonah says. "Since that's something you struggle with, try to maintain focus on it along with your other tasks."

"Right."

She squares her shoulders and with a flick of her hand, the cold sensation begins to creep along my skin. My clothing, along with everyone else's, starts to change. It morphs and fits to my form. But my scrubs are quite a lot darker than Pierce's—and Rosalie's and Jonah's are blue. Keith's, on the other hand, are perfect. We lock eyes again, and I can feel my face turn pink.

Vianne's hands begin to tremble as her face screws up in concentration. The cold tickles my arms and legs, and the shape of my scrubs change, sharpening into the cornered seams from the memory.

Then, with a burst of movement, everyone's hair slicks back. I gasp at the sudden tug. Vianne spreads her fingertips and widens her stance, moving her hands in an even rhythm. My hair elongates, pulling up and twisting itself into a neat bun. Rosalie's vibrant red hair dulls into a copper brown, and it changes its style to match mine. The boys look like they've all taken a swim in the river.

Vianne's arms are shaking now, and sweat is pouring from her brow. I can physically see the amount of power this is taking her—but the group is almost perfect. Shocking white hues dance onto everyone's scrubs, spreading through the fabric in bursts.

For a moment, Vianne looks like she's going to be sick. Her face takes on a reddish tint, as if she were holding her breath. And then, with a violent explosion of color, her hair changes from purple to green to yellow and then back again—and scars erupt across her face and neck. They throb in the sunlight of the clearing. Deep and raw.

She relinquishes her power, all of us transform back to normal, and her hands fly to her face. With scarlet cheeks, she pulls the collar of her shirt up over her nose and turns away from us, sprinting through the trees.

I take off after her. "Vianne, wait!"

"Hollis, no!" Rosalie shouts. "Don't!"

But I'm already gone. I rush through the forest, hot on Vianne's trail. Leaping over gnarled roots and pine cones, I keep up with her pace, and after a minute or so, we emerge onto the riverbed. I'm panting, clutching at the stitch developing in my side.

"Wait!" I call out.

She starts marching down the side of the water. "Go away, Hollis."

"Vianne, you don't—"

"Leave me alone!"

"It's okay," I say, catching up to her. I grab her arm. "You don't have to hide—"

She spins around with an alarming look. "*This* is okay?" she shrieks. "*This?*"

Her scars shatter across her face again—terrible and taunting. I stagger back at the intensity of it. Her bloodshot eyes and beating wounds are horrifying. A near-animal aggression emerges from her and she yanks her arm from my grasp.

"You don't know what you're talking about," she hisses, her teeth bared.

She continues to march upstream, stomping across the damp earth.

"Wait!" I say, chasing after her again. "Vianne, please. I'm sorry."

"I said leave me alone!"

I run past her and stop, holding my hands up to block her path. "No."

She glares at me, and her hands curl into fists. It looks like she might hit me, but I stand my ground, keeping my hands aloft. Considering what she did to Ashton back at the old compound, I'm surprised at my boldness. She distorted his appearance for stealing her artbook. She could easily transform me into some kind of mutant if she wanted to.

"What do you want from me?" She demands, venom in her tone. "You want to make this okay?" She points to her face and her scars pulse as the light throws them into sharp relief. "Because this will never be okay. So save your breath."

Angry tears smear her delicate features, and her face falls to her chest. She brushes a hand through her hair and it changes to match the deep blue of the stream. Her scars melt away into a porcelain complexion, and she turns to face the water, hugging herself.

"This will never be okay . . ." she repeats, her voice stricken.

I stare at her, troubled. The deep anguish on her face is disturbing. She's broken—completely defeated. Do I dare ask? But something deep within compels me to do so.

"What happened?"

The question is soft and filled with all the compassion I

have. I can almost feel Jonah's calming presence take over in my mind. He's good at this kind of thing, and somehow, he always knows what to say. I only hope that in this moment, I've learned enough from him to do the same.

Vianne doesn't say a word. She sniffles, peering out across the river, and wipes her nose with the flat of her hand. We both stand in silence as the soothing water trickles past our feet.

The chilly air prickles my arms, and I rub them to keep warm. It doesn't seem like Vianne is going to talk. But I can see something in her face, so I wait.

"It happened when I was fourteen," she says. She traces her thumb under her eyes, wiping away the tears. "We aren't the only ones that find people with abilities. Sometimes the government finds them too..."

My lips part, and my eyebrows turn upward, but I don't speak. Again, the rippling water fills the quiet, and I keep still, waiting for her to continue.

"My parents and I were living in this abandoned car park. Things were hard, but we were managing it fine. My dad was hoping to find others like us so we wouldn't be alone..." She blows air out between pursed lips. "The government likes to sweep isolated areas for trespassers, so we never stayed in one place for very long. But that night..."

Vianne closes her eyes.

"I woke up to their screams," she whispers. Fresh tears spill down her face, and she sips the air, the grief deepening in her brow. "They found us... and they sent in dogs."

My mouth opens in shock, and my eyes begin to water, but I dare not interrupt.

"My parents were screaming. I couldn't find them. It was so dark," she whimpers. "And when I got up, one of the dogs found me. And it started biting me—clawing at my face and neck, ripping my skin off. I remember pain—white, hot, blinding pain. I was screaming for my mom. I couldn't get away from it. I . . . I thought I was going to die."

Tears make their way into my open mouth, but I rub them away, transfixed on Vianne's beautiful, sorrow-filled face.

"And that's when it happened," she says. "My ability came for the first time. Right then and there. And I killed it . . . with my hands. I don't know how. I just remember this loud bang, and it stopped moving. It was lying on top of me, so I pushed it off, and its face . . ."

Vianne shudders. Her hands comb through her hair.

"It was deformed and bruised, like I had smashed its skull in with a club. But I had never even touched it. And I was bleeding—I couldn't see straight. I tried to go to find my parents. They were still screaming because the rest of the dogs . . ."

Her lips are trembling as she fights with her words.

"But I was terrified. It was like every muscle in me locked up, and I was stuck next to the dead dog, petrified. I couldn't move—no matter how much I tried. And I tried over and over again. They were dying, shrieking in agony, struggling for their lives. Then everything went quiet, and my parents . . . were dead."

She's crying now, red patches cropping up under her puffy eyes. I reach my hand out and place it gently on her back.

"So this will never be okay," she says, angry tears replacing her sad ones. Her tone deepens, and her hands curl up in fists. "I hide my scars because I'm a coward. I hide my scars to forget about that night. I hide my scars because all they do is remind me of the kind of world I live in and the kind of person I am. Who just sits there while their parents are torn to shreds? What kind of monster does that make me?"

She kicks out at the ground, scuffing the sole of her shoe in the mud. A pebble flies to the right and splashes into the water with a distinct plop.

"Vianne," I say, and my voice breaks. "I am so sorry."

"I deserve to look the way I do. I'm just too much of a coward to show everyone," she whispers. "The government took everything from me, and I did nothing. I *am* nothing."

I shake my head. "No. That's not true. If there's anything I've learned, it's that you can never let the government define who you are," I say. "You're not a coward, Vianne. The government did this—not you. You were just a kid ... *I* was just a kid. Don't let them define you because that's when they win. That's how they've won for a hundred years. They label us because we're different—bad blood, diseased. They name us, but you don't have to accept that."

"But I can't just forget," she says, turning to face me. She's furious. I can see it. "I can't take back what I did. I should have helped them. I should have done something!"

"You don't have to forget. This is part of who you are," I

say. "But don't let the pain of it keep you from being the best you can possibly be."

"I can't. I don't know how."

I nod, my brow furrowing. "I understand what that feels like. I did a really messed up thing, and I'm going to carry that with me for the rest of my life. But it's the choices I make *now* that define who I become—not what I did in the past."

Vianne's head falls to her chest, and her scars spread back across her features. "How could I ever wear these? Just look at me. I'm hideous."

"But you're not," I say. "Do you want to know what I see? I see someone who's doing an incredible thing to help a little boy who's just like us. You're making a difference—a real difference, and I think your parents would be proud of you. And you want to know the best part?"

She sniffles. "What's that?"

"When we rescue that kid, we're really going to piss off the government. And I can't wait."

She gives a dry laugh through her littered tears and looks at me with curious eyes. She wipes her face off with the sleeve of her sweater and shakes her hair out. It cascades over her shoulders, brightening back to teal, and her scars melt away.

"Just know that if you're ever ready to show them, I'll support you," I say, giving her a warm smile. "You're beautiful, scars and all. Don't let anyone ever tell you otherwise."

"You're different now," she says. "You've changed."

"Yes. I have."

"You're alright, Hollis. You know that?"

"Thanks," I say. I point back over my shoulder. "Are you ready to go back and help? We need your kick-ass powers."

She lets the smallest fraction of a grin slide. "I think I need a minute."

"Okay."

"And Hollis?"

"Yes?"

"Thanks for chasing me," she says. "No one's ever done that."

"What are friends for?"

She crinkles her nose, and we continue our banter. But as we gaze out beyond the river, my mind moves to the one task left. It's the only thing we've yet to achieve: finding that little boy in my memories.

I've never wanted anything so badly. As it stands, he's the only weapon against us, and if we can steal him away, then the government's means for removing the biomarker is gone. They'll have a blood test without insurance. I know more needs to be done to free people with powers, but this rescue operation is a major first step. It might just be the crack the system needs to start crumbling. There's a reason Area 19 houses the Capitol City's Testing Center—a reason they never taught us in school. That boy. We're going to find him. And when we do, we'll have started something bigger than all of us.

19

IT'S DAY TWENTY-FIVE OF MY PROBATIONARY PERIOD, AND once again Jonah, Rosalie, and I are pouring over my memories. I'm exhausted beyond belief. Every day I help train the team, and every day I fill my quota of firewood. If I keep this up for much longer, I'm going to burn out.

"Teleport yourself back," my misty figure commands.

Tiffany vanishes from the scene, and the woman towers over me, victory in her black eyes. "You've done the right thing, Hollis. I can see the pain you carry, but you don't need to suffer anymore. Two of my men have gone to get the boy, and then this nightmare will be over."

"Okay."

"It will be quick and painless. Easier than falling asleep. I promise."

I groan in frustration, kicking the dirt. I'm sick of this. I don't want to watch it anymore. I can't. There I am, standing in the middle of the clearing, transparent and shimmering in the sunlight. I'm waiting for the boy, thinking how great it's going to be to finally free myself of my power and go back home. I thought I was ending it by removing the beast, but it was only the beginning, and the tantalizing promise of my old life was nothing but a lie meant to find and destroy the only people who ever cared about me.

I turn away, unable to bear witness. Striding over to the tree line, I climb the boulder and take a seat, keeping my eyes averted from the scene. I thought we would have found him by now—that Jonah would have deduced the meaning of his gut instincts. He said he had a feeling, but this is turning into the most futile of endeavors. I don't want to give up, but maybe this was a lost cause all along. I just don't have the heart to say so . . .

"Jonah!"

Rosalie's flustered voice sends a shock wave through my body, and I slip from the boulder. I land on my feet just in time, but not before scraping my elbow against a jagged zigzag on the rock's face.

"What's wrong?" Jonah asks, alarmed.

"Stop the memory!"

Jonah pulls his hands apart, and everything freezes. She scampers up to the Chief Overseer, staring at her with wide eyes. Her mouth is askew.

"Rosalie, what is it?"

She bats her hands furiously, keeping her gaze glued on the woman. "Give me the memory," she says. "Give me control!"

Jonah obliges her with a flick of his wrist. Rosalie appears to catch an invisible object from mid-air. Her fingertips dance, the scene rewinds, and then it resumes.

"Teleport yourself back," my twin says again.

"Rosalie, what—" I begin.

"Shh!" She scolds, brandishing her hand like a sword.

"You've done the right thing, Hollis. I can see the pain you carry, but you don't need to suffer anymore. Two of my men have gone to get the boy, and then this nightmare will be over."

The woman wears her motherly facade.

"Okay."

"It will be quick and painless. Easier than falling asleep. I promise."

Rosalie's hands fly through the air, and the memory rewinds again. With a flick, it begins anew with my command to Tiffany. She's gaping at the woman, utterly transfixed on her face.

"She's thinking of him," Rosalie whispers. Her palms move again, and the lines replay. "Oh my God . . . she's thinking of him."

With a tug, Rosalie slides her hands apart to bring the woman into sharp focus. She splays her fingertips and pauses. Then, she walks straight up to the woman until she's less than a few inches from her.

Her hands snap and the memory continues, but now it's trained on the woman. I can hear my voice, but my misted counterpart is no longer standing in the clearing. Then, Rosalie gasps so violently that she almost topples over.

"Jonah!" She exclaims.

"What?" I say, looking between them. "What is it?"

"I know where he is! I know where the boy is!"

"What?" he says. "How?"

"The answers aren't in Hollis's memories. They never were." She points to the woman. "They're in hers."

A tense moment follows this, but I break it. "In hers? But how . . . how can you see hers?"

"I've never watched a set of memories this extensively," she replies. "I've never had to. But when the woman talks, I can see the room where they keep the boy. It's a memory within a memory." She rewinds the scene yet again, locking eyes with Jonah. "Here. Take it back. See for yourself."

Jonah's hands center at his chest, and he faces the Chief Overseer. His movements are fluid and calculated, and as the scene plays, his features light up with understanding.

"I can see it," he says. "He's on the top floor, but I'm not sure where."

"His nurse!" I say. "Move the memory ahead to the nurse."

"Excellent idea." Jonah motions his pointer finger, and the memory speeds forward. It halts as the boy enters the room.

"Further," I say, shaking my head. "When she takes him to leave."

The peppery mist lingers in the air, expanding and breathing like an animal as it zooms through the part with the golden light. The trees brighten as the boy's power shines, and with a jerk of motion, everything stops and then continues at a normal pace.

"Alright sweetheart. It's time to go," the nurse says.

"Here," I say. "Right here."

Jonah stops the memory and rewinds it. His fingers drum the air, and the section repeats.

"Alright sweetheart. It's time to go."

He steps back, aghast. "There's a thirteenth floor . . ."

"What?" I say, my mouth dropping open.

"The boy is on the thirteenth floor."

I shake my head. "But the floor plans never showed that."

"How clever of them," Rosalie muses.

"But how do we . . ." I trail off as something occurs to me. The panel in the lift: twelve silver buttons, and one perfectly polished white one standing out of place above the rest. "The white button in the lift!" I cry. "That must be the button for the thirteenth floor."

"We did it . . ." Rosalie breathes. "We found him."

The three of us look at each other in astonishment. The magnitude of what's just happened is crashing over us. We found him. Those three words reverberate in my mind, swelling into an anthem—a war cry against the government. This whole operation just turned from impossible to almost certain. The boy will be rescued.

"We did it," Jonah says. "Let's start again. Let's look at every facility worker. I want to get a clearer picture of this room. Rosalie, are you ready?"

"Oh, I'm ready."

And together, they throw their hands forward and my memories explode into the open expanse. The force of their combined power hits me like a shock wave and I brace myself, triumph in my heart. This is the moment we win.

"Ah, Miss Hollis Timewire. Big day."

"No kidding," I say under my breath.

■　■　■

The rest of the afternoon speeds by. We've pored over every shred of memory I own, and after four hours of intense review, Jonah has what he needs.

I peer up at the sky, noting the sun's position. "Jonah, I have to cut some wood," I say. "The sun won't be out for much longer, and I haven't even started."

He squints up at the tree line. "You're right. Rosalie, I think that's enough for today. You did remarkable work."

"I didn't know my ability could do that," she admits, rocking up on her toes.

"I didn't either."

"I guess your hunch was right," Rosalie says, nudging Jonah. "Who knew watching a memory that many times would do the trick."

Jonah smiles. "You have a whole new part of your ability to explore, young lady."

She wrinkles her nose. "That's a lot of memory watching."

"It is."

"You were amazing, Rosalie," I say, giving her a smile.

She beams at me, and with a wave over her shoulder, she starts back toward the dome. Her red hair bounces in step with her stride, and then she disappears into the forest.

I grab the axe, grimacing at the amount of work I need to do. Today went longer than I expected, but it was the best possible victory. I set a log up and chop it into fourths. It's muscle memory now. My body is strong and my hands have calluses. This kind of work hardly phases me anymore.

After what seems to be no time at all, the sun sets in the horizon, casting blue shadows across the clearing. Stars hang above us, glittering in the black sky. It's getting darker earlier now, and the moon's sliver wanes into the inky night.

"Hollis, it's time to call it," Jonah says. "I know you're not done, but that's okay. Let's go back to the dome. We've had a long day."

"Alright," I say. I yawn and stretch out my arms, rolling my shoulders out.

My grip on the axe tightens. I don't want to drop it. That wouldn't be good. Knowing my luck, I'd probably drop it on my foot or something...

I join Jonah as he slides off of the boulder.

"Ready?" he asks.

"Ready."

Darkness sweeps over the trees like the shadow of a bird's wing. I squint, trying to make out the path back to the compound. It's a new moon tonight, and visibility is low. All I can think about is getting a bowl of steaming vegetable soup. My mouth waters as we trudge along, and my stomach grumbles.

A thought occurs to me. I look down and laugh. "Jonah, I still have the axe. Hold on. Let me run and put it back."

"Alright," he says. "I'll wait here."

I jog back through the trees, keeping my vision sharp so that I don't trip over the uneven earth. When I make it back to the pile of wood, I lean the axe against its side and turn around to head back up the path. The stars provide just enough light for me to see a few feet ahead.

In the distance, a distinct thud causes me to halt in my tracks. My eyes strain through the near darkness, and my heart hammers against my chest. I take a few tentative steps, my ears on high alert.

"Jonah?" I call out.

The crickets chirp, playing out their medley, and my blood turns to ice.

"Jonah?"

Nothing.

The hairs on the back of my neck stand on end as I move further into the trees. Branches brush my arms and roots catch at my feet, and all the while, the silence pushes me closer and closer to panic.

"Jonah? Where are you?"

I emerge past two thick pines and they tower over me, blocking out the stars. I stand there peering around. I don't see him . . . My fear spikes as a crisp breeze tosses my hair. Where did he go? Why isn't he answering me? Something is not right . . .

Three hooded figures in black masks erupt from the trees, jumping onto me and arresting my arms. Before I can even gasp, a huge hand presses over my mouth, and I'm lifted from my feet.

I scream, but it's muted—completely muffled. I tear at the hands holding me, kicking out at my assailants with every muscle I possess. They stagger, and the one holding my upper body drops to his knees.

"Hold her!" someone snarls.

"I'm trying to!"

They lift me up again, dragging me through the trees. I'm fighting them tooth and nail, screaming and screaming, but I can barely hear myself. I sound faint—almost inconsequential against the ambient noise of the forest, and I'm suffocated by the hand pressed over my face.

I kick my right leg, hard, and the person holding it lurches backward, giving me just enough time to yank my ankle from his grip. I recoil and slam my foot into his jaw. His hands fly to his face, and he shrieks, but it's not enough to shake him. He grabs me again, vicious in his intent, his nails digging into my flesh.

We struggle through the pines, and my adrenaline-fraught attempts at freeing myself grow wilder. The sound of the riverhead thunders in my ears, and terror rips through me like a hot knife. They're dragging me downstream. I can hear the rushing of the rapids.

I let out a strangled yell, scraping at the arms around me and twisting my body. The grip over my mouth tightens. I can't breathe.

The group of three force me through the remaining stretch of wood, and as we emerge struggling onto the riverbed, the mud causes one of them to slip. Panic sends me into a frenzy. I flail, and my teeth sink into the hand covering my mouth.

I taste blood, and the attacker holding me from behind yelps, dropping me with a resounding thud. My hands slam into the rocky earth, and pain spasms up to my shoulders. Stars blind my vision.

"Somebody help me!" I screech, thrashing out at the other two.

My back scrapes against the ground as I'm yanked to my feet. And now a new set of hands clamps over my mouth, and a wad of cloth is shoved between my teeth. I bite down on thick fabric.

The group hauls me to the edge of an outcropping that hangs over the roaring rapids. The assailant holding me from behind pulls me close, his mouth an inch from my ear.

"Thought you could just get away with this?" he hisses, teeth bared. "Thought you could turn us in to the government, huh?"

I'm crying—yelling through the gag and struggling with everything I have, but my muted screams are inaudible over the torrent. The three push me further, forcing me to the bitter edge of the shelf. White water tosses itself menacingly, churning in the depths below.

"The Council should have executed you," he growls. "Nobody wants you here. You're a traitor."

I claw at the hand pressed over my mouth, hopelessly trying to pull it away.

"And traitors deserve to die!" he spits. "Push her over!"

With a tug, I'm thrown around, and I nearly topple over

the edge. But I'm vice-like upon their arms, clinging to them with all of my strength.

"Come on!" one of them shouts. "Get her over!"

"I'm trying!"

I gasp as my feet slip precariously on the rim.

"Push her over!"

My fists clamp down on their wrists, refusing to relinquish their grasp.

"Grab her hands and push her over!" he screeches.

Their fingers move to mine, prying them up one by one. I can't let go. If I let go, I'll die. My feet slide, and my grip begins to slacken. With a jerk, they wrench my hands up. I try to grab them again, but my sweaty palms can't find purchase. My fingertips scrape against rough fabric. I'm going to fall. I can't hold on any longer.

"HEY!"

A commanding voice booms from behind the group of masked figures.

In unison, the three of them turn their heads, and this gives me just enough time to pull myself away from the outcropping. My heart soars. I know that voice . . .

My assailants are pulled from me, toppling backward onto the rocky ground, and I fall to my knees in tandem. Caught by surprise, they attempt to stand, but not before they are knocked down with several powerful blows. Fist on flesh echoes through the night, and my rescuer attempts to snatch off one of the masks. At this, the trio scrambles up, running back through the thicket of trees and vanishing into the night.

"Cowards!" the newcomer yells after them.

I'm kneeling in the mud, trembling and terrified. I pull the wad of cloth from my mouth and look up into the face of my liberator.

"Keith!" I cry.

He grabs me and pulls me to my feet. I'm coughing and sputtering, unable to stand. I collapse into his arms, my knees buckling under me. Keith catches me and his strong hands hold me up.

"Are you okay?"

I can't find my voice. I clutch onto Keith's jacket, leaning my head against his chest. He hugs me, and for a moment, we stand in the darkness. I can feel his arms around me, warm and safe. But the distress of the situation returns as a thought assaults me: Jonah.

"C-can you h-help me?" I stammer, wide-eyed and quivering.

"Hollis, what is it?" he says, staring into my face.

"Jonah," I say. "Help m-me find h-him."

"Okay." He nods, keeping a firm support on me.

We make our way back through the hooded forest, and the shadows creep with our every step. Keith's arms are around me, guarding me. I'm wheezing, and my mind moves to the worst. Where is Jonah? Why didn't he answer me? What did they do to him?

"Jonah?" My throat constricts. I'm trying to keep from sobbing. "Jonah, w-where are you?" I'm beginning to worry as I strain my eyes along the ground. "Keith, do you see him?"

"Over there!" He points to a spot several yards off.

My eyes dart across the twig-strewn earth, where the crumpled form of a man lies still in the starlight.

"Jonah!" I scream, pulling myself from Keith's grasp and running to him. I drop to my knees beside him, and fresh tears spring to my eyes. I'm crying so hard that I can't see. Sobs rack my body as I lean over him. Salt and snot mix with my saliva, and a tingling sensation enters my face.

Keith's hand is on my shoulder. He presses his fingers up to Jonah's neck. A few seconds pass before he removes his hand.

"He's alive. I can feel a pulse. It's okay, Hollis. Jonah's alive."

20

"ORDER, PLEASE. ORDER!"

It's the middle of the night, and I'm bound to the wooden chair in the Council room. I face a sparsely populated semicircle of tired, old men. Libbie's enchanted wooden cuffs bite into my wrists. I look up at my captors, unable to breathe.

Eli Stone peers down at me with grim eyes, adjusting his cracked glasses. "We are here to address the events of an hour previous," he says. "And to discuss Miss Timewire's actions against Mr. Jonah Luxent. In addition, we will review her performance over the past twenty-five days and come to a verdict on her place here."

At this, the Council erupts into a chorus of chatter. Eli bangs his fist on the table.

"Order! I say order!"

I'm shaking in my restraints. My actions against Jonah? *My* actions? I flush with anger, seething at the injustice. After

Keith and I found Jonah, he woke Eli Stone, who promptly called an emergency meeting of the Council. They rushed Jonah into an alcove, asked Keith to help attend to him, and then arrested me on the spot—no questions asked.

"Miss Timewire," Mr. Stuart says, leaning over the table with disgust. "After all we've done for you? After giving you a second chance? Why have you assaulted Mr. Luxent?"

"I didn't! I would never attack him! There were three—"

"Jonah sustained blunt force trauma to the back of his head," Mr. Stuart says, cutting across me. "Perhaps, with the flat of an axe?"

"No!" I yell. "I didn't attack him! I put the axe back in the clearing and that's when I heard—"

"Do you have anyone to corroborate your story?"

"My story?" I repeat, aghast, raising my voice even higher now. "It's not a story. I'm telling you the truth!"

"Miss Timewire," Eli Stone says, holding a hand up. "Answer the question. Do you have anyone to corroborate your story?"

"Yes. Keith," I say. "When I was in the clearing, someone attacked Jonah, and when I went to investigate, they attacked *me*. There were three of them. They grabbed me and tried to push me into the river. And then Keith saved me."

A spattering of grunts moves around the room. At this, I expect to hear someone announce that they should bring Keith in to verify his account of the attack, but Mr. Stuart continues his questioning. He puffs his chest out.

"So, according to *you*, three of our own attacked Jonah and then tried to kill you?" he says, his eyebrows raised. "By pushing you into the river?"

"Yes! That's what I've been trying to tell you," I say, exasperated.

"Alright then, who attacked you?"

"I don't know. They wore masks. I couldn't see their faces."

A gruff voice from the back joins in. "How convenient."

My stomach writhes. It's Mr. Thomas. He clutches his mangled arm and stares at me with menace—as if he knew that this would happen all along.

"It seems to me that you've concocted a tale to save your own neck," Mr. Stuart continues.

"Concocted? I'm telling you the truth!" I say, looking around the semicircle. I twist my arms in the cuffs, straining against them. "Why don't you believe me? Just ask Keith. He'll tell you the same—"

"Miss Timewire, lower your voice," Eli Stone says.

"No!" I hurl my words at him, my brow wrinkling. "Lead Council, you will *not* silence me. I didn't attack Jonah! If you would just—"

"Miss Timewire!" he shouts above me, slamming his fist down. "You will stop yelling so we can proceed in an orderly manner!"

My heart rams itself against the inside of my chest, and Mr. Stuart takes the moment as an opportunity to jump in again.

"Were you and Jonah alone tonight?" he asks.

"Yes, we were."

"And do you not have access to the axe for your work assignment?"

"Yes, I do. But, sir—"

"Now, let's review your progress these past twenty-five days," he says, refusing to let me speak. He pulls a sheet of paper toward him with a malicious look in his eye. "Recently, the production of firewood has significantly dropped."

I shake my head in disbelief. "How does that have *anything* to do with what happened tonight? Jonah is hurt! *I* was almost—"

"Additionally, you have been spotted on several occasions wandering off through the dome without supervision, and—"

"I'm stacking the wood! I've never wandered—"

"—and on one particular occasion, you recklessly jumped into the river, endangering the lives of yourself, young Jamie Harvey, and Mr. Luxent—who, if I'm not mistaken, charged into the water after you."

"I saved that boy's life!" I cry. "Jamie fell into the river!"

"Didn't Mr. Luxent pull you and the boy out?"

"Yes, but that was only after—"

"I think I've heard enough," Mr. Stuart's voice surges over mine. "It seems clear to me that you've been reckless with your time here, and this incident with Mr. Luxent further proves your mental instability. It was a mistake to give you this probationary period."

My blood boils over, and hot rage intensifies my retort. "My mental instability?" I flail against the armrests of the chair. "I didn't do this! Jonah and I were attacked, and Keith was a witness! I'm not the criminal here, and if it weren't for your blatant vendetta against me, you'd see that."

Mr. Stuart looks as though he's been slapped in the face. "My vendetta against . . . ?" he sputters, clearly beside himself. His face turns a nasty shade of scarlet. "*You* are the reason we're here, Miss Timewire. Yet *again*."

"That's only because you arrested me before letting me speak. You dragged me here, and then proceeded to interrupt me at every turn," I say, teeth gritted.

"That's because you're a *liar*," he spits.

"Caleb—" Eli Stone interjects.

"I am *not* a liar!" I say, speaking over the lead Council member. "I have done nothing but the work required of me *every* day since my trial. I've done *nothing* to jeopardize my place with this community! And if Jonah were here, he'd say the same."

Just then, Keith bursts in through the doors of the Council room, and relief, like an overwhelming wave, floods me. He meets my gaze, and his mouth falls open. His eyes dart to my restraints, and then he marches past me—straight up to Eli Stone.

"Lead Council, there's been a misunderstanding."

"Young man," Mr. Stuart says. "What is the meaning of this?"

Keith ignores him. "Hollis was attacked by three people in the woods tonight."

Mr. Stuart cranes his head over his seat, glaring at Keith. "You have been quite helpful, but I demand that you leave at once. This hearing does not concern you."

Keith turns to Mr. Stuart with a piercing look and speaks with deliberate venom. "With all due respect sir, this hearing concerns me very much."

There's a few seconds of tension that follow this, and sweat collects on Mr. Stuart's forehead. Keith gives his attention back to Eli Stone and then points at me.

"Three people tried to push her into the river, and if I hadn't been there, Hollis wouldn't be tied to that chair, she'd be dead."

A hush falls over the Council, and curious eyes move from Keith to me. I'm breathless with parched lips, and my eyes begin to water. Do they believe me now?

"And you saw these... these so-called attackers?" Mr. Stuart asks, his tone tentative. He appears indignant that his proceedings have been interrupted.

"Yes. Three of them," Keith says. "But I didn't see their faces. They had masks."

"Did you see them attack Jonah as well?" the lead Council member asks.

"No, sir," he replies. "Hollis and I found Jonah lying on the ground. He was already unconscious. And if you still don't believe me, then call Rosalie Simmons in here and she can show you Hollis's memories."

My heart flutters with gratitude. Rosalie. How did I not think of that? Mr. Stuart's eyes widen, and his nose turns up. He runs a hand through his grey mane. His accusatory demeanor is deflating. "Yes, well I . . . I hardly think that's necessary."

"You can even have Rosalie pull up Jonah's memories," Keith adds.

"Mr. Luxent is indisposed," he quips.

"I'm quite aware of that," Keith says, equally as cold.

"Is Jonah okay?" I ask, straining in my seat.

Keith turns to me with a gentle nod. "Yes. He's going to be just fine."

I let out a whimper, bowing my head and closing my eyes. I just want this nightmare to be over. I'm spent. The bruising from my assault is starting to crop up across my arms and legs, and it aches to the bone.

"Well, I suppose—since you're a witness," Mr. Stuart begins. "I hardly think that looking over her memories is . . ."

"He's lying!" Mr. Thomas interjects. He stands to his feet and sticks his finger out at Keith. "He's lying to protect her. Fighting off three assailants? You're strong, boy, but not that strong."

"I caught them off guard, sir. The moment I went for their masks, they fled," he says. "There wasn't much of a fight."

Libbie Lizette stands as well, her mousy brown hair falling askew. "Mr. Thomas, I can't vouch for the girl, but I can certainly vouch for Mr. Keaton. His character is above reproach. But if you're absolutely opposed to his testimony then by all means, take his suggestion and call Rosalie Simmons to this hearing to see for yourself."

Mr. Thomas scowls, craning his bald head around as the rest of the panel looks to him. "I suppose . . . that it's not necessary." He folds himself up, sneering at me with his crooked teeth.

"Hollis didn't do this," Keith says. "She would never hurt Jonah. I'd stake my life on that." He walks over to me, placing a hand on the back of the chair. "Are the restraints really necessary?"

The lead Council member considers me for a second and then turns to Miss Lizette. "Libbie, will you release her?"

"Certainly." Her hands flower open and the cuffs slink back into the woodwork. I rub my wrists, sitting up and holding my arms close to my chest.

"Miss Timewire," Eli Stone says. "Due to Mr. Keaton's testimony and Mr. Luxent's absence, we will resume this hearing at a later time. We will return you to your cell, and you will remain there until such proceedings can be arranged. Libbie, will you escort Miss Timewire to her room? I think we'd all like to get some sleep."

Libbie dips her head. "Yes, lead Council."

"This meeting is adjourned," he announces.

Chairs scrape against the floorboards of the room. Disgruntled Council members stand, some stretching, some muttering under their breath. They move toward the exit, filing out in a single line. Libbie approaches me with a stern countenance.

"Miss Timewire, if you would follow me."

"Yes, ma'am," I whisper.

I fall in step behind her, and to my surprise, so does Keith. Neither of us speaks as we make our way from the Council room to my cell—the quiet is torture.

When we reach it, I pull the door open and shut it behind

me. Libbie's hands move in an arc, and the branches twist around the frame, sealing me in. She turns about, and without so much as another glance, she stalks off.

I grab the thin blanket and curl up on the cot. I never thought I'd feel this way, but I'm glad I'm locked in here. Knowing that my door is hopelessly twisted shut is the most comforting thing I possess. If I can't get out, then no one can get in.

Keith stands by the bars, peering at me with his tender, sky blue eyes. "Hollis, are you okay?"

I sit there unable to think. The only thing I can do is shake my head. I wrap the blanket around my shoulders and pull it tight, anchoring myself to something real as the buzz of thoughts crowds my mind.

I tuck my chin up on my knees, hugging myself. Three people tried to kill me. Did I really think things would get better? Over a hundred people are dead because of me. Was this fate's way of trying to bring about justice? Should I have died tonight?

It's as if Keith can read my thoughts, and his soft voice picks my head up. "You don't deserve to die, Hollis. I don't care what people say. You don't."

A tear slides down my face. I'm shivering, unable to keep the intensity of my emotions at bay.

"And what you're doing now," he says. "What you've been doing to help Jonah and the team . . . I think it's amazing. The rescue mission was your idea, right?"

I nod, sipping the air to stay calm, but tears keep trickling down my cheeks at a steady rate. I lock eyes with Keith, sniffling. "How . . . how did you find me?"

"I was upstream. I like to sit on the riverbed at night. It's where I go to think now. And . . . I heard you screaming for help."

I grasp the folds of the blanket between my fingers, feeling the soft fabric on my skin. If Keith wasn't there tonight, I'd be dead. It's as simple as that. And if he hadn't come to the Council room when he did, who knows what else I'd have been accused of. He was my protector—twice. I own him more than my life.

"Thank you," I whisper. It's all I can manage to say.

Keith leans his head against the bars and gives me a reassuring smile. His dark hair falls across his forehead, and his eyes meet mine. "Any time."

21

"HOLLIS, IT'S TIME," A SOFT VOICE SAYS.

My eyes flutter open. I'm tucked under my blanket, cocooned and wonderfully warm, but I sit up. Jonah is standing outside of my cell along with Libbie Lizette. I swing my feet off the cot and stuff them into my boots. The branches fall from the door with a swipe of Libbie's fingertips, and I emerge into the crisp morning.

It's been four days since the attack, and I'm on my way back to that dreadful room. But this time, it's of my own volition. I've requested this meeting. Today is the day I'm presenting the rescue mission to the Council.

The identities of the three attackers are still unknown. The day after the incident, Rosalie reviewed my memories. She also looked at Jonah's, but it was too dark to see anything useful. The black night mixed with the masks and the peppery nature of Rosalie's power didn't afford much clarity. So for the time being, the Council has recruited Rosalie to the investigation. But going through the memories of every person in the compound is no small task. It will take time to catch the people who did this.

I glance at Jonah to still the butterflies in my stomach as we trek across the dome. He gives me a nod of encouragement. I'm so glad he's okay. According to Keith, he regained consciousness shortly after my interrogation. Keith, after being asked to help attend to Jonah, wanted to check up on me. But when I wasn't in my cell, he figured I'd be in the Council room—which is why he burst through the door in the middle of the proceedings. He wanted to make sure I had someone on my side. I'm grateful to him. I don't know what I would have done otherwise.

I keep in step behind my teacher. After a few days of rest and recuperation, Jonah is doing quite well. He looks tired, but considering everything that's happened, I don't blame him.

Yes, my attackers are still out there, but never mind that. I'm under intense supervision now. I doubt they will have another opportunity to get to me. I almost died. Twice. So I'm fired up for this meeting. Jonah and I have talked everything through, and nothing is going to stop me.

The chilly morning air dances on my skin, and goosebumps flesh out across my arms and legs. Twigs crunch underfoot against the brittle ground. I rub my hands together, blowing into them to keep warm. Winter is falling fast, and I can't help but notice that Jonah has gloves. I wish I had gloves. Unfortunately, there weren't enough in the ready packs to go around. I pull my jacket tight, but its thin material isn't made for this kind of weather.

I push these thoughts away. I need to focus. Today is an important day. I must convince the Council to sanction a rescue mission, and I hope to show them that I *do* belong here, and I *am* on their side.

When we enter the Council room, no one speaks. Rosalie, Vianne, Keith, and Pierce are already there, standing to the side of the semicircle. The room is packed to capacity, all waiting for me.

I meet Eli Stone's dark eyes, and his cracked glasses slide down the bridge of his nose. He brushes a hand through his greying beard and then addresses the room. "Members of the Council, we are here today at the request of Miss Timewire and Mr. Luxent." He glances down at a piece of paper. "I was informed that you have something to propose to us? Is that correct?"

"Yes, sir," I say.

He gives me a stiff nod. "The floor is yours."

I walk to the center of the room, facing the semicircle. The wooden chair is pushed off to the side. I catch it out of the corner of my eye, and my stomach whirls. This is the first time I've been in here without restraints. Jonah gives me an encouraging nod, so I clear my throat and begin.

"One month ago, I went to the Area 19 Testing Center," I say. "And the government took away my ability."

Stern looks cast down on me from every angle, but I disregard them, gearing up for my statement.

"They took away my ability with the help of a little boy," I continue. "He has an incredible power, and a hundred years ago the government kidnapped him. Ever since then, they've been using him to get rid of people like us. The boy takes away the victim's power, and then the government kills them. The blood test. It's a process that almost took my life six months ago. It's the foundation of society. It's how people graduate from school. No biomarker? Then you have a job, a spouse, a home, and a life. Otherwise, it's death."

I take a deep breath, keeping my posture upright and my eyes forward.

"This little boy is one of us, and without him, the government has no weapon," I say with conviction. "So, I propose that we rescue him."

At this, the Council bursts into an uproar. Scattered voices fly around the panel—some incredulous, some downright angry—but I keep my expression unphased. Jonah told me that this would happen and that I shouldn't let it bother me.

"Yes, Miss Timewire," Eli Stone says, raising a hand to quiet the room. "We are aware that your ability was taken away by this boy, but I'm afraid that a rescue mission is out of the question. The logistics of attempting to break into a government facility are far too complex, and frankly, quite impossible under the circumstances."

Chatter breaks out again, and a pit forms in my stomach. I step forward, holding my head high. I raise my voice. "It's not impossible, lead Council."

The room dies down, and every eye falls on me.

He peers over the table. "I'm afraid it is."

"I believe you're wrong," I say.

Gasps come from the back of the panel at my gall. Mr. Stone's eyes widen beneath his spectacles. He leans forward, cocking his head to the side. "What is the meaning of this?"

"I can show you," I say. "And after my proposal is done, you can decide if it's impossible for yourself."

"Miss Timewire, perhaps I should have been more clear," he says, sitting back in his seat. "The answer is no."

"Jonah has selected a team of people to go on this mission," I begin. "And if you'll allow me to—"

"I'm not interested in the team of people Mr. Luxent has selected," he says, cutting me off. "He's in no position to—"

"You're not even letting her talk," Keith interjects. "With the utmost respect, sir. At least hear her out. You still have the authority to say no."

"Young man, you will hold your tongue," Mr. Stuart says.

I glance between Keith and Mr. Stuart, taking the fleeting lapse to begin speaking again. "For a hundred years, you've searched the globe for people with abilities and given them a home. You've rescued them from the world, and I'm not an exception. You gave me a place and a purpose, even when I couldn't see it—even when I didn't deserve it."

Mr. Stuart shakes his head. "Miss Timewire, this boy resides in a high-security government facility guarded, I am sure, with the best technology and security the world has to offer. The chances of pulling off a successful rescue are slim at best."

"Since when has our purpose changed?" I ask. "Isn't this exactly the kind of thing we should do?"

"This is not a matter of purpose," Eli Stone states.

"Of course it is," I say. "We know where someone with an ability is. It's that little boy, and he's at the Area 19 Testing Center on the thirteenth floor in a large, metal room where he's kept cryogenically frozen until he's called upon to take away someone's power. He's their weapon—not a person. No one deserves that."

"It would be reckless and dangerous," Mr. Stuart adds. "Not to mention that if anything were to go wrong, there would undoubtedly be loss of life."

"Why should this boy's circumstances change anything? He's one of us. He has an ability, and that should be reason enough for you to hear me out."

"It's not worth the risk."

"There are only a few hundred of us left!" I say, anger cropping up in my tone. "That's it. A few hundred. And that's on me. What happened back at the old compound was my fault, and I take full responsibility for my actions. But that shouldn't change what we're meant to do. If anything, I'd say that as a people, we're obligated to take the risk."

"Obligated?" the lead Council member repeats.

"Yes, obligated."

I'm not backing down. I stand there, determination bolstering my resolve. No one seems to have anything to say to this, but my eyes haven't left Eli Stone's. He's the one I need to listen.

"Very well, Miss Timewire. I'll humor you," he says. "How do you plan on breaking into the Capitol City's Testing Center?"

"Thank you, sir," I say, bowing my head. I turn to the left. "Vianne, if you will."

Vianne, Keith, Pierce, and Jonah all step forward, and with a flick of her fingertips, Vianne transforms the four of them into facility workers. Sharply sewn white scrubs blend with slicked back hairstyles—and they even wear blank stares to match. I smile to myself. Vianne has mastered this. They look flawless. It's almost chilling.

A surprised murmur trickles through the room.

"Vianne will transform the team into Testing Center employees," I say, walking across the panel. "And Pierce's ability will help them avoid any unnecessary interactions. With him, they'll be able to walk straight through the front doors. And from the extensive study of my memories, we know the boy's exact location—even down to the security measures they've taken to conceal him."

Everyone is watching me, rapt into my dialogue, so I forge ahead.

"Keith's ability will provide an easy means of escape, should they need one. And Jonah can double on any power," I say. "If the team needs more of a disguise, he can help Vianne, and if they need a little more suggestion to avoid workers, he can assist Pierce. And when—"

"You claim that the government is using this boy as a weapon," Mr. Thomas says, interrupting me with a toothy smirk. "How can we be certain of this? Considering your track record, you're aren't exactly reliable."

His patronizing smile boils my blood. Part of me knows that Mr. Thomas is only looking to get a reaction out of me, but I don't care. I'm done with this. If that's what he wants, that's what I'll give him. I glare across the room, speaking with spite.

"It's not a claim. It's a fact. The government took away my ability, and they've done this to countless others," I say, my eyes narrowing. "But you already knew that, didn't you? Because the Council's already seen my memories from that day. Mr. Stone requested it after my trial. Every one of you saw what I did. So, you can't seriously be asking me if the boy is being used as a weapon. Because that would mean that you're so incredibly stupid that you didn't understand what you watched. You saw the videos, you saw the twins, and you saw the man that murdered the little girl. I'm done being questioned about my past. And if you had any shred of decency at all, you'd stop wasting everyone's time."

Mr. Thomas's mouth drops open.

"How . . . how dare you speak to me like that." He cradles his injured arm, turning to Eli Stone. "Lead Council, are you going to let this blatant defiance for authority stand?"

My hands turn clammy. I've gone too far. Did I just ruin this because I can't keep my mouth shut?

Eli Stone raises an eyebrow, glancing between me and the piece of paper in front of him before saying, "Mr. Thomas, while Miss Timewire's cheek is distasteful, she is correct.

Questioning her about what we already know isn't helpful."

My lips part. Did he just—

"And Miss Timewire?" he adds.

"Yes, sir?"

"Watch your mouth."

"Yes, sir."

Mr. Thomas leans back, folding himself up with a murderous look. I catch Jonah's eye, and the smallest hint of a smile hides in the corner of his cheeks. That's all the approval I need. I continue my address.

"A hundred years ago, the girl was killed," I say. "But her brother is still alive, and he's been a prisoner all this time. If we rescue him, we'll be saving one of our own *and* dealing a serious blow to the government. Without him, the guise behind the Test doesn't exist. They can take people's blood, and they can detect the presence of the biomarker, but without the secret weapon, the government has no way of dealing with someone's ability. That's how I escaped. My power came before they could take it away. Don't you see? They claim they've won— that they've eradicated the Diseased Ones—but they've been hiding behind someone with an ability all this time. The government has taken enough of our lives. Let's do something about it. Let's take back what's rightfully ours."

I stand there, slightly breathless. I'm proud that I was able to articulate myself. No one from the panel has anything to say, and for a moment, I think I've convinced them. But Mr. Thomas stands, and his words shatter my resolve into a thousand pieces.

"The boy grabbed the man that killed his twin sister and took away his ability," he says. "You're right. I watched your memories. The kid was scared and under stress, and he did exactly what a scared kid would do. He reacted. He removed the man's power. So tell me something, girl. How do you propose to deal with this?"

I stare at him, my mouth askew. "I . . ."

"A rescue mission will cause the boy to become unstable, resulting in the removal of one or all of the abilities we send to him. What about that? Is he worth the abilities of the four people here?"

My tongue turns dry, and my palms begin to sweat. I brush the hair from my face, trying to come up with an answer.

"And Ashton Teel can't go on this mission because his ability is compromised," he says with a wicked grin. "Your little outburst in the common room made sure of that."

Mr. Thomas leers at me with triumph, relishing in his victory. He takes a seat and gestures to the rest of the panel. His glee makes my stomach twist. I stand there for a few seconds before turning to Jonah, but it seems that he is just as baffled as I am. How did we not think about this?

"Miss Timewire?" Eli Stone readjusts his glasses. "What do you have to say?"

"I . . . I don't . . ."

Several Council members shake their heads at one another, and the murmuring bristles back up. It rises in volume, framed by Mr. Thomas's horrible smile. My heart is sinking.

"Miss Timewire, I'm afraid that Mr. Thomas has a valid

point. I'm sorry, but this is too risky. You have made excellent strides. I can see all the work you've put in. Truly, I can. But we can't proceed. There is too much at stake. Not to mention additional exposure for our people if the rescue were to go wrong. The answer is no."

My hands fall limp to my sides, and I lower my head. How could I have missed this? In all our time with the memories, why did it never occur to me? Of course the boy can take away their powers, and then what? I try to keep my breathing even. I can't even bring myself to look up at them. I thought that I could finally make a difference, and I can't believe that after everything, it's all come to nothing—absolutely nothing. I've lost everything...

"I lost everything," I whisper, but the second I say the words, my heartbeat picks up, and a brilliant thought comes to me. "That's it! I've lost everything!"

The group appears perplexed at this, so I continue, too excited to remain still.

"Lead Council, I don't have my ability anymore! If I go on the rescue mission, then I'll be able to interact with the boy. And even if he does use his power on me, I can't lose my ability again. It's already gone."

At this, understanding blossoms across the room as well as an eruption of voices.

"Order!" Eli Stone shouts, banging a fist on the table.

"Miss Timewire," Mr. Stuart says. "You can't seriously believe we'd allow you to go on this mission. You're in our custody."

But now Jonah has stepped up, moving in front of me to address the panel. "And why not? Hollis is the perfect solution. She can be the buffer between our team and the boy. With her, we can accomplish the rescue without ever having to touch him. She knows the layout of the city and the Testing Center better than any of us. And she'll remain in *my* custody."

Mr. Thomas leaps to his feet, his eyes blazing. "This is crazy! She's a reckless individual who turned us in to the government and tried to kill you! She'll do it again!"

"Mr. Thomas," Jonah says, raising his voice in an alarming fashion. "You know very well that's a malicious lie. We have already cleared up the matter of the attack, and Hollis was found to be innocent. Now, if you will please keep your juvenile outbursts to yourself. I'd like to resume discussing this with the rest of the adults."

"I—how dare—I never," he sputters, seething.

"Hollis has displayed nothing but determination to fulfill her role here. She has repented of her actions and maintained the highest possible degree of integrity during her probationary period."

"Enough of this!" Eli Stone says. "Enough!" His wrinkled brow furrows. "Jonah, this is simply unprecedented. We can't. We don't have reason to."

"We have every reason to. Hollis has provided the Council with plenty of them."

"How will the team get there?"

"I'd like to request the military truck we salvaged from the wreckage of the compound. We can use the vehicle to drive to the Testing Center and back after we've secured the boy."

This idea is met with much protest as several Council members raise their fists. The noise in the room grows to an uncomfortable level until Mr. Stone demands everyone's silence again.

"Friends, when did we become like this?" Jonah asks. "Why are we afraid to do what is right? We have stood firm against the government time and time again. When did that change? Why did that change? Because of our circumstances? This boy is suffering at the hands of a cruel institution, and if we can end that, shouldn't we?"

Curious and pondering eyes follow Jonah as he paces the length of the room.

"I know there is risk involved. In all our rescues, we've never attempted a break-in—even when Hollis failed her Test—but in that moment, we considered it. Why? Because Hollis is one of us. She bore the disdain of history simply for having the biomarker. And if we do nothing to help this boy, we are condemning him to a life of imprisonment. We shouldn't do nothing if we have the ability to do something. Hasn't that been our mindset since the beginning?"

He pauses, holding his arms out with his palms extended toward the ceiling. Deep conviction settles in his brow.

"Friends, please consider what this would mean. As Hollis said earlier, if we do this, the entire facade of the Test will crumble. As it stands, they have the technology to find the biomarker and the means to eradicate it. What if we took their means? One boy carrying the weight of society on his back—

unseen and hidden away. This could be our chance. We've never planned an act of open rebellion against the government. We chose to hide and to help others like us—and that was the best possible choice. It preserved our species. But I believe the time for passivity is over. We need to take an active role in our own destiny, and rescuing this boy is the first step. Let's be brave enough to do what needs to be done. Let's reclaim what's rightfully ours, and continue the fight. And maybe one day, we truly can end this."

Eli Stone sits back in his chair. He leans over to Mr. Stuart, and the two of them exchange hushed words. Something is happening, and my heart leaps. I hold my breath, waiting in earnest for them to speak. It's so quiet that any movement at all would thunder through the space.

Mr. Stone adjusts his glasses and clears his throat. "Let's put this to a vote, shall we? All those in favor of the rescue attempt, please raise your hand."

I chew on the inside of my cheek, clasping my sweaty hands together behind my back. I'm pulled into the moment, peering around the semicircle with eagle eyes. Please. It's all I can think over and over again in my brain. Please. Please . . .

And then, as if someone flipped a switch, hands spring up one by one. They join together like a victory waltz, and as I scan the room, I count every one—every single one. Adrenaline kick starts my body, and the biggest grin spreads over my face.

We're starting the revolution.

22

THE MORNING OF THE RESCUE MISSION COMES WITH
nauseating nerves.

I get up and eat a hasty breakfast with the team. The sun
isn't up yet. We sit around the firepit, and the scrape of utensils
replace our words. The steaming lentil stew isn't appealing, but I
force myself to finish it. The crisp forest air seems heavier today.
I can see it in everyone's face. We are about to do something that
no one has ever done before—and we have to do it perfectly.

My stomach feels worse than it did before the Test, and my
dreams didn't help. They were a mix of nightmare upon
nightmare: hands holding me down, a mob throwing me into
the rapids, the boy lost, my friends dying, and the rattling blue
orb from the forest attacking me with painful shocks of
electricity. To be awake, even on this day, is a blessing. I remind
myself that our meticulous training is done, the plans are set,
and this is it.

Today I help change the world.

It's ironic that the last phrase of the pledge is on my mind. Back then, I thought becoming a society member was the highest honor. I thought passing a blood test made me valuable, but I was never meant to be a cog in the machine. My destiny is wrapped up in that last phrase. I just didn't know it at the time.

After our meal, we grab the supply packs and start hiking up the trail to the salvaged military truck. My breath comes out in puffs, visible in the chill of the morning. I adjust the strap slung over my shoulder so that it doesn't dig into my skin.

Keith walks by my side. His hand keeps brushing mine, like he wants to take hold of it, but he doesn't. I wish he would. It would calm my butterflies and tell me what I'm desperately longing to know. Ever since Jonah and I were attacked, Keith's been talking to me, and sometimes it feels just as wonderful as it did back at the old compound, but I'm too scared to make the first move. I can't mess this up again, and thinking about it is driving me crazy. It's not the right time. But I keep lingering on his fingertips as they sway an inch from mine.

Half an hour later, we reach the military truck, huffing and cold. Keith's ruddy cheeks and Vianne's pink nose glisten in the rising sun. Pierce and Jonah are the only ones who look warm. They have gloves.

I blow into my hands, rubbing them back and forth as Jonah pulls open the rear door of the vehicle. He ruffles in the folds of a duffle bag, withdrawing a large map. He spreads it open on the trunk, and the four of us gather around him. A gust of wind catches the corner, and Jonah grabs a couple of rocks to weigh it down.

"The Area 19 Testing Center is 327 miles north of this section of the forest," he says, tracing his finger across the map. "I don't know how fast this thing can go, but I'm hoping we can make it to the outer edge of the city by midday. After that, we'll walk to the Testing Center." He looks up at the group. "Are we ready?"

All of us nod, murmuring indistinct phrases under our breaths. I'm sick with anxiety. I tuck my hands under my armpits in the bitter cold. I'm shivering so much that I almost lose my balance as I climb into the truck.

Inside, there are two benches. They face each other instead of the front of the vehicle, giving the truck a fair amount of floor space. As everyone piles in, Vianne and Pierce sit across from me and Keith.

"Jonah, how does this thing run?" Vianne asks.

"Solar power." He jumps into the driver's seat and slams the door, frightening a yellow warbler into flight a few yards off. "Everyone in?" he asks, peering back over his shoulder.

"Yes," Keith answers. "Pierce, can you get the side door?"

Pierce grabs the inside handle of the slider and pulls the vehicle shut. I sit there, hugging myself and clenching my jaw tight to keep my teeth from chattering.

"Here," Keith says, putting his arm around me.

My butterflies spring into a dance. "Thanks."

The truck comes to life and jerks forward, sending us sliding in our seats. I grab onto Keith so I don't fall.

"Sorry," Jonah calls out. "I'm a little rusty. I haven't driven in . . . well, I haven't driven much."

"You've driven before?" Keith asks.

"Once," he says.

"Really? When?"

"A few weeks back. The Council sent a group to salvage what we could find from the wreckage of the compound, and they returned with the truck. I couldn't resist. I always wanted to learn how to drive. I figured it was time, so I tinkered around with it."

I smile, imagining Jonah out on a joy ride.

Vianne shifts herself to look up front. "How are you going to drive this through the trees?"

"Libbie maneuvered a path with her ability when we brought the truck back from the old compound," Jonah says. "We'll just follow the gaps in the forest. I've mapped it out."

The vehicle bounces over the ground, hitting roots and rocks, so I lean back in my seat. Keith's arm is still around me. It's wonderful and warm. I'm happy he finally initiated. I catch Vianne's encouraging smile. She's noticed us and tries to pass off an under-the-radar, flirty look. I shake my head, glancing off to the side with my eyes.

She grins, her hair shimmering to an icy white. It's amazing how much her command of color has changed over the past few weeks. There's budding confidence in her. Our conversation by the river made a difference. She wears determination like a cloak now, and it's inspiring.

"You're going to do great," I say.

She nudges my boot with the toe of her shoe. "*We're* going to do great."

The front tire hits an uneven rut, and we bounce toward the ceiling. I imagine that this is what it feels like to be on a kiddy ride from an old-fashioned amusement park. I picture the roller coasters from my school textbooks. I always thought they were odd.

"Once we're out of the trees, we'll see how fast this thing goes," Jonah calls out. "It shouldn't be too long."

But getting out of the forest proves to be an arduous task. Libbie left very little space between the trunks. It's just enough to clear the truck, and Jonah moves it at a crawl. Each turn is slow and painstaking, and after two hours of bobbing along, we emerge into the open expanse.

It stretches for miles. I look through the front window, staring out at the desolate plain. Besides the outline of the compound's wreckage in the distance, it's barren.

"Alright everyone. Hold on!" Jonah shouts. "Let's see what she can do."

I grip the edge of my seat as we lurch forward. With a burst, the military truck explodes across the ground, and my stomach flips over. The increase in speed is formidable. The terrain blurs by us, and the forest shrinks, growing smaller and smaller until it's a green line in the distance.

"How fast are we going?" I ask.

Jonah taps his hand against the wheel. "A hundred and forty miles per hour."

Keith's face screws up in concentration, and he counts on

his fingertips. "That means we should be there in a little over two hours."

My nerves are back, firing like hot pokers and searing my insides. I keep hold of Keith's arm as my mind zips through a host of thoughts. We can do this. We're going to be fine. We've scrutinized it from all angles, and everything is going to be okay. It has to be.

The truck lurches again, charging forward across the ground. I'm surprised it's working so well after the bombing. The government left little behind that night, and today we're striking back.

We don't speak much after this. The somber mood from earlier fills our group to the brim. Considering the gravity of the situation, small talk seems pointless. Soon we'll be at the city limit. Soon we'll walk through the doors of the Testing Center. Soon . . .

The truck decelerates, snapping me out of it. I look up from my lap, craning my head around to see through the window. "We're here already?"

"Yes," Keith says.

I brace myself against the seat as the vehicle glides to a stop. It springs over a deep rut in the earth, and my feet scrape against the heavy-duty plastic flooring. The four of us look at each other, and something seals. We're in this together. We've got each other's backs. We can do this.

Jonah exits the driver's side, walks around the vehicle, and pulls open the slider. It thuds against its hinges, and we pile out into the grey afternoon. Dark clouds obscure the sun, stretching for miles in every direction. We're out in the open, but far enough away from the city to remain innocuous. Even if someone were to see the truck, it would be a black speck in the distance. It's safer for us to walk from here.

"Vianne, let's transform everyone," Jonah says, moving to her side.

"Okay."

In unison, they raise their hands, and white scrubs snap against my skin. My hair pulls itself into a bun, lengthening and twisting up, and after a few seconds, our group stands together as facility workers. Vianne's work is flawless.

The wind picks up, tossing dust around us, and its chill digs down to the bone. I hug myself, watching the city's edge. Its dark outline rises up against the colorless sky. I swallow the knot in my throat. It's strange to come back to my old home. I thought I would feel sad, but I feel nothing but disgust. What I had here wasn't a life. It was cold and unfeeling oppression driven by power.

Jonah approaches me. "I'm going to change some of your facial features," he says. "I don't want anyone to recognize you."

I nod, shivering in the wind. Jonah's hands move delicately, hovering over my nose. My face begins to tingle, and a warm sensation spreads from between my eyes. It travels down to my lips, and my skin stretches.

"There," he says, backing up and tilting his head to the side. "Perfect."

"How do I look?"

"Older." Jonah surveys the group. "Everyone ready?"

"Ready."

And with that, the five of us begin to march.

"No emotion," I call out over the gusts. "None at all. Remember what we talked about. Keep your face blank. Relax every muscle. It's easier that way. Everything you do has to be controlled and perfect. Every word. Every action. And think twice before you say or do anything."

The sky continues to darken, and even though it's high noon, the weather has taken a turn for the worst. A storm is brewing over the tall buildings in the distance. The sunshine from this morning feels like it's a million miles away.

"And no touch," I continue. "None. And if we pass anyone on the streets, don't look at them. You're not supposed to."

We continue our trek through the barren wasteland, and ten minutes later, we arrive at the flanks of the outer block. The smooth street is deserted. Boxy housing units span the length of the pavement, cut neatly into place against the muted sky.

There's no wall to fortify the outskirts. I smirk. With all the government's might, they never considered the possibility of a band of Diseased Ones walking right in. Why build a barrier when you have the world convinced there's no danger?

I look back at our group. "Follow me, and remember, absolutely no emotion."

I turn from them, dropping my expression back to the mindless drone I was raised to be. Years of practice makes it easy. My face is void of anything—absolutely perfect. My mother would be proud.

We walk down the empty streets at a brisk pace. In the distance, a street transit stop flashes with advertisements. The pictures cycle through, buoyed by their pitch lines:

Sit better with **ErgoBack!**

Have you considered **Sleepmax**?

Get the latest **Holo-Tablet**.

Does your **Smart Vacuum** need an upgrade?

What's next for **Presto-Fold**?

I'm reminded of my citizen's card splashed across the screens for all to see. The Testing Center isn't far from here— my housing unit too. Are my parents home? Do they still think about me? Do they believe I'm a terrorist because President Alvaro Camille named me the leader of the second Terror War? If only they could see me now. If only they knew . . .

I shiver. The breeze of the brewing storm picks up leaves around the sidewalk. Just ahead, a burly man in a dark blue jacket strolls along, and my heart kick starts my body, flooding it with a deep desire for caution. He's walking toward our group on the same side of the pavement.

"Pierce," I say, keeping my voice low.

The man is only a few yards off. Pierce moves directly behind me, and with a twitch of his pointer finger, the deed is done. The man stops, scratches his head, and looks across the street. He turns to the left and the right, checking for vehicles. Then, he scurries off.

I breathe a sigh of relief, keeping my posture and face collected. We round the next block, and together, my four companions and I raise our heads to gaze upon the towering heights of the Area 19 Testing Center. It looms under the dark clouds, overshadowing the city. Its marble grandeur and glass architecture taunt me. I'm back, but this time I've shed my delusions. Society's symbol for purity and worth means nothing to me now. I'm here to steal their secret weapon.

With determination in my heart, I start the climb up the steps. At long last, after days of deliberation, hours of pouring over my memories, and many sleepless nights, we're standing at the entrance. The doors are before us. I look back over my shoulder, checking each face to ensure perfection. Then, with trembling fingertips, I take hold of the ornate handles and pull the doors open.

There's no turning back now.

23

Our footsteps interrupt the quiet of the lobby. The safety of the forest is gone. It's real now.

We walk into the foyer, keeping close together. The receptionist perks her head up and scans over the five of us. Her chestnut hair gleams in the synthetic lighting framed by the red pen tucked behind her ear. She opens her mouth, but Pierce's hand moves, and her eyes light up with surprise.

"Oh!" she squeaks, turning from us to rummage in a large file folder. She ducks under the desk, pulling open several drawers—no doubt searching for some important document that needs attention.

Just ahead, a heavy-set man in a white suit approaches the lift carrying a briefcase and tablet.

"We need his fingerprints," I murmur. "Let's go."

I glance back at the desk, but the receptionist is still busy at work, delving through the contents of a box. The group follows me as I walk straight up to the man. His stance shifts, and his face displays a near imperceptible amount of concern.

"May I help you?" he asks.

My nerves spike. It's the man who drove me to my Test. I nearly lose my composure, but Jonah steps in front of me, his hand splayed open at his side. "We're waiting for the lift."

It's as if Jonah cast a spell. Calm overcomes his features, and he nods. "Oh. Of course. Allow me."

He adjusts his grip on the handle of the briefcase and presses the button on the wall. We stand back, waiting for the doors to open. With a click, the lift admits us, and our odd group files in. It shuts, and the soft musical voice issues from overhead.

"Identification please."

The man places his thumb on the bioscanner above the button panel, and it flashes.

"Identification verified."

He goes to press the button for the fifth floor, but Pierce's fingertips shudder, overtaking him with his ability. "To the thirteenth floor, please."

The man scratches his chin, staring at the panel with wide eyes. After a few seconds of this he says, "Ah yes. That's right. The white button." He pushes it with his stubby forefinger.

"Identification please," the voice chimes.

"Pesky lift." He scans his thumb again, tapping his foot against the metal trim.

"Identification verified."

The lift zooms up, and I grab the handrail, keeping my eyes

averted and my posture closed off. Even with my facial reconstruction, I can't run the risk of him recognizing me. The ride only takes fifteen seconds, and then the doors slide open.

The five of us file out. The man clears his throat, appearing to scold himself, and my heart jumps out of my chest. But Pierce's palm is still facing him.

"I need to get to the fifth floor," he announces, troubled. "I'm very late. If you will excuse me."

He jams his thumb over the panel and the doors close, taking him from our sight.

The ambiance of the hall ahead is chilling. No sound. No color. No furnishings. No doors. I don't even want to breathe. There's an eerie lack of any stimulus at all. For a moment, none of us move. We simply stare into the void of the white corridor.

"This way," Jonah whispers, moving to the front. "His room is all the way at the end."

We begin down the hall, but we don't get far before Vianne's spooked voice stops us in our tracks. "What is that?" She points ahead.

I didn't notice it at first, but a faint, cream-colored substance lies along the tiles a few yards from us. It looks as though someone spread white tar in a thick line around the floor, walls, and ceiling. Its outline forms a large ring—almost like a portal—with no way around it.

"It looks like some kind of rubber adhesive," Keith says.

"Careful. Don't touch it," I say.

We approach the ring cautiously, peering through it to the hall beyond.

"We have to step through it," Vianne says.

"Wait." Keith holds his arm out. "Just wait. This could set off an alarm."

Jonah exams the left wall, tracing his fingers along the white tar outline. Then he moves to the right wall and repeats the process. He steps back, putting a hand to his chin. "I think it's a sealant for some kind of door."

"A door?" I repeat. "But there's nothing there. It's just a ring."

"What do we do?" Pierce asks.

"There doesn't seem to be a tripping mechanism, and there's no place for a fingerprint scan. I don't think crossing it will do anything."

Fear jumps down my throat. "Jonah, wait."

"Hollis, it's okay," he says.

I hold my breath as his foot hovers over the threshold. He crosses the line, stepping over the adhesive. I look up, half expecting shrill alarms to pierce my eardrums, but nothing happens. I breathe a sigh of relief.

"Let's go," Jonah says. "Quickly now."

At Jonah's words, the four of us cross through the white tar ring, moving further down the hall. I steal one last glance at it, and a pit forms in my stomach. Something doesn't feel right, but I shake it off and force my attention ahead. We're almost there.

The hallway is expanding now, growing wider with every step. At its end, it arcs to the right, and as we round the corner, we come face to face with an armed facility worker. A machine gun is slung over his chest, and he's standing in front of an enormous metal door.

He looks at us with curious eyes, and then something more sinister falls across his features. To my horror, his gun begins to move. Jonah and Pierce step in front of us, raising their hands simultaneously and advancing on the man.

"You don't want to do that," Pierce says, his hand in the man's face. "Just open the door. The Chief Overseer has requested the boy. We were sent to fetch him."

Half dazed, he lowers his gun and places his hand to the center of the door. He holds it there for five seconds. The scrape of deadbolts sliding out of place sets my teeth on edge.

"Access granted," the automated female voice says.

With a rush of decompressed air, the huge metal door lifts straight up, folding itself into the ceiling with slow, mechanical clicks.

Pierce grabs the man's weapon and strikes him in the face with the butt of it. I gasp as the worker crumples to the floor. Pierce slides his gun away from him with the tip of his boot. "Let's be quick about this," he says gruffly.

"Okay Hollis, let's go get him," Jonah says. "The rest of you stay out here. Pierce, keep that guard down. We'll be out in a minute. And remember, no one but Hollis is to touch the boy. We don't want any accidents."

Jonah and I lock eyes, and without hesitation, we enter the room. It's dark and covered in plastic. A coffin-like, glass chamber protrudes from the back wall with a flat control module hooked up to it. It's lined with buttons, each backlit and shining like a beacon.

"There he is," I breathe.

I approach the chamber, peering within. The boy's eyes are shut and his arms are crossed. His skin, perfectly preserved, is frosted over with ice. He looks peaceful, like he's imagining a wonderful fantasy.

My eyes dart over the buttons on the module, running through the dozens of labels on its surface. "Revive," I say, turning to Jonah. "This button says 'Revive.'"

Jonah's brow furrows as he examines the options. "That's got to be it."

"Okay," I say. "Here goes."

Heart pounding, with sweat collecting on my brow, I press 'Revive.' Hissing issues from the panel, and I jump back. It lights up and a display appears in the upper righthand corner with a timer.

"Revive initiated," the female voice chimes. "Please wait."

"Three minutes," I say, glancing from the panel to the open door. Keith, Vianne, and Pierce are huddled together, all peering within, but remaining where Jonah asked them to stay.

My head is starting to spin.

2:47 . . .

We're going to do this. We're going to pull this off. We have to.

2:17 . . .

I grab the folds of my jacket to wipe off my sweaty hands.

2:00 . . .

The blaring red numbers tick down with agonizing beats.

1:38 . . .

We're going to rescue him.

0:47 . . .

He's almost here.

"Ten seconds," I say, unable to take my attention away from the screen.

Then, with a loud pop, the chamber opens, and white fog floods into the room. It's cold on my skin, skittering past my ankles and dissipating over the plastic. Jonah backs away, and the little boy sits up, blinking in the dim light.

I step forward, peering in, and the boy's blue eyes find my hazel ones.

"Hi," I say, speaking softly. "My name is Hollis. Do you remember me?"

He angles his head to the side, and then nods slowly, clasping his tiny hands together.

"What's your name?" I ask.

"I'm Maddy." His sweet voice carries up to the ceiling. He's staring at me intently, and his fingers move to my cheeks. He holds my face in his hands, studying me.

"Oh," I say, caught off guard by this. "Hi Maddy."

"You're not my nurse," he says, giggling.

"No, I'm not your nurse."

"Are you going to take me to someone so I can use the golden light?" he asks, removing his hands from my face and tucking himself up into a ball. He rocks back and forth playfully.

"No," I say. "I'm going to take you to meet some very

special people. These people can do things like you can."

At this, his whole demeanor brightens. "They can use the golden light too?"

I smile. "No, not the golden light. But they can do other wonderful things, and they would like to meet you."

"They would?" He leans forward with innocent eyes.

"They would," I say. "I'm going to bring you to them. Can you take my hand?"

I extend my arm to him, but Maddy pauses, rubbing the top of his head. Something ignites behind his features, and he stares at me.

"You're the girl," he whispers, transfixed. "They told me you were special."

"I . . . Yes, I am the girl," I say. I hold my hand out again. "Maddy, will you come with me?"

He puts his cold hand in mine. My fingers close around his, warming him, and I help him down from the chamber. I look to Jonah, a sad smile flickering across my lips.

"Let's go," I say. "Jonah, you first. I'll follow."

"Okay." He walks back through the room, crossing over the threshold to join the trio in the hall. The moment he leaves, the automated voice comes alive.

"Exit identification required."

I stop dead in my tracks, grasping Maddy's hand. Adrenaline shoots into me, and blinding panic chokes my senses.

"Exit identification required," the voice repeats.

"Jonah . . ."

"Exit identification required."

"Grab the guard!" I cry, looking to Pierce. "Put his hand to the panel! Hurry!"

I pull Maddy through the door, backing away from the interior, but the moment we're clear of the room, the halls explode with shrill alarms. Lights flare up across the entire ceiling, and the large metal door to Maddy's room begins to close. It's too late . . .

"We have to move!" Jonah shouts.

Maddy screeches, clapping his hands over his ears. His face contorts, and he begins to cry.

"The white ring down the hall!" Vianne screeches. "It's a door! It's closing!"

My body douses itself in adrenaline. I'm vice-like upon Maddy's arm. "Go!" I cry. "Everyone ahead of me. Now!"

The group hurls down the hall, charging toward the ring. It's closing from above. A thick pane of glass is descending down to the floor below.

I grip Maddy, running with all my might, but with a sudden jerk, my hand is pulled from his. I fly forward, smacking my wrists against the tile. Maddy has stopped running. He's standing still as if in shock, a terrified look on his face.

"Maddy!" I scream, launching myself up and running back to him. I try to pick him up, but he fights me, squirming himself out of my grasp with a surprising amount of strength. I pull at his arm, trying to coax him forward. "Maddy, we have to run!"

My sweaty hands slip, and I stumble to my knees.

"Hollis! The door!" Keith yells. "Hurry!"

A moment later, Jonah is at my side. He pulls me to my feet and pushes me forward. "Go!" he roars. "I've got Maddy. Go!"

With only seconds left, I obey. Running with every fiber of my being, I sprint down the remaining strength of hall. The glass is sliding down, certain in its end. Vianne, Keith, and Pierce are already on the other side, waving their hands and screaming at us.

With a burst of speed, I dive under the door, sliding a little and landing on my hands and knees. I can feel Maddy at my back, pushed under at the last moment. His tiny frame lands on mine, and I'm flattened by his weight.

The loud hiss of the glass seals behind me, thundering over the alarms. We made it. I can't believe it. We actually made it.

I stand to my feet, keen to keep moving. The military men will be here any minute. But my companions stop me in my tracks. Their mouths are parted. Vianne's hand is to her face, Keith's brow has turned upward, and Pierce's usual stoicism is sobered.

"What is it?"

But the instant I turn around, I understand, and my heart shatters into a thousand pieces like it's on fire. Jonah is standing trapped on the other side of the door, his palm resting gently against its surface.

"No . . ." Tingling enters my face and knees. I shake my head, running to the door and pushing my hands against the glass. I try to lift it up, but it won't budge. "No!"

I slam my fist against it, and pain shoots up to my elbow.

"Hollis . . ." Keith's soft voice issues from behind me.

"There has to be a way to open this door!" I shriek. "No!"

I'm shaking—barely able to keep myself upright. I push at the glass again, desperately trying to pry it up. I strike at it with my fists.

"Isn't anyone going to help me?" I cry. "Help me open the door! Please!"

I hit the glass again, turning to my friends with a wild look.

"Hollis," Keith says, approaching me and taking hold of my shoulder. He's shaking and his face is white. "The door isn't going to open. We have to go. We've triggered the alarms. The military men are going to be here any—"

"No!" I push his hand away, redoubling my efforts. "Jonah!"

I meet Jonah's eyes. I can see his tired expression—as if he had accomplished a wonderful work. I stare at him, holding my palm up against the glass across from his. He studies my face and smiles, giving me the most loving look—one that says he's proud of me and of who I've become. We stand facing one another for a few moments longer. He bows his head, and then removes his hand from the door, turning away from me to walk back up the hall.

"No! Jonah, no!" I hit the glass over and over again. "Please!"

"Hollis, we have to go," Keith says, pulling at me, but I shake him off.

"Jonah!" I sob, pressing myself against the door. I sink to my knees.

Keith's strong hands are around my waist. I flail in his grip, but he doesn't relinquish it. "We have to go. I'm so sorry, Hollis, but we have to move."

"No!"

"If we don't leave now, then we'll all die," he says, his tone constricting. Tears have wetted his cheeks. "Don't let Jonah's sacrifice be in vain. We have to go. Right now." Keith's hands are on my face, and he pulls my forehead against his own. "You can't fall apart right now. You have to be strong. Do you understand? You have to do this. Okay?"

I clutch onto his arms. I'm shaking so much that my chest is heaving.

"You can do this," Keith says.

I grit my teeth, trying to gain control of my legs. Keith's right. We have seconds left. If we don't leave now, we'll die. I pull away from him, and take hold of Maddy's hand, looking into his frightened face and choking back a sob.

"Let's go," I say.

And with one last glance at Jonah's retreating back, I plunge down the hallway, leaving him behind.

24

"THIS WAY!"

Vianne halts at the doors of the lift, slamming her hand against the wall.

"Not the lift!" Keith shouts. "We don't have fingerprints. This way." He darts off down a small corridor to the right, and Pierce follows.

"Where does this go?" Vianne asks.

"No idea."

Maddy and I follow at the rear. I'm breathing so hard that the stitch in my chest is nearly unbearable.

An eruption of noise echoes from behind us as the lift clatters open. Military men with machine guns fly from the doors. They move in a straight line, running down the hall toward the white tar ring where Jonah stands trapped.

My tears are starting to dry on my face. I'm holding myself together with everything I've got. I'm numb with grief, but

we're getting out of here if it's the last thing I do. Keith's right.
I can't fall apart now.

Maddy is shaking, so I scoop him up in my arms. I have so
much adrenaline that he doesn't feel heavy. We pelt down the
remaining stretch of tile to the base of an ascending staircase. I
grab the railing and scramble up the steps. A heavy metal door
is straight ahead, and Keith reaches it first.

He smashes his hand against the push bar, and the door juts
open to reveal a dark and stormy sky. We've reached the
rooftop of the Area 19 Testing Center. Pierce and Vianne spill
out after Keith, nearly knocking him over. Men are shouting
from the hall beyond. They've spotted us.

"There they are!"

I leap up the last step, lunging through the door into the icy
wind. It whips around us with force, and I stumble.

"They're coming!" I scream, and Pierce and Keith push the
door closed and lean against it to hold it in place.

"We're trapped!" Vianne says, her hands to her forehead.
She walks in circles, a wild look on her porcelain face.

Pounding shakes the door on its hinges. The military men
are here. Pierce and Keith strain against the metal to keep it
shut, and Vianne runs over to help. She throws herself in, and
the crack of the seam closes.

"What do we do?" Pierce yells, grunting in his efforts.

I look around the rooftop, trying to come up with a way for
Keith to get us out of here without anyone getting shot. A crazy
idea comes to me. I set Maddy down. He's crying, shivering, and
holding his hands up to a mouth covered in snot.

"Maddy, I know you're scared," I say, kneeling to his level. "Everything will be okay, but I need you to stay right here. Can you do that for me?"

He nods, sniffling into his shirt.

"Okay," I say. "I'll be right back. I promise."

I run to the edge of the roof, scanning the depths below. We're on the side of the Testing Center facing the city sidewalk. Housing units begin across the street. We have to get down there. I race back to the group. The battering at the door is ear-splitting—sounding even over the roar of the wind. Muffled shouts come from within.

"Keith!" I yell. "You have to fly us down."

"What?" he shouts, struggling against the door.

A huge clap of thunder resounds through the sky, making all of us jump. Vianne's slick white hair shudders and then changes back to teal. My hair falls from its bun, and with a snap, everyone's old clothing returns.

Maddy is sobbing, shaking in the storm, his face contorted. I hurry over to him, picking him up again. I return to my friends but keep my distance.

"Keith, you have to fly us down to the housing units."

Boom.

Thunder explodes, cracking over us like a bomb, and the wind picks up. It's hard to keep my footing.

"Pierce and Vianne can hold the door!" I shout. "Fly me and Maddy down and then come back for—"

Boom.

Another clap of thunder, but this time, rain cascades down

from the heavens, soaking us. I hug Maddy, keeping him close to my body.

"—for Pierce," I continue.

"Are you serious? What if he freaks out?" Pierce yells, pointing to Maddy. "Keith could lose his ability!"

"Do you have a better idea?" I ask.

He stares at me but says nothing.

Boom.

The noise rips through the torrent, and I look to Vianne, swallowing the knot in my throat. "Vianne, this next part depends on you," I say. "When Keith takes Pierce, the military men are going to burst through that door and start shooting."

Boom.

Lighting flashes, lighting up the sky. It strikes so close to us that I can feel the electricity in the air, and its power almost knocks us to our knees. The hairs on the back of my neck stand on end.

"You need to transform their faces so they can't shoot you," I say

Vianne shakes her head. "But I—I can't," she stammers. "Hollis, I can't."

Her hair changes from teal to black, and the metal door shakes again.

I set Maddy down once more. "Maddy, stay here. Don't move!" I rush over to Vianne, staring her straight in the face. "Yes, you can. You're the only one whose ability can help. Pierce can't take them all, but you can." I cup my eyes, squinting through the sleet. "Transform them like the dogs.

They can't shoot you if they can't see you."

Her face is flushed with cold. "I . . . Hollis . . . I can't. I don't know if—if it will work. That was an accident. I don't know how I did it! I don't—"

"Look at me," I say, grabbing her shoulders. "You can do this. You've grown more in your power than anyone here. I've seen it. Your ability is incredible, and so are you! You can do this, Vianne. You have to. It's the only way we're getting out of here."

We lock eyes and something seals in her resolve. "Okay." She digs her feet into the roofing with her back to the metal. "Pierce, hold the door with me. Together."

I turn back to Maddy, scooping him up.

"Okay," Keith says, straining still. "Do you guys have it?"

"Yes, go!" Pierce says. "Go!"

Keith abandons his efforts, runs to me, and hooks his arms around my waist. I'm lifted from my feet, and my stomach clenches at the staggering height. With a nosedive, Keith plunges us over the edge of the building, and I scream. The whirling rainstorm blinds me, so I shut my eyes, holding Maddy tight.

"The housing units!" I cry. "Get behind them!"

Keith touches down a few seconds later, and my feet slip against the wet concrete. I find my balance, buffeted by the gale-force winds. Keith's hands are still around me, but I push them off. Maddy's screeching is heart-breaking.

"Go get them!" I say, pointing back up at the sky. "We'll be okay."

Keith nods and then rockets back into the torrential downpour. I squint around, shielding my face with the flat of my palm.

"Come on, Maddy," I say, walking down the front of one of the units. "It's okay. We're almost done. Everything will be okay."

I'm sopping wet—soaked to the bone and shivering. Maddy is too. I can feel his little body heaving against mine. I'm colder than I've ever been in my life, and my numb fingertips are beginning to throb, but I trudge on, keeping Maddy up on my hip.

I duck into the alley between two units, standing up against the wall. I suck in gulps of air, attempting to gain composure over my erratic pulse. My hair is plastered to my cheeks, so I swipe it away with my free hand.

"It's okay, Maddy," I say through his sobs. "It's okay."

Rain dumps in buckets over the earth, pouring down without mercy. Every part of my brain feels suffocated by thoughts of Jonah, to the point where I'm beginning to see stars. But I can't do this to myself. I can't. I need to focus on getting out of here alive.

Maddy clings to my neck, his wet nose burying into my skin.

"Shh," I say, rocking him gently. "We're almost done. Okay? I promise." Thunder booms over the city again, striking like clockwork. "Come on, Keith," I whisper, peering up into the sky. "Come on."

The scrape of wet shoes against pavement sends me bolting

from the alley. It's Keith and Pierce. Vianne is the only one left.

"Go!" Pierce shouts, shoving Keith from him.

"Pierce, this way," I call, slinking back between the housing units.

He follows me, removing himself from the open view of the street. I meet his eyes, but he doesn't say a word. He looks like he's seen a ghost. I want to ask, but I'm too fearful, so I wait with him as the storm continues on.

Boom.

The earth shakes again, and Maddy squeals. "It's okay," I say.

Pierce holds his gloved hand to the sky, searching in a zigzag pattern. The wind intensifies, whipping over the streets with angry gusts. It whistles past the gap between the housing units.

"Do you see them?" I ask.

"No."

My heart is thrashing in my chest. Fear is creeping into me—slow and seeping. They have to make it. I can't lose anyone else today. I can't handle it.

"Come on, Keith," I say. "Please."

I jump, electrified by the last set of feet landing on the road. I run from the alleyway, and to my relief, Keith and Vianne are there, white-faced and trembling, but very much alive. Vianne looks like she's going to be sick. Her pale skin and wide eyes overtake her colorful hair.

"We have to go," Keith says. His complexion is ghastly, and the dark circles under his eyes match his shellshock. What happened on that roof?

"Vianne, you have to change us back," I say. "We can't walk through the city like this. We don't look like facility workers."

She nods, holds her hands up, and the sodden scrubs appear. My hair pulls back too. Vianne's arms fall limp to her sides, as if she were going to collapse, but Keith keeps a firm grip on her.

"Follow me," I say.

Adjusting Maddy on my hip, we embark onto the pavement. The street is deserted because of the storm, but that doesn't mean we're safe. I should know best of all. My parents turned me in. Someone is always watching . . .

The street transit stop flashes in the gloom, lighting up its surroundings. We're almost to the end of the first block.

"Walk," I say sharply. "Just walk."

If we can make it a few more blocks, we'll be outside the city limit. The military truck is waiting there, and we can escape.

I look up, and my anxiety heightens. There's a man with an umbrella walking toward us. I clutch Maddy and maintain my pace. The footsteps of my companions shuffle behind me, splashing through the puddles. The man is only a few yards from us now. Maybe he won't look . . .

But to my dismay, we meet eyes, and he stares at me. He's noticed that I'm carrying Maddy, and the oddity of our group makes him stop. Five people in a rainstorm—one of them holding a child. No touch—the golden rule of society. And even with the severity of the storm, I doubt the man in front of me carries any compassion for the boy at all. He's staring at me because I'm touching him.

I don't know what to do other than break eye contact and continue on my way. I try to pass myself off as emotionless, but I know I'm failing.

We're almost to the corner...

With a shrill tone, the street transit stop lights up in red, and the advertisements vanish, replaced by a screaming alarm. Every light on the city block blares red, and I gasp, turning about to face my friends. Dread is filling me. I know what this is.

"It's a lockdown!" I screech. "They're quarantining the city! We have to run!"

I spin back toward the block's end, catching the man's slipping expression. He knows.

"Go!" I hear Keith holler. "Run!"

Without hesitation, I charge the man. He ducks out of the way, falling into a row of bushes in front of a housing unit. Keith, Pierce, and Vianne run ahead of me. Maddy is becoming heavy in my arms, but I lock my fingertips together to support him. My chest is exploding and the stitch in my side grows to an agonizing pain. If we get locked in, I don't know how we'll escape. A city quarantine is a death sentence. We have to beat the military to the city's limit.

"Keep going!" I scream at Keith's hesitation. "To the left!"

He turns, sprinting around the next corner. Every second, the alarms become more piercing. They screech, reaching an uncomfortable pitch. I wish I could cover my ears, but Maddy is having a fit, and it takes every muscle in my body to keep a grip on him.

We round the last block, and the end of the sidewalk looms into view. It protrudes from the housing units into the muddy expanse of the plain. Our escape is in the distance. We just have to get to it.

But ahead, Vianne slips in the mud and lands with a sickening crack. She screams, clutching onto her ankle, and her initial shock turns to an ear-splitting cry of agony. She grips her leg, rolling into the fetal position, and the rest of us snap back to our street clothes. With no disguise and the rumble of dozens of military tanks at our backs, I panic. We're running out of time.

"Keith!" I cry.

He falls back, running to Vianne's side and pulling her up into his arms. "I've got her!" he yells. "Get to the truck!"

I press on, my feet sliding across the mud. Pierce is in front of me. He charges toward the truck, reaching it in less than a minute. Throwing the doors open, he shoves our supply pack aside, and then stands back to avoid Maddy.

"Get in!" he says to me.

I step into the vehicle, placing Maddy on the bench. He is fussing so much that it's hard for me to get him situated. I wrap him in a thick blanket we brought and kneel in front of him. "Stay right here," I say. "Okay? I'll be back."

I skid across the plastic of the interior, ducking my head out into the rain. Keith is flying toward us, carrying Vianne. He lands a few feet from me and sets Vianne into the back of the truck.

"Take her," he says.

The moment we're clear of the doors, Keith slams them shut. Vianne is shaking, her breathing shallow. I catch a glimpse of her ankle and gasp. Deep red bruising is already starting to creep across her skin.

"I broke it," she grimaces. Tears trace her face, and I can tell that she's actively trying not to pass out. She turns to me with wild eyes.

"How does this thing work?" Pierce yells from the driver's seat.

"Move over!" Keith shouts. "To the passenger seat."

A different kind of noise rumbles across the storm, and my ears turn sharp. I move to the rear window, peering out into the torrent. Military trucks—dozens and dozens of them. They spill from the city like ants from a hill, and they're all headed toward our stationary vehicle.

I turn to Vianne, and panic closes my throat. A moment later, the truck jerks forward, sending me to my hands and knees. Keith floors it, and Vianne lets out a shriek. She rolls to her side, and I catch her, shifting my weight to keep her from slipping further.

Then, I pick up a new sound, and my fear soars: machine guns. The trucks tailing us out of the city have opened fire, and a spray of bullets skims across the roof.

An idea comes to me. "Vianne, can you hide the truck?"

"What?"

"Can you make us blend in with the storm?" I cry. "Camouflage!"

She stares at me, her lower lip quivering. Bullets ricochet off the metal of the truck.

"If they hit the wheels, we're done," I say.

"I've never transformed an object before," she says, clutching her ankle with both hands. A grey hue is working its way into her skin.

"You've got to try! Please! Try to make the truck blend in."

Vianne's hands extend from her chest, and with a piercing cry, she pours herself into her palms. A clear substance streams from her skin, hitting the roof and spreading across it. Vianne is screaming, crying out with everything she's got, and slowly our surroundings begin to lighten. The metal is changing from black to transparent.

"You're doing it! Vianne, you're doing it!"

The vehicle rumbles on, darting across the mud, but now we're a watery grey, and almost imperceptible against the storm.

I raise myself just high enough to peek out of the window. The pursuit has turned to confusion. The trucks following us have fanned out, many turning off in the wrong direction.

"They can't see us," I say. "You did it. Just keep focus on it, okay?"

Vianne nods, tears streaming down her face. Her teeth are bared and her fists are raised. This is taking every piece of her to maintain.

"Keith, get us out of here," I call up front. "I don't know how much longer Vianne can hold it."

"I'm on it," he says.

The truck picks up speed as I stare out at the storm. Victory is settling in me. I lean back against the bench, scarcely able to believe it. What a feat. We took the government's secret weapon. The boy is ours.

The rain beats against us, pounding over the translucent roof, but nothing can stop us now. The search party behind us is at a loss. Our camp is only 327 miles away. I survey our ragged group, and the glaring absence hits me in the stomach with the force of the raging storm outside: the escape vehicle meant for six is only carrying five.

25

WE SIT IN STIFLING SILENCE. I HELPED WITH VIANNE'S ANKLE by splinting it with some cloth from my supply pack and a metal rod I cut out of the supporting frame of Jonah's duffle bag. It's not much, but it will have to do. It's swollen and turning purple. She's suffering. I can tell. But she doesn't say a word. Instead, she keeps her jaw set, and her eyes forward, clearly keen on making it back to the forest without a single complaint.

She saved us. Without Vianne, we'd all be dead.

I sit next to Maddy, my arm wrapped around his cocoon of blankets. He's stopped shivering now and is sleeping against my shoulder. Poor thing. I can't imagine how terrifying this must have been for him.

The rain has thinned out, and we've been driving for a couple of hours. The mud is proving to be a formidable travel companion. The journey back is turning into a longer ordeal than I anticipated. Every minute I find myself wishing this was done.

My eyelids droop, and exhaustion settles in the pit of my abdomen. I'm grieved beyond what I can express. I can't stop thinking about Jonah. Is he dead? Did they shoot him on sight? Did he manage some kind of miraculous escape? The deepest part of me clings to this, but I shouldn't imagine such foolishness. I close my eyes as a tear slides down my cheek. They were going to shoot me on sight when I failed my Test. Why would an intruder be any different?

I want to weep, but I have nothing left in me. I can't right now. It feels like an impossible task. To start this horrid process all over again? I'm not done grieving for Tiffany. How can I even begin to grieve for Jonah?

"The trees," Keith says, turning over his shoulder. "Just ahead."

My eyes flutter open, and out front, the tall pines shimmer between the broken clouds. We've moved away from the storm's epicenter, and the sunshine feels like an incredible gift. Mist drizzles down in patches, throwing a rainbow to our right.

"Drive as far as you can," I call up. "The less walking we have to do the better. Vianne will need help."

"Got it," Keith says.

The truck bumps over the uneven ground. The ride is far from over. I hold Maddy in my arms, leaning my head over his. He's still fast asleep. Good. He needs sleep after a day like this. We all need sleep.

The motion of the vehicle jerks me forward on the bench,

and my heels hook the rivets in the floor. I'm still damp and cold, and the farther we drive, the sicker I feel. My skin is pruned and my fingers are cracked, and the freezing air doesn't help. My brain is stuck on a loop. The glass door descends from the ceiling of the hallway over and over again in my mind's eye. I'll never forget Jonah's face—the way he looked at me.

I bow my head, holding in a sob. Maybe they didn't... maybe they . . . I can't do this to myself. I have to stop.

After what feels like three hours, the military truck slows. The rain is gone, and the pine trunks glisten in the patches of sun. I slide my arm forward, gently coaxing Maddy from his slumber.

"Hey," I say softly. "Time to wake up."

Maddy blinks, rubbing his nose with his fist. "Hi."

I smile at him. "Hi."

"Are we where the special people are?"

"Almost. We have to take a short walk. Okay?"

"Okay."

His sweet voice calms me. It's what I needed. Everything about this moment is trying to tip me over the edge. I have to stay focused—just a little longer. Our purpose was to bring Maddy to the camp safely, and we're so close.

I hold out my hand and he takes it, jumping down from the bench.

"That's it," I say. "Are you ready to see the special people?"

"Yes," he giggles. Sleep must have put away the trauma of Maddy's day.

"Good."

I lift him into my arms, and his hands wrap around my neck. Meanwhile, Keith exits the driver's side and pulls open the slider. I step down, moving aside, and Pierce follows.

"How are you doing, Vianne?" Keith asks.

She grimaces, shifting herself on her hands to make it easier for Keith to help her. "Not great. It's broken."

"You were amazing," he says. He helps her out of the vehicle, supporting most of her weight so she can stand on her good ankle.

Pierce gives a stiff nod. "Yes, thank you. And to you, Keith, for driving. You have a knack for electronics."

"Here, Maddy," I say. "I'm going to set you down so I can take off this jacket."

I lower him to the ground and begin unzipping my soggy clothing. My hands are still numb. What I would give to be dry and warm right now.

"Good idea," Pierce says, following suit.

He pulls his soggy sweater over his head. It catches on his arm, clinging to him. For a moment, he struggles with it, tugging until the sleeve slides down his right arm. It snags his glove, and the glove inverts, slipping off of his hand.

Red puncture wounds line his palm, deep and curved into an arch, and my heart jumps into my throat. "What is that?"

Pierce stuffs his hand into the sweater, holding it away from me. "Nothing."

"What is that?" I demand, advancing on him.

"Hollis, what are you—" Keith starts, but I interrupt him.

"Pierce, what's on your hand?" I ask, grabbing his sweater.

Pierce yanks it from me so forcefully that I lose my footing. I slip on the wet ground, landing on my hands and knees.

"Hey!" Keith shouts. "What is going on?"

Vianne removes her arms from Keith and grabs the nearest tree. Keith approaches Pierce, and he backs away.

He clutches his sweater near his chest. "It's nothing."

Keith lunges, snatching the sleeve and yanking it away to reveal the wound. It flashes in front of me, raw and slightly infected. Teeth marks. *My* teeth marks.

I stand to my feet, my mouth open. "You?"

Pierce Bodegard was one of my attackers? I feel like I can't breathe. My hand is to my face. For a second, no one moves, but the moment breaks as Keith launches himself at Pierce, punching him in the nose.

Vianne and I scream, and the two of them topple over, struggling in a fit of fists across the pine-littered ground.

"You gutless—"

Wham.

"—worthless—"

Wham.

"—son of a—"

Wham.

Before Keith can finish, he's thrown into the air, landing on his back. Pierce jumps on top of him, slamming his fist into Keith's jaw.

"Stop!" I screech. "Stop it!"

I charge Pierce, grabbing his shoulder, but my small frame isn't a match for his large one. He shoves me back with ease, and I skid in the mud, catching myself on a branch. It jabs me in the back, and I gasp. Pain travels up through my chest, knocking the breath from me.

"Pierce! Keith! Stop!" Vianne cries, clinging to the tree, unable to help.

The two roll around, and now Keith is back on top, pummeling Pierce with several fierce blows. They echo through the forest, and the sound of flesh on flesh sends me into a panic.

Wham.

"Who else—"

Wham.

"—was with you—"

Wham.

"—you cowardly piece of—"

Pierce shoves his hand up, splitting open Keith's lip, and Vianne squeals. I have to do something. I spin around, looking for some kind of weapon, and I spot a snapped off branch. That will do.

But before I can rejoin the fray, a flash draws my attention away from the fight. Maddy is standing a few yards off. He's shrieking, and his hands are glowing. The golden light pulses from him, illuminating the trees. It expands from his skin, growing larger and arching high above us.

Keith and Pierce scramble to their feet, abandoning their attempts to hit each other. They retreat from Maddy in a fright as the light seeps toward them. This isn't good. If the light touches them, I don't know what will happen.

"Maddy," I say, dropping the branch and holding my hands out. I step in front of the others, shielding them with my body. The light is a foot from me. "It's okay."

Maddy's arms are shaking. "What's happening?" he cries, bobbing his head between me and his hands. His eyes are streaming.

"Hey, look at me," I say, slowly inching my way toward him. "It's alright. The golden light is good. It's not going to hurt you."

"I don't like this," he says, his little brow turned up. "I . . . I don't . . ."

And even though he can't express it, I know he's talking about the fistfight. He turns his hands around, and the light expands again. His eyes move behind me, landing on Keith and Pierce.

"Maddy," I say gently. "They won't fight anymore. Okay? I know it's scary. But they're done."

I shoot a vile look behind me.

"Why . . . why is the light—" he whimpers.

"It's just the golden light. It's what makes you special, remember? You don't have to be afraid."

He sniffles, nodding, and the light begins to shrink.

"That's it," I say. "Good. Can you take a big breath? Like this?" I inhale and blow air out between my lips.

Maddy keeps his eyes on mine and then copies me. He clenches his hands into fists, holding them out in front of his chest.

I smile. "Good. Just like that. See?" I point to the light

above our heads. The sparks start to flicker, some dissipating back into his palms. "You're doing really good, Maddy. Just breathe."

And with one last nudge of encouragement, his power vanishes altogether. I close the gap between us, scooping him up into my arms again. I wipe the tears from his dirt-smudged face with my thumb, and I turn back to face our group. Pierce backs away, as if he were going to make a run for it, but Vianne holds her palm up, spreading her fingertips wide and glaring at him.

"Don't even think about it," she snarls. "You saw what I did to those men on the roof. Don't think for a second I won't do that to you too. You tried to kill Hollis, and you're not getting away with it."

Pierce scoffs but doesn't move. A horrible smirk crosses his face, and he stares at me without saying a word. My skin crawls and I back away from him, hugging Maddy close.

"You win, metamorph," he says, raising his hands above his head. "I know when I'm beat."

Keith walks over to his pack and rummages within. His split lip is bleeding profusely, and he spits into the dirt. He withdraws a length of cord and then approaches Pierce, grabbing his upraised arms and pulling them behind his back. He secures his wrists together and pushes him forward.

"Walk," he says viciously. He moves to Vianne, supporting her weight again. "Hollis?"

"Yeah," I say, moving out of his way.

Vianne's hand is still aloft. "I've got you all the way," she calls up to Pierce. "So don't try anything stupid. You can't suggest your way out of this one."

The five of us begin the hike back to the dome. Pierce leads the group, followed closely by Vianne and Keith. Maddy and I bring up the rear, but I keep my distance. The scare we just had was close. If Maddy had removed anyone else's ability, even by accident, I don't know what we would've done. I'm glad I was able to calm him down. I miss my power, and I wouldn't wish its absence on anyone—even Pierce.

Our trek is slow. Vianne limps along, supported by Keith, but her hand stays out in front of her, trained on Pierce's back. I can't believe it. Pierce tried to kill me. I'd never even met him before our first training session. But like many of the others, his hate for me runs deep. Before the attack, it never occurred to me that anyone would go that far . . .

An hour later, we're back. The twisted dome towers before us, but I'm not relieved. Once again, I feel the weight of my grief, and my thoughts return to Jonah. Tears brim in my eyes until they sting, and I don't wipe them away.

The moment we enter the dome, dozens upon dozens of eyes find us. Everyone stops their work to stare, and it only makes me feel worse. Shock falls over the onlookers, and I don't blame them. Pierce is bloodied and beaten, tied up and leading us—and Keith looks just as horrible. Dried blood trails from his chin, and red bruising buds across his jaw. Vianne is as pale as a ghost, sweating and clutching onto Keith. Her ankle is swollen and throbbing. And I'm at the end, holding the government's prized possession. We're quite a sight. It only takes a few more seconds for people to see that Jonah is nowhere to be found.

I look down at my feet. It's like before. I can't meet anyone's accusing gaze. What if they think I did this too? Some of them already believe that *I* attacked Jonah that night.

"To the Council room," Keith says, directing us forward.

The five of us walk through the center of the compound, filing into the empty room a minute later. Keith shuts the door, helps Vianne to the wall, and grabs the wooden chair. It traces a path in the dirt as Keith hauls it over.

"Sit," he growls at Pierce.

Pierce complies, taking a seat. His dark eyes never waver from me, and my stomach squirms. He's acting like he's not a captive, and it's making me nervous.

"I need to gather the Council," Keith says. "Vianne, do you have this?"

"I've got him," she says. "Go. We'll be fine."

"Okay." He pauses before exiting the room. "Hollis, are you alright?"

I nod, readjusting Maddy on my hip. "Are you?"

"It's just a busted lip."

"It looks bad."

He appears grim but chuckles anyway. "I've had worse." I give him an incredulous look. "A story for another time. I'll be right back."

"Okay."

Keith whips out of the door, leaving us alone. Vianne maintains a steady stance on her good leg, but she's shaking, and her hair is a blend of grey and white. Perspiration creeps across her brow, but she isn't backing down.

Pierce, on the other hand, seems unphased by Vianne's presence. He hasn't stopped staring at me. An eerie expression slips over him—a mix of malice, loathing, and hostility—as if he would love nothing better than to finish me off.

This upsets Maddy, and he begins to fuss in my arms. "It's alright," I say, setting him down. He clings to me, hiding behind my leg, and Pierce's gaze follows. "Stop looking at him," I snarl.

"My sister would have liked meeting Maddy," he says.

"Your sister?" Vianne repeats, but Pierce doesn't acknowledge her.

"It's a shame the Council didn't do the right thing."

"And by that, you mean my execution?" My hands curl into fists. I know I shouldn't engage him, but I can't help it. "You and your friends attacked me in the dark. You hurt Jonah to get to me. You're a coward."

"And so are you." He tilts his head around the room. "Why do you think we're here?"

"I've changed."

"Have you?"

"Yes," I say, putting a definite edge to my tone.

"Well," he says, and his deep voice carries through the room. "I hope you can live with yourself. Because everyone else here has to. And the funny thing is, my sister would have forgiven you. She was *that* person—too good for this world. But thanks to you, she can't do that anymore. She can't do anything anymore. So that's great that you think you've changed, but don't expect anyone to care. The only person who ever cared about you was Jonah, but he's dead now, and that's your fault too."

The door to the Council room opens, slamming against the wall. Keith and a scattered group of Council members pile in. Eli Stone doesn't even wait for anyone to sit. He charges up to the front, looking like he's been hit in the stomach.

"First things first," he says, adjusting his glasses on the bridge of his nose. "The boy?"

"Here," I say, my voice cracking.

I squeeze Maddy's hand, bringing him out from behind my leg. My heart rate rises as a fresh dose of adrenaline drowns me. If the Council hadn't arrived the moment they did, I would've launched myself at Pierce the way Keith did back at the truck. My eyes are teaming with angry tears, but I pull them back, wiping them away with the flat of my hand.

"Hello there, young man," Eli Stone says.

Maddy looks around the semicircle, his big, blue eyes framed by his mess of curly blond hair. "Hi."

"And what's your name?"

"I'm Maddy," he says, clasping his tiny fingers together and smiling. "Are you the special people?"

"Yes, Maddy," Eli Stone responds.

He waves at them. "Hi!"

A few of the members chuckle, waving back. Maddy hangs on my arm, becoming shy. He dips behind my leg again, holding me like his favorite stuffed animal.

"Miss Timewire, what is the meaning of this?" Mr. Stuart says, pointing to Pierce.

But to my relief, Keith steps in and addresses the room. "Pierce was one of the three people who attacked Jonah and Hollis, sir."

A murmur rumbles through the Council.

"What?" Libbie says, staring at Pierce like she's never seen him before. She brushes a hand through her mousy hair. "How do you know?"

"I bit one of my attackers," I say tersely. "Pierce's hand has my teeth marks."

"Mr. Bodegard . . . you attacked them?" she says. Her lips thin out into a line, and her brow crinkles. With a snap of movement, her fists clamp shut and branches spring from the chair, wrapping around Pierce's torso.

At this Vianne collapses on the floor, utterly spent.

"Oh my," Libbie says.

Keith kneels by her side. "She broke her ankle, and she's been using her power all day. She needs medical attention."

"Of course," the lead Council member says. "Can I have—"

But several volunteers have already stepped in, lifting Vianne up and carrying her from the room. The door shuts behind them, and I turn back toward those of us who remain.

Mr. Stuart appears to be beside himself. His face is red and his mouth is pursed. He looms over Pierce. "You dare attack a Council member? Who were your accomplices?"

"Caleb, not now," Eli says, holding his hand up. "We will deal with Mr. Bodegard in a moment."

Pierce doesn't speak, and his silent victory mocks me. Why aren't we addressing this now? I look between Eli Stone and Caleb Stuart, unsure of what could be more pressing than this. But Mr. Stone's expression is enough to quell my protest. He's pale and shifty, his hand continuously returning to adjust his glasses. Something isn't right, and as I survey the room, I see the same look on everyone's face. Melancholy eyes meet mine.

"Libbie, can you show Miss Timewire?"

"Show me what?" I ask.

Libbie withdraws a tablet from her bag, her face stricken.

"Show me what?" I repeat, dread filling me. "What is it?"

"We received this four hours ago," she says, tapping on the tablet and then handing it to me. She's crying, and this sends numbing panic down to my toes. The tablet sparks to life, and a video feed begins to play.

President Alvaro Camille stands behind his podium in a pure white suit. The gold-encrusted seal of the Capitol City's emblem blazes in front of him. His jet black hair is tidy, slicked back to perfection, and he stares into the lens as cameras flash.

"Citizens of the world," he begins. "It is my solemn duty to bring to light the recent events of this day. As your leader, I want to be transparent with you. What I am about to tell you is shocking, but I implore you to listen and listen well."

He pauses to consult a piece of paper, before looking back up. His black eyes ignite behind the screen.

"Today, the Diseased Ones infiltrated our city, and stole a valuable item from us—an item we have possessed for a hundred years. They broke into a government facility and slaughtered our workers. They attacked us in a place we call home, at an institution we hold most dear—the Area 19 Testing Center."

Still perfect in his societal control, the President sobers his tone.

"But take heart when I tell you that this alarming event has not come without victory. The Diseased Ones stole a precious item from us, but we have procured a priceless item from them in return."

The President's demeanor changes. His features intensify with a sinister victory, and he addresses the camera, radiant in his words.

"And now, Hollis Timewire, I address you. First, I want to acknowledge your cleverness, for cleverness and guile can be found even in the most hateful and murderous of creatures. I underestimated you—a mistake I will not make again. And I am willing to admit this openly. But I want everyone to understand that the cleverness of an evolutionary mistake is nothing compared to the might of our united order. You have accomplished nothing."

The President lights up, speaking slowly, as if addressing someone stupid.

"Return what you took to the Capitol building, or I will dispose of *your* cherished item publicly. Everyone in the world will watch. Trust me when I say it will be painful and slow, and I will take great pleasure in it. That was a touching moment at the door, Hollis. You have twenty-four hours to meet my demand."

The feed cuts to black and I'm left standing in a heart-pounding silence. Jonah. Jonah is still alive. But Maddy tugs on my arm, bringing me back to my senses, and I peer down into his precious face.

26

"WE HAVE TO GO BACK."

The words tumble out of me before anyone speaks. My hands are shaking, I can't think, and my knees are weak and tingling. I scan the room, hoping that someone will agree with me, but the dejected faces that meet mine plunge me into despair.

"We have to rescue him!" My voice constricts. "We have to save him!"

"Miss Timewire... we can't," Libbie says, holding a hand up to her mouth. Her puffy eyes glitter with fresh tears.

I round on her. "But he's going to die! They're going to kill him. We can't just leave him there. They're going to execute him!"

"We don't even know if Jonah is truly alive," Eli Stone says, stricken. "Chances are they've already killed him and they're using this broadcast as a means of luring you back to the city. I'm sorry, but—"

"No!" I roar, my chest heaving. "We have to rescue him. He's alive. Jonah is still alive. There's got to be a way. We still have twenty hours left. We can come up with a plan! We've got to. There's still time!"

"Miss Timewire, I know this must be difficult for you. Given the nature of your relationship with him, I understand—"

"No, you don't understand!" I say. Bitter tears fall against my cheeks. Jonah was the only person who spoke for me. He was the only one who could even look at me after what I did. These people were ready to kill me, and I deserved it, but he saw something in me—even when I couldn't see it in myself. He believed in me, and he made me better. "I owe him *everything*! I can't abandon him. I won't."

I stumble forward, every nerve in my body on fire. I've never felt so helpless. The horror of it plays over in my mind— Jonah set to be executed by the people who've taken everything from me.

"Jonah is going to die!" I scream at them. "We have to do something!"

The room's silent grief mirrors mine. I turn to Keith, desperate for support.

"Keith?" I approach him and take hold of his hands. "Please? We have to go back. We have to rescue him. We can't just ..."

But he gives me the same look he did back at the Testing Center: one that bears no hope. "I'm so sorry, Hollis. But we can't."

"No," I say, shaking my head. I drop his hands and back

away from him. "I refuse to accept that."

"Miss Timewire," Eli Stone says, but I cut him off.

"You have powers!" I cry, spinning around. "There must be something you can do. Why can't you—"

"No one here has an ability powerful enough to help him. I'm sorry, but that's the reality of it. Sending another team to the Capitol would be suicide."

I stand there at a loss, my mouth parted, and a cruel thought enters my mind: my ability. If only I still had it.

"*I* could have helped him," I whisper, choking back a sob.

Eli Stone sighs, putting a wrinkled hand to his forehead. His cracked glasses slide down his nose. "You could have. But you made your choice, Miss Timewire. Now you have to find a way to live with it."

His words are like a slap to the face. I look around. No one can meet my gaze, and the worst kind of sorrow fills me. Its cold grip seeps into my heart, suffocating me. I can't accept this. How is it that my grave mistake is still the reason I'm losing everything? Overcome by anguish, I bundle Maddy up in my arms and sprint from the Council room.

"Hollis, wait!" Keith calls after me, but I ignore him, running through the enclosure. I have to get away from them.

I hold Maddy tight, bolting past my cell until I reach the exit to the clearing. I trample over roots and rocks, making my way up the path. When I arrive at the clearing, the pile of wood lies neatly in place, soaked through from the rain. It mocks me, like it's ready for the axe, but I push past it, coming to stand on the riverbed a few minutes later.

The gritty mud crunches under my boots, and the sunlight dips off the water in the late afternoon. The breeze picks up, unforgiving in its winter glory. I stop at the water's edge, setting Maddy down and collapsing in the sludge. I curl forward, tucking myself into a ball.

At last, after quenching every urge to fall apart since sun-up, I let go, and the reservations within me shatter. I'm sobbing, clutching my chest and sucking in ragged breaths. It hurts. Everything hurts. It's all pain. To what depths can the human mind sink when grief is the only thing you think you'll ever experience again?

A soft hand touches my shoulder, and I pull myself up to see Maddy's curious eyes.

"Why are you crying?" he asks. He stands right in front of me, tilting his head to the side. His blond curls slide across his forehead.

I wipe my face with both of my hands, sniffling. My head is throbbing. "I'm crying because I'm sad, Maddy."

"Why are you sad?"

I stare out across the river. It was at this spot that I stood next to Jonah, talking to him about rescuing this sweet boy. It seems like yesterday, like I could turn around and Jonah would be standing at the tree line watching me skip rocks with my friends.

"I'm sad because a very good man is going to die today," I say.

"Die?"

I fight another bout of tears. "It's when someone goes away, and they don't come back."

"What man?" he asks. He sits down by my side, never taking his attention from me.

"The man who was in your room," I say. "The man who helped wake you up so that you could come here. His name is Jonah."

"Jonah," Maddy repeats.

I nod, crushed with misery. What if Maddy hadn't stopped running? What if Jonah didn't go back for me? What if the door stayed open? If only there was more time. I bury my head in my arms.

"Don't be sad," Maddy says, leaning over me with a hug.

"Maddy, what happened in the hallway? Why did you stop running?" It feels futile to ask him this. It doesn't change anything, but I have to know. I lift my head, peering down at him. "Were you scared? Is that why?"

"My head told me to stop," he says, pulling on my arm.

"Your head . . . what?"

"My head told me to stop running."

I stare at Maddy, and my lips part as understanding crashes over me like a ruthless wave. Jonah was never meant to get trapped behind the glass door. Pierce meant that for me. How hideously perfect. What did it matter to him if the team failed to procure the secret weapon? He saw the opportunity to finish what he started, and he took it. Seal the leader of the second Terror War and the secret weapon into the Testing Center. How simple. How neat. But Pierce never counted on the wonderful man who came back for me—the man who gave up everything so we could escape with Maddy.

Jonah is going to die in my place . . .

I lower my head, too stunned to bring myself to say anything more. It's over, the mission is complete, and there's nothing I can do to change it. Eli Stone is right. I have to learn to live with this—all of it—every broken piece. Jonah got caught in the pit of my destruction, and even I can't save him from that.

Little hands move from my arms to my face, and Maddy picks up my head by lifting my chin.

"Don't be sad," he says, looking at me intently.

I sniffle, wiping my face with the sleeve of my jacket. Maddy holds his hands together into a bowl, and his palms shine gold. A tiny orb materializes, pulsing and hovering there. It expands, and Maddy smiles at me, setting the golden light into my lap.

"Don't be sad," he says again.

I gasp as the light seeps into my skin. It travels up through my chest, filling me with incredible warmth, like a fire that's been stoked back to life. The light pulsates around me, rising up through my arms and moving into my face. It's electric, more wonderful than bliss itself. It's every happy moment in a lifetime, all surging together in one compelling symphony. I'm exhilarated beyond words as the surge continues, plunging me to the brim of ecstasy with a sensation far beyond joy. Energy fills every sinew of my body, and my eyes widen as the last set of dancing sparks dissipate into my chest.

I stand to my feet, gaping at my hands. They begin to tingle, and for the first time since the Testing Center, I feel that irresistible sense of control. It seeps through each pore, powerful and poignant, taking root at my core, and I finally understand why this is me. I feel whole again. I've reunited with the companion I never knew I needed. I'm a puppet master once more.

"M-Maddy," I stammer, turning my hands over. "My ability . . . how did you?"

"The golden light!" he giggles, clapping and jumping up and down.

I laugh, choking back tears. "The golden light," I repeat. "Of course!"

Maddy is beaming at me, so I kneel, taking in his button nose and messy hair. He puts his hands up to my face, and I crinkle my nose at him. He laughs, and I scoop him up, hugging him. His arms wrap around my neck.

"Thank you," I whisper. "Thank you so much."

The trickling river slides past us in the distance, and I gaze across the beauty in the setting sun, breathing in the air with new lungs. My ability roars in my chest, ready for my command, and I welcome in the tingling like an old friend.

"Maddy, do you know what this means?" I say.

"What?"

"I'm going to the Capitol, and I'm getting Jonah back."

27

I MARCH BACK TO THE DOME, DETERMINATION KINDLING in my heart. Maddy tags along, his hand in mine. He bobs up and down with the energy of a firecracker, and it makes me smile. In my haste, I pass my cell. The door hangs open in the dust, empty and forgotten. There's nothing there for me now.

First things first. I can't bring Maddy. There's no way I'm giving him back. I'm ending this on my terms, and that means the government will never see him again—not as long as I have breath in my lungs and power in my hands.

I poke my head into the alcove on the far left. It's the designated medical cubby, and sure enough, Vianne lies in a cot surrounded by three women. They scowl at me as I enter, and Maddy hides behind my leg.

"Vianne, I need to talk to you," I say. "Alone."

The women turn their noses up at this, and the one nearest

the back, whose bony features remind me glaringly of a malnourished horse, scoffs. "She's resting."

I ignore her. "It's urgent."

"It's alright," Vianne says to the women. "Can you give us a minute?"

The second woman wags her stubby finger at me, giving me a scathing look, but they oblige Vianne, shuffling out and muttering to themselves. When they're far enough away, I sit at the end of the cot, bringing Maddy in front of me.

"Hollis, what is it?" Vianne asks. "What's wrong? You look . . ."

"Jonah's alive," I say. "And I'm going back for him."

"What?" She sits up, and then winces, bracing her leg. "He's alive? How do you know?"

"President Camille sent a broadcast," I say. "They're going to execute him in twenty hours. I don't have much time. I need you to watch Maddy. I can't bring him with me, and you're the only other person he knows. I don't trust the Council to do it, and if something were to go wrong then—"

Vianne shakes her head. "Hollis, are you crazy? You can't go back there." She looks to Maddy and then lowers her voice. "You know what could happen. How are you going to—"

I hold my hand aloft, pointing it at Vianne, and with intention, I channel my ability into her. She freezes, and the moment she does, her eyes light up. I pull my ability back, releasing her, and she gapes at me.

"Your power?"

"My power," I say.

"But . . . how?"

I squeeze Maddy's hand, and he chimes up in my place. "The golden light!"

I smile at him. "That's right. The golden light."

"I'll watch him," she says, shifting herself forward.

"Thank you." I stoop down, turning Maddy around to face me. "Maddy, this is Vianne. She helped rescue you today. Do you remember?"

He nods and waves at her. "Hi."

"Hi Maddy," she says.

"Good," I say. "Now this is very important, Maddy. I need to go, but I'll only be gone for a little, and then I'm coming back. Vianne is going to watch you, and I need you to stay with her. Okay?"

Maddy pulls on my arm, looking between Vianne and me. "Okay."

"Okay," I say, standing to my feet. "I'll be back. I promise."

Vianne and I lock eyes, and the same silent understanding we shared before the rescue mission seals between us.

"Go get him," she says.

"I will."

And with that, I exit the alcove. The three women give me another round of nasty looks, but I disregard this, making a beeline to the Council room. I barge in, interrupting what I'm sure is an arduous amount of discussion regarding Pierce's fate.

Everyone looks at me, and Mr. Stuart's mouth presses into a thin line. "Miss Timewire, what are you—"

"Keith, meet me in the clearing in five minutes," I say.

I turn from them and walk out, the garbled protests of Mr. Stuart and Eli Stone ringing in my ears. I continue back across the dome, keen to find the rest of my friends. A minute later, I spot Ben, Candice, and Darren sitting at the farthest firepit, chatting away. I approach them and interrupt their conversation.

"Meet me in the clearing in five minutes," I say.

Darren gives me a scornful look. "No. I think we'll stay here."

"This is important," I shoot back, glaring at him.

Candice perks her head up. "Hollis, what's wrong?"

"The clearing. Five minutes," I say. "I'll explain there."

I walk away, scanning the scattered compound for Rosalie's vibrant red hair. People can't help but stare—like I'm an animal—but it doesn't faze me anymore. My mind is set on the task at hand. I catch sight of her at one of the tables near the kitchen alcove—a place I'm not allowed. All of my meals were given to me at the clearing or in my cell. But I haven't the time for the Council's rules.

"Rosalie," I say, striding up to her. The girls at the table stop talking, giving me the 'you're-something-disgusting' glances I've come to know so well. "I need you in the clearing. Right now."

She stands up without questioning me, disentangling herself from the bench, and the smallest part of me understands that this would only come from a friend.

"Rosalie!" The stout, brunette side-saddling her seat scoffs, contempt written into her tone. "Seriously?"

"Seriously," she says, joining my side. She turns her back on them and walks with me down the length of the dome. "Hollis, what is it?"

"It's Jonah," I say. "I'll explain in a minute."

Part of me thinks I shouldn't say anything at all. Why worry my friends when ignorance would be easier? Even with my power, going back to the city will be dangerous, but I want to let them know what's happening. Jonah is their teacher too, and they're the only people I can talk to. They'd want to know. It's the right thing to do.

We trudge through the trees, and when we arrive at the clearing, I find Keith standing by the pile of wood.

"Hollis, what's going on?" he asks.

The crunch of footsteps follow behind me, and to my relief, Candice and Ben emerge from between two trunks.

I wave them over. "You came."

"We did," Candice says.

"What's happening?" Ben asks. "You look awful."

Candice punches him in the arm.

"Ouch! What was that for?"

"I don't have much time, but long story short, the government's got Jonah," I say. Candice and Rosalie put their hands to their face in sync, and Ben's mouth drops open, but before any of them can speak, I forge on. "I'm going to the Capitol building to get him."

"Hollis," Keith says, pulling me aside. He grasps both of my hands, squeezing them tight. Grief still resides in his face. "You can't. It's suicide. If you go back there, they'll kill you, and I'm not going to let that happen. There's nothing we can do for Jonah. I'm sorry, but this is over."

"No," I say. "It's just getting started."

I pull my hands from his and step back, raising both of my arms and flaring out my fingertips. My ability encases the four of them into perfect statues, and distinctive gasps escape them. I swipe my hands, and they fall from their positions, stumbling about.

"You—you have your ability?" Keith says, aghast. "But how?"

"Maddy. He can give abilities too. It was incredible!"

"Who's Maddy?" Ben asks, clearly at a loss.

"The boy!" Rosalie says, pushing her mess of hair over her shoulder.

My hands curl into fists. "The government is going to execute Jonah in less than twenty hours, and I'm going back for him. I wanted to tell you because . . . well, because you're my friends, and I know all of you care about Jonah." I pause, taking a deep breath. "Keith, I need you to drive. Will you come with me?"

"Yes," he says without missing a beat.

I grab his hand. "Thank you."

"I'm coming too," Candice says, pulling her dark brown hair up into a ponytail.

"I'm in," Ben says. He rubs his hands together and tosses his head side to side.

"Me too," Rosalie adds.

I stare at them, momentarily shocked, but I shake my head. "No. It's too dangerous."

Candice laughs. "I can produce fire from my hands. I think I'll be fine."

"No!" I say. "Even with my power, this isn't going to be—"

"Hollis, we'll be fine," Ben says. He jabs his thumb at his chest. "Me especially."

Candice pops a flame into her pointer finger and then blows it out. "Why you especially?"

He rolls his eyes. "Well, it's not like the bad guys can catch me. Super speed. Duh."

"This isn't a game!" I say, exasperated. "The military men have machine guns. They will kill you if they get the chance. This isn't like training where you get another go if you mess up. This is real."

"I'm coming," Ben says flatly. "And I know it's not a game. If Jonah's in danger, then I'm in."

"Okay, then it's settled," Rosalie says before I can get another word in edgewise. "We're coming."

Now I wish I hadn't said anything. But the determined looks my friends wear calm my nerves. Perhaps it wouldn't hurt to have a few extra powers along for this venture.

"Fine," I say, gritting my teeth. "But we need to go. Right now. Jonah doesn't have much time."

"Hollis," Rosalie says with a tentative step forward. Her brow furrows. "What if Jonah . . . what if they've already . . ." She can't bring herself to finish.

I shake my head. "No. I refuse to believe that. They want Maddy, and Jonah's the bait. But Maddy is staying right here. There's no way we're giving him back. The government has taken enough. And I swear on my ability, if they've killed Jonah, I won't ever stop."

"Won't ever stop?" Candice repeats.

My power rears up in my fingertips like a caged animal ready to break free. "I'm not scared of this anymore, but they certainly should be."

Keith steps up to my side, grabbing my hand. "Let's go get him."

"Let's."

28

HALF AN HOUR LATER, KEITH, BEN, CANDICE, ROSALIE, and I are sitting in the military truck, and we're on our way through the forest.

I've hardly said a word since the clearing. Anger is pouring through me, spurring me onward. This will be over soon. The government has burned us one too many times. I know the truth of history, I have my ability back, and there's nothing that can stop us.

The truck rumbles through the trees, bouncing over the ruts, but this time my stomach isn't churning. This time, I'm vibrant with the power at my core. I train my attention out the front window, taking in the surrounding terrain, keen to break free of the woods. And, in what feels like no time at all, we make it to the edge of the pines. I speak up, and my voice cracks from lack of use.

"Floor it," I say to Keith. "Let's see what this thing can really do."

The vehicle launches forward, and I grip the bench. My stomach flutters at the speed as we tear across the plain. Mud spits up at the rear, and the forest shrinks behind us until it's nothing but a line. At this rate, we'll get to the city in a few hours.

It's dark now, and stars litter the sky. I lean back in my seat, my fingertips itching to try on my power, as if all the days I lacked my ability were teaming together in revenge. The tingling sharpens, each moment more poignant than the last. It's bursting at the seams of my being, alive and hungry. The government pushed me too far. Their mistake. I'm seething with the energy building inside of me, and soon—very soon—I'll unleash it.

The black night zooms by, blurring around us. Now that the rain is gone, we're moving quickly. I catch sight of Keith in the mirror. His complexion is ghastly: pale skin and sunken eyes set against a mess of dark brown hair. He's exhausted, and his hands clutch the steering wheel so tightly that his knuckles are white. As we travel farther, the mood of the group sobers. Still, I'm not afraid. Fear is no longer my devilish companion. My only concerns are saving Jonah and getting everyone out of this safely. I'm going to do everything in my power to protect my friends.

"We're almost there," Keith says. "It's just ahead."

The outline of the city towers up in the distance, and the glow of street lights obscure the stars. As we hurl toward it, something unsettles me, and I squint through the window. The outskirts of the city limit are deserted.

"It's empty," I say. "Why is it empty?"

A pit forms in my stomach. Why would the government pull back the military? Earlier today they quarantined the city, and trucks flooded the plain beyond the sidewalk. It was a full lockdown, so why are they gone? Where did they go? It's been less than half a day. I was expecting to have to fight my way in, but this seems like an all-too-easy welcome back. What game is President Camille playing?

"Slow down, Keith," I say. "We're close enough."

Keith hits the brakes, and we come to a halt just outside the first block. The boxy housing units stand still in the abandoned street, alight with the city's lamp posts. I grab the inside handle of the vehicle, throw the door open, and leap from the interior. My hands ignite, buzzing with power, and the others pile out in my wake. We're ready to go.

The quiet of the city is chilling, and as we step onto the sidewalk, nothing dampens our footsteps. It's the only sound— not even the hum of street transit stops is present. They've been turned off.

"Stay behind me," I say. "Something isn't right."

"Hollis, where are the military men?" Keith whispers. "Why aren't they here?"

"I don't know, but let's move. The Capitol building is past the Testing Center. Follow me."

Without hesitation, I start down the block, marching up the long street. It's strange to be back here yet again. My old life and my new one are both coming together in a storm, but this time, I'm going to win. The pristine pavements I've walked my entire life feel foreign, and the housing units I've come to know so well are unwelcome. Everything about my past hurls itself at me. Its unfeeling aura extends its tendrils, but the feeling inside my chest overpowers it, propelling me toward the Capitol—toward Jonah.

We continue, block after deserted block, heading for the heart of the city, and still, I see no one. Not a soul. The city is barren, and this doesn't bode well.

"Keep your guard up," I instruct my friends.

We turn down the second to last street. Not a sound chimes up, except for our footsteps. They reverberate in my ears, booming like cannons announcing a procession, and when we round the last corner of the final block, the reason for the city's utter desolation explodes into view.

I halt at the end of the road, throwing my hands up to stop everyone. Before us, the towering Capitol building is aglow with floodlights. Military men line the steps up to its entrance. Row upon row stand at the ready—easily a thousand strong, if not more. They cascade down into the street, extending along either side of the pavement, blocking the housing units in and barricading the entrance for a hundred yards.

The five of us stand there, suspended in the moment. The Council was right. No one has an ability powerful enough for this. No one but me.

I look up the steps, spotting the double door entrance amidst the crowd. The men have noticed our group, small and insignificant against the vast sea of weaponry.

I step forward to shield my friends, lifting my hands out in front of my chest. No one is going to die today. Not if I have anything to say about it. My ability surges through me, but I wait, like a lion playing with a gazelle. I watch as hundreds of guns raise across the throng, and for the first time in my life, I yield to the force in my fingertips without any lingering restraint. And with every fiber of my being, with every lie I've been told, with every feeling I've experienced, every sorrow I've known, and every friendship I've forged—with all the strength I can muster—I allow my ability to explode from me with the force of a bomb.

Enough.

The dark voice is back, but this time, I welcome it in. Power shatters from me, and I scream into the torrent as my hands grasp control over every person before me. The nerves in my body are on fire. Every part of me is in pain, but I don't stop. I'm pouring myself in, filling the cup of my wrath until it's quenched. I lower my fists to the ground, kneeling in the dust, and as I look up, the men are to their knees, completely under my control. Every single one of them.

I stand to my feet, panting. Blood drips from my nose, and I wipe it away with the back of my hand. Disheveled strands of my hair dance across my forehead, and I turn to my friends, who are all staring at me like they've never seen me before.

"Let's go get Jonah," I growl, and my ability rears up with my words.

I face the Capitol building once more, swiping my hands to either side. The sea of men parts down the middle, providing a path up the steps. We walk through their midst, and all the while I can feel them writhing under my grip, but I've silenced them, and this time, I know I won't slip. Rage is fueling me, and no one can escape it.

As we climb, I scan the crowd and select the nearest man, seizing him with my fingertips. "You," I command. "Bring me to President Alvaro Camille."

He walks over with mechanical steps, powerless to refuse me. His bloodshot eyes and pressed lips spell fear, but I revel in it. He should be afraid of me. In this moment, I own him. I own all of them.

At the top flight, my hands reach for the golden doors, and I throw them open, charging into the foyer. Ruby nylon carpets, a crystal chandelier, and rose marble artistry decorate the space. It sets a tone of rich decadence. It's different from the Testing Center. This feels warm, almost welcoming, like I've stepped into a lavish dream. Taupe walls frame a double spiraling redwood staircase that extends up either side of the room, and a first-floor inner balcony hangs above our heads. The stark white signature of the government's architecture is gone. This time, it's personal. I've entered the President's home.

My hands flare, and the man under my power moves ahead of me to the left staircase.

"Let's go," I say.

The five of us follow him up, treading lightly. I've never seen such extravagance. Even the craftsmanship of the Testing Center dulls in comparison. But as we continue up the spiral, an alarming display stretches into sight. Five marble statues of wild animals are set into the wall at intervals: a bear, a lion, a wolf, a crocodile, and a viper. All of them have their mouths open and their teeth bared, and as we reach the top of the balcony, a sixth statue resides. It's much larger than the others, and it's a conglomeration of the five creatures. Their heads are all carved into one, and they're coming off of the body of a man who stands with his palms open to the heavens.

"Hollis, what is this?" Rosalie whispers, eyeing the final statue with revulsion.

"I don't know. But keep close to me. We're almost there."

We follow our guide, moving past the final statue and coming to a set of doors at the back, center of the balcony. The man pulls them open, and a long, carpeted hallway with no windows or doors extends in front of us. Instead, paintings line the walls, all of them depicting one of the five beasts from the previous room. A bear feasting on fish. A lion tearing open a gazelle. A wolf with a bloodied lamb. A crocodile swallowing the head of a boar. And a viper engulfing a mouse.

I take my eyes away from the gruesome portraits, an uneasy sensation twisting my stomach into a knot. A single door lies ahead, and as we approach it, the same eerie quiet from the city returns. The carpet muffles our footsteps, and when we reach the door, the man under my control places his hand to the panel on the right. It flashes, and the door opens into a lift.

"Get in," I say, shoving the man forward.

Everyone follows me, and the lift clinks shut. The man presses the button marked for the top floor, and we zoom up. My stomach whirls at the change in momentum, but instead of grabbing the rail, I keep my hands out, channeling my fury into the puppet under my control. We're almost there. Within moments, the lift slows and then comes to a stop, sliding open to either side.

"Move."

The man obeys me, tottering out into a second hallway. It's smaller than the first, and bare to the bone with sheer white. Now it feels like the Testing Center. The sterile cleanliness of the government's facade is back. Two large, white double doors glare at me from the end of the hall, and my hands ball into fists.

"This is over," I say, my teeth grinding against one another.

We reach the doors, and our escort pulls them open to reveal the vast presidential suite from the broadcasts. It's even grander in person. Golden tapestries carrying the President's seal hang from the opposite wall above a large, half-moon desk. A massive bookshelf towers from floor to ceiling to our left, and wall screens mirror this on the right. President Alvaro Camille sits in his chair, his fingertips pressed together, as if in thought, like he's been waiting for me. He wears a white suit and tie, but his jet black hair matches his eyes. His chiseled features and broad shoulders carry an impression of youth, but his face holds the cunning of decades.

His security detail stands around him, and every gun in the room moves to me, but I grip them without effort, gagging them with my ability and pushing them down to their knees. With a flick, I leave them there and approach the President, wrath coursing through my veins.

"This ends now," I snarl, staring into his cold eyes. "I'm

taking Jonah back and I'm leaving." I raise my hand, pointing it at the President's chest, and with all the force I have, I throw authority behind my command. "Tell me where he is."

Nothing happens. The President simply looks at me, quite calmly. His eyes burrow into mine. He's frozen to the spot, unmoving, and yet, he smiles at me.

"You came," he says. His black eyes move down the length of my body and then back up to my face. "Curious."

"What?" I say, taken aback. My hand falters, but I keep it aloft. I gave him an order.

"And the boy?" he asks, his tone even. "I don't see him."

The mere mention of Maddy boils my blood. "And you'll never see him again. He's safe now, and there's nothing you can do about it."

"Curious," he muses, still perfectly poised. "Very curious."

"Tell me where Jonah is!" I demand, flaring my fingertips again, but still, nothing happens. My heartbeat thunders through my chest at the President's next smile—a wicked and deranged one with the potency of glee a society member should never express. I stand there, alarmed. Why isn't my power working? "Where is he?" I ask again.

"You intrigue me," Camille leers, speaking slowly. "How . . . interesting."

I step back, my lips parted. Why isn't he obeying me? My power is tingling in my fingertips. I can feel every person under my grasp, but not him.

"And why is that?" I say, responding with more boldness than I feel.

The President tilts his head. "Because I've never met anyone else like me."

"What?" My voice fractures. "I . . . I'm nothing like you."

"Tell me something, Hollis. How does it make you feel?" he asks, still frozen in place with his fingertips pressed together. "Having all that power coursing through your veins?"

I open my mouth, but nothing comes out.

"Is it frightening?" he continues, but his tone is growing in energy, building with a sinister excitement. "Or is it thrilling? Does it make you feel alive? Does it make you *hunger* for more?"

And to my horror, President Camille stands to his feet, and with a flash of his hands, the military men break from their statues, and their guns rise in unison. A violent tug pulls through my palms, and I'm thrown to my hands and knees as the control of the room is wrenched from me. I turn behind me to find my friends, rigid and bound to the spot, their mouths pressed shut. I stare back at the President with wide eyes.

"Y-you? You're a—"

His fingertips dance through the air and my four companions move into a straight line, looming over me. Their faces hold fear, and terror blossoms from behind their eyes. They're all looking at me, helpless to do anything but obey.

"My dear girl," he says, his demented smile growing. "I'd have thought that you, of all people, would recognize a fellow puppet master's handiwork."

I scramble backward, standing to my feet and clutching my chest. I stare open-mouthed at President Alvaro Camille, and he advances on me, holding his hand up by his wicked grin.

"Let me tell you the story of Hollis Timewire," he glows, and the might of his power fills the entire suite, expanding into every corner of the room. "This is the story of how you lose . . . everything."

29

My hands spring forward, and my friends jerk within my grasp, but Camille swipes his palms, taking them back from me with ease. He chuckles, wild amusement playing into his tone.

"Not quite."

"Let them go!" I say.

The President walks around me, placing himself between me and my companions. His eyes narrow, and then he says, "You intrigue me, Hollis." His fingertips slash directly over my heart, and I flinch, but nothing happens. I stand with the bookshelf to my back, completely unaffected. He draws his hand back. "I can't make you still. How interesting."

Perspiration collects on my brow. He can't control me either.

My ability rears up in my fingers, and for a second time, my hands cut through the air as I reach for control, but the

President yanks it from me once more, and his tug sends me to my knees.

"Silly girl. I've had decades of practice."

I look up at him, fear ripping through me. Tingling thunders up my arms, but the confidence I felt on the steps of the Capitol is fading fast. Camille has all the power.

"Stand up," he says.

And even though his ability isn't commanding me, I obey. My hands find the shelving and I cling to it, paralyzed. My friends are in danger, I can't take them back, and I still don't know if Jonah is alive.

"What an interesting pair," he contemplates, placing a hand to his chin. "The leader of the second Terror War and the leader of the world, unable to touch one another."

"Where is Jonah?" I ask. "What have you done with him?"

"It's been a long six months," Camille says, disregarding my question. His eyes bore into mine. "I've been waiting for this moment, Hollis, ever since you failed the Test. Six months ago, I watched the footage of your escape, and I couldn't believe what I saw. Another puppet master. So young. Frightened by the beast."

"You knew what I was?" My knees turn weak.

"I failed my Test just as you did yours," he says like it's nothing of consequence. "But history doesn't remember." He smiles, flourishing his hand. "Beasty took care of that."

I gape at him. "*You* failed the Test?"

"Yes. But unlike you, I was quicker on my feet. I never ran from society. I embraced it despite my biomarker. I saw my power's potential, and I imagined a brighter future—one with me at its heart to curb the chaos." He sneers as if relishing in the memory of his accomplishment.

I shake my head, dumbfounded. He rose to power amidst the World Order's hunt for Diseased Ones?

"I knew it was only a matter of time before we met," he continues. "I just had to wait for the destruction, and follow it. A power as strong as ours leaves casualties, as I'm sure you're aware. But I didn't anticipate the depths of yours."

Camille cocks his head to the side, his black eyes growing hungry.

"You've made quite a mess, haven't you? Exposing the remaining Diseased Ones. Bravo. Even *I* haven't been able to accomplish that."

"But you're a Diseased One."

He hisses, exposing his teeth, and his black pupils expand. "I'm nothing of the sort. I have dedicated my life to the preservation of one united order. I am the emblem people look to for peace. I am the face of perfection. I am the height of what it means to be a society member, and my ability gives me that. I am obedience. I *am* control."

He prowls up to me, a wicked smirk distorting his features.

"How lucky I am that Jonah fell so conveniently into my possession," he says. "Because I didn't anticipate meeting you face to face so soon. But here you are, puppet master, at my doorstep."

The delight in his voice is terrifying.

"Did you kill him?" I ask, my teeth gritted.

"Let's play a game," the President says. "I want to see what you've learned, young puppet master."

His hands flick, and four of the military men move in sync. Their coordination is flawless. Two of them grab me, arresting my arms and pulling me to the side of the room. The other two exit the suite, and the doors slam shut behind them.

I'm shaking. My entire body is tingling, raw with the power I can't use. I struggle against the men holding me, but they keep an iron grip, one hand on either shoulder and one on each wrist. I wince at the unnatural angle.

Camille walks over to his desk, opens a drawer, and withdraws a slim, golden case the size of my forearm. He unfastens the lid and pulls out a hunting knife. Its handle is engraved with the Capitol's insignia. Closing the case, he slips it back into the drawer.

My breathing turns shallow as my eyes track the knife. But to my horror, the President doesn't move toward me. Instead, he moves to Rosalie, sticking the blade up under her neck.

"Chin up," he says, and beads of blood spring from her skin.

"Stop!" I scream, throwing myself forward, but my captors pull me back. The tingling in my hands intensifies, but still, I can't overcome Camille's grip.

The President's eyes gleam, and he removes the blade, walking down the line of four. His hand cascades over each shoulder. Rosalie . . . Ben . . . Candice . . . He stops in front of Keith, staring at him.

"This one is a fighter. I can feel him." Camille flexes his dominant hand. "Strong-willed."

My heart throws itself against my ribcage like a bird desperate for flight. "Don't touch them!"

"Oh, I won't." The President dips his head. "You have my word, Hollis."

He turns to face the double doors, and on cue, they burst open. The second set of military men have returned, dragging a limp and half-conscious Jonah. He is bound and gagged, with his arms tied behind his back and his feet fastened together at the ankles. Bruising and deep cuts extend across his face, and dried blood is clotted into his hair. The men release Jonah onto the floor, dropping him to his knees. He slumps sideways, unable to catch himself.

I shriek. "Jonah!"

I thrash against the hands restraining me, and my ability erupts. For a few seconds, the men are back under my control, and I'm free of them. But it's short-lived. Camille takes them from me, and their hands clamp back over my arms.

"That a girl, Hollis!" he says, an unhinged smile kicking in. "Good. Fight back. Take the power from me. How did Beasty feel?" He approaches me with crazed energy, inches away. "Do you feel the hunger?"

I spit into his face. His hand moves to my saliva, wiping it off, and for a moment, I think he might stab me, but he stands back, turning to my friends instead. He points the tip of the blade toward them.

"Pick one."

My eyes widen, and I shake my head. "No."

"My game," the President says softly, "my rules. Pick one."

"No!"

He sneers and then walks over to Jonah, who appears so badly beaten that he isn't fully present. He slumps, blood caked to his face. He's in no condition to put up any semblance of a fight.

Camille drops to his knees and takes hold of the top of Jonah's head. Grabbing a fistful of his hair, he yanks him into a sitting position and forces his head upward, pressing the blade to his throat.

"Stop!" I scream. "Please stop!"

"Pick one," he says again, nodding toward my friends.

My hands flex in an attempt to gain back the room, but my ability can't overpower Camille's. It's like I'm a mouse trying to fight a lion. I'm smothered. The President chuckles, the blade still pressed into Jonah's throat, but it falls away, and he stands to his feet, approaching me again. He comes close, his stale breath in my face.

"You're stubborn," he says, and his slippery tone ignites his dark eyes. "I admire that."

"Let them go."

"Oh, Hollis," he says. "You and I both know that's not how this ends. Pick one."

"No."

"Then perhaps I need to break you a little before we play."

His hands twitch, and my four friends move in unison. They surround me, dragging me to the center of the room and forcing me to my knees. In a snap, they move back, encircling me. Their movements are smooth and calculated. I stare up at them, and they begin to speak with animalistic energy, forced to talk by the President's prancing fingertips.

"We're Diseased Ones," Candice taunts.

"Diseased Ones," Rosalie echoes.

"We murder," Ben hurls at me.

"Murderers," Keith says.

I leap to my feet, my hands out, but the moment I'm up, Keith and Ben launch themselves at me, forcing me down again. They retreat back into circling.

"On your knees, Hollis," the President says, a daunting glint in his eye.

"We hate you," Keith jeers. "You're worthless."

"Worthless," Candice sings, chiming in with her brother.

"You're a traitor!" Rosalie screeches, slapping me full across the face, and the sting she leaves sends another wave of panic through me. But nothing I do pulls them back to me, even though I can feel the power building in my chest.

"You turned us in," Ben hisses. "We're not your friends."

"Who would ever want to be friends with you?" Keith adds. "You're disgusting."

"Stop!" I command, channeling my ability through my hands, but this only seems to fuel Camille's fun. He closes the circle in on me, forcing my friends to speak faster.

"You're an animal."

"We hate you!"

"A beast."

"Monster."

"Filth."

"Worthless."

"Vile."

"Diseased One!"

I clamp my hands over my ears, but Ben and Keith grab my wrists, forcing my hands away from my head. They twist my arms back and I shriek in pain. And now, all of them speak in unity, and their voices amplify each other.

"Hollis Timewire, the girl who turned us in! The girl who exposed us! The girl who ruined us! The girl who murdered us!"

I fight their grip, but they hold me still, screeching at me with unearthly notes.

"Hollis Timewire, the leader of the second Terror War! Murderous, traitorous, Diseased One!"

They throw me, and I skid across the floor, skinning my elbows and landing on my stomach. The four of them move back into the line, and the President points two of his military men to my side. They lift me to my feet, restraining me again. Camille approaches, placing the tip of the blade up to my chin. It digs into my skin, but I refuse to grimace. Instead, I stare at him, throwing all the contempt I have into my expression. I'm terrified, but I can't fall apart. It's what he wants.

The President's eyes narrow. "You didn't pick, so I shall." He turns from me and walks directly up to Ben.

"No!" I shout, twisting my arms.

"And I encourage you, Hollis," he says, bowing to me. "Do try and put up a fight."

To my surprise, the President hands Ben the knife and then

steps to the side of the line, splaying his hand forward. Ben grips the blade. The President's hands move again, and Rosalie falls from her rigid form, collapsing on all fours and gasping for breath. She's free of Camille's power, and tears spring to her eyes. The President flicks his hand at Ben.

"Kill her," he commands.

Ben jumps forward, lunging at Rosalie, who shrieks and rolls out of the way. She clambers to her feet, running around the desk. "Hollis!" she shrieks, stumbling over the President's chair and knocking it over. "Help me!"

"Stop!" I say, pleading with Camille. I throw myself forward, but I'm no match for the two detaining me. Their grip tightens, fingernails digging into my flesh. I have to use my power. My hands flare out, making an attempt for control, and the tingling intensifies. I'm grasping for Ben, the energy at my core electric.

Ben leaps over the discarded chair, advancing on Rosalie. The knife glints in front of him, held aloft and poised to strike.

"Please!" I cry, flailing. My ability sears my fingertips, but every time I reach for the command, the President overpowers me.

Rosalie runs from the desk, sprinting to the door, but Keith and Candice block her path, pushing her with so much force that she falls. She skids to the floor, scrambling backward on her hands and feet. Ben stalks up to her with lightning speed.

"Hollis, help me!"

Ben dives, grabbing her ankles and dragging her across the floor. The knife flashes, Ben plunges it into Rosalie's stomach.

She gasps, and her face lights up, lips parted as if caught in surprise. Ben wrenches the blade from her flesh, and she curls over, sputtering for breath. Her body shudders, and a pool of blood starts to seep onto the white tile.

"No! Rosalie!" I screech.

Ben moves back to the line, still clutching the knife in his fist. It's crimson and dripping. Horror resides behind Ben's eyes, but he is still bound under the President's will, unable to do a thing.

Camille walks over to Rosalie, placing his foot on her shoulder. He rolls her onto her back so that she's looking up at the ceiling. Her labored breathing intensifies, and she whimpers, clutching her stomach. Tears streak down her freckled face.

"That wound is deep," he says.

My chest is on fire, and another powerful wave of my ability surges through me. I scream, spreading out my hands, and the room is mine. All of the military men sink to their knees, and I stagger forward, finally free.

"There she is!" Camille taunts in a singsong, slow clapping. "Good girl, Hollis."

"Rosalie!" I run to the center of the suite and drop to my knees at her side. She's wheezing, pale with perspiration. Blood, in copious amounts, is spreading across the floor, and I press my hands to the wound. "I'm sorry! I'm so sorry! It's okay! Everything will be fine, do you hear me? You're alright!"

"Yes, lie to her," Camille says, snapping his fingers.

His hands extend to take back the power, and his men

move in unison to drag me away from Rosalie. But this time, I'm ready. Before they can grab me, I launch myself at Camille, and my fingernails find purchase across the left side of his face. He screams, staggering backward, and his guards seize me, pulling me off of him.

I kick out, Rosalie's blood smearing against my clothing. "Let me go!"

Camille's hand is on his face, and the feral look he wears says he never expected me to do that. He shakes himself off by pulling the trim of his suit straight. Just under his left eye, a deep mark beads with blood. But his alarm passes all too quickly, and pleasure splays across his features once more.

He walks over to my friends, towering over them. Then, with a flick, he pulls Ben forward. Ben holds the knife at the ready, and Camille, with an icy glare, says, "So, who's next? Pick one."

My lower lip trembles as I meet his cruel gaze. I'm quivering, rage and terror battling within me.

"Pick one," he states again.

I bow my head, my eyes tearing up. I can't beat him. He's too strong. So I say the only thing I can. "Me."

Camille angles his head to the side. "Speak up, Hollis."

"Me," I say louder. "Pick me."

The President purses his lips in distaste. "That's not the game. Pick one."

"Me," I state again.

"Pick one!" he growls, madness infused into his tone. He approaches me, his beady eyes inches from mine. The grip on my wrists tighten, but I stand straight, refusing to back down.

"I will not have any more blood on my hands," I say. "And no one, not even another puppet master, can force that on me. I don't want to play your game. Kill me. I'm the one you want. I'm the leader."

Camille's face curls into a terrible smile. "Let me hear you say it," he hisses.

"I'm the leader of the second Terror War," I say, and my voice breaks. "Take me in their place. I'm the face the world knows. I'm the death that will end this. So kill me, but let them go. Please."

He pauses, curiosity replacing his insanity, and then he speaks calmly, the crazed man from moments ago gone.

"From the moment I saw you, I only wanted two things. One, to know that my power is stronger than yours—and from what I've seen tonight, that is abundantly clear. You have no understanding of the entity beneath your fingertips. You're an infant: juvenile in your control, and rash in your emotions," he says. "And the second is this: to end your life. I can't allow your power to grow, Hollis, because you will become like me. It's inevitable. Given time, you would come to understand the beast—to cultivate it. We are different from the others, Hollis. Our ability isn't as simple as the biomarker, but I think you already knew that. Does it speak to you yet? Have you tasted its power?"

The President's pupils increase until the whites of his eyes are gone, and he bares his teeth at me, the monster within lighting back up his features.

"Tell me, Hollis, are you afraid of it? Or does it make you thirst for greatness?"

I pull back from him, gasping as his composure slips into insanity once more. He stares directly into my face.

"Make no mistake, Hollis Timewire," he replies, and my full name rings in my ears. "I intend to kill you." He leers. "And the best part? I want you to know that every moment we stand here you have the capacity to stop me. You're just too weak."

He turns from me and moves to the back wall of the presidential suite. The military men shuffle me around to face him. He opens a white panel on the left side of the wall behind his desk. A golden button lies under the cover.

"It's fitting, isn't it? Our fates coming together so soon," Camille says, his excitement growing. "We're the unseen ones, Hollis, cast out by society, ostracized even by those who claim to be our allies. They don't really *see* us, do they? They don't understand. Our power is greater—superior in every way—but to harness its potential, it must go unnoticed. You were a good student, weren't you? What is society's mantra?"

My jaw clenches, and I stay silent.

"Oh come now, Hollis. You haven't forgotten your schooling, have you?" Camille asks. "Say it."

I stare at him defiantly.

"Why must you make this difficult?"

He casts his hand toward Jonah, and Jonah begins to writhe in his restraints, his limbs forced back at odd angles. He gasps through the gag, his back arching in excruciating pain.

"The path to a perfect society is perfect obedience!" I say, my eyes watering. "Stop!"

"Indeed." Camille pulls his hand back, and Jonah falls limp again, curled onto the floor. "And therein lies our power. How do you think I got here?" He gestures around his office. "I am what it means to obey. I am control. You chose to run from the beast, but I chose to embrace it. And here we stand, me at the precipice of my existence, and you and at the end of yours. There can only be *one* puppet master."

And without warning, Camille slams his hand into the golden button, and the large, half-moon desk begins to slide to the side of the room. The floor trembles with the power of an earthquake, and before us, the outside of the Capitol building opens to the city below. The walls shrink, tucking themselves up by sliding down into the floor, and the ceiling rises like a lid.

The President turns to me, straightening his tie. "It's time to end this, Hollis," he says. "And I'm going to do it in front of the whole world."

At the twist of his pointer finger, the remaining military men step up to Keith, Candice, and Ben, arresting them and bringing them to stand next to me. Rosalie is still shuddering on the tile, pale and discarded. And all the while, the room continues to transform, converting itself to a massive platform that raises up to the heavens.

Rough hands pull me forward until I'm at the edge, looking down at the depths. The city is lit with floodlights that smear out the stars, and a thousand men gather at the steps, peering up at us as a screen the size of the clearing unfolds from the side of the Capitol. The moment it finishes assembling itself, a live feed begins. It reflects off the glass of the adjacent building, flashing into view.

The feed zooms out, capturing the entire platform. Me and my three companions detained in place, and Rosalie and Jonah lying still on the floor. President Alvaro Camille steps up to his podium, facing the masses. He clicks something on his collar, and his voice booms out over the city—and across every screen in the world.

"Citizens," he announces. "I have wonderful news for every man, woman, and child. We have captured Hollis Timewire and her fellow Diseased Ones."

A roar comes from the crowd below. I'm struggling again, desperate in my attempts for freedom. With what little motion I'm allowed, my hands spread wide, vying for control, but Camille's power swells with every word. My heartbeat thunders within me, and the tingling grows until I'm bursting at the seams. All that I am is straining to fight him.

"Their reign of terror is over!" he says. "And they will pay for their crimes with their lives. It is my solemn duty, as your leader, to publicly put an end to this. Their defiance and hateful destruction of all we hold dear will not stand. Hollis Timewire and her accomplices will die, and once again, the world will be at peace. True and lasting peace!"

The military erupts into a warcry, saluting their supreme leader. I stare at the feed's reflection. Candice's face is littered with tears, Ben and Keith are shaking, Jonah is beaten and broken, and Rosalie is dying in a pool of her own blood. And suddenly, my hands relax in the men's grip. It's over. All of it—the struggle, the pain, and the wonder. I don't have to fight anymore. I don't have to love, or hurt, or laugh, or cry, or feel. I've lost. We're going to die, and there's nothing I can do. I couldn't save them. Tears streak my face, and I choke back a sob as the barrel of a gun is placed at the back of my head.

"Citizens," the President shouts. "Let this night be a reminder to all. Deception and guile never win. It is always power, and those who are brave enough to take hold of it."

I close my eyes, resigning myself. I'm going to die, but this time I can't imagine a better way to perish—standing with the truest and bravest people I know. Standing on the right side of history, though no one in the world can see it. Standing proudly for who I am: a Diseased One.

Shrieks echo from the mob on the steps. The commotion is so abrupt and cacophonous that my eyes fly open. I gasp, staring at the reflection of the screen. A massive blue orb of pulsating light glints in the feed. The hands restraining me vanish, and my captors scream in terror, retreating from the anomaly. I turn around to find the orb directly in our midst. It hovers on the platform, rattling like some bizarre, electric creature.

"The orb from the forest," I whisper, wide-eyed. "What?"

The orb expands, perfectly spherical, encasing Candice, Ben, Keith, Rosalie, and Jonah within its depths. It fills the platform, engulfing me, and its gentle embrace floods the air with warmth. For the smallest fraction of a second, I catch President Camille's enraged look. His hands launch forward, attempting to clutch us within his power again, but in a brilliant flash of blue, the orb collapses around us, and we are all plunged into darkness with a jerk of motion.

30

I'M THROWN TO MY KNEES, AND MY SKIN SCRAPES AGAINST hard concrete. It's like I've been dunked under icy water. The sensation travels into my stomach and down to my toes. The orb contracts and then vanishes in a blinding flash of blue, leaving black spots in my vision.

I'm disoriented and faint, but I leap to my feet, ready to fight anew. So much adrenaline is in my blood that I'm hyper-aware of my surroundings, and as my vision clears, I take an account of who's with me. The orb took us all. To my relief, everyone is here, battered and lying on the floor, but alive.

I scan the high walls that encapsulate us. It looks like we're in an aircraft hangar. Steel arches tower above, and a balcony juts out from the back of the massive space.

My ability buzzes beneath my skin, thriving with energy. From the side of the room, a door crashes open, sending me into a frenzy. Two people approach our ragged group. I can only decipher their silhouettes in the dim lighting. I throw my hands out, capturing them in my grasp.

"Who are you?" I demand, desperate to keep my footing. I'm trembling, still gripped in the panic of our impending death.

"Wait, Hollis!" a girl's voice calls out. "It's okay!"

I squint at them, unable to decipher who's speaking. Do I know them?

"It's okay. We're like you!" she says. "We have powers!"

"You're . . . what?" I repeat, bewildered. I twitch my fingers, pulling the two strangers into my view. It's a man and girl, but I've never seen them before. The man stands tall and lanky, his ginger hair pressed flat against his forehead. The girl looks to be my age and height, and her short, black, curly hair complements her dark skin.

"Who are you? What happened?" I say rapid-fire, keeping my ability on them.

"We have abilities too," the man says. "We're like you."

"Prove it," I say, unwilling to let my guard down.

"May I?" the girl asks, looking down at her frozen body. She seems completely unfazed by the fact that she's bound under my power, as if she's seen it before.

I release her with more force than I anticipated. She stumbles, almost falling over, and my eyes dart to her deep brown ones. I keep one of my hands directed toward the man, as my other one tracks the girl. She moves a few steps from me and then flourishes her fingertips. The blue orb from the forest expands into existence. It hovers for a moment, bobbing in the concrete room, and then, in a burst of intense light, it vanishes.

"I rescued you from the platform," the girl says. "My name is Olivia Turrick, and this is Terrace DuPont." She points to the man. "We're not going to hurt you, Hollis. We're on your side."

My mouth hangs open. "There are more of us?"

Olivia gives me a curious smile. "Of course there are more of us."

ACKNOWLEDGMENTS

Whew, what a journey! This novel was a whirlwind of fun to write, but it also taught me more about myself and the craft of storytelling. Hollis's story is near and dear to my heart, and I can't thank you enough for being part of it. It means the world to me that you've read my book.

Some big thank you's are in order.

To my husband: Steven, you've been my rock through this whole series. Crafting the world together, reading every version of every chapter, encouraging me when I get discouraged, and loving me through it all. I wouldn't be where I am without you. You're an amazing human, and I'm so happy you're my forever.

To my editor: Holly, wow! I have no words. You're so good at what you do. You know how to point out what I do well, while providing incredible insight into where I can improve. You've taught me so much, and I feel confident in my writing because of you. Thank you for taking a chance on me and mentoring me. I'm honored to be an Acorn author.

To my beta readers: Sky, Gabby, Molly, and Gemma. You ladies are queens. Thank you for your enthusiasm! You've brought joy to this project, and you've helped me develop the finer details that have enriched many scenes. I value you and your feedback.

To my family: Your support is what keeps me going. Mom and Dad, I love you to the moon and back. Thank you for teaching me to chase my dreams. Michelle, Luke, and Gabby, I'm so blessed to have you in my life. You're the best siblings! Thank you for being a part of the world-building, storytelling, beta reading, ARC round, marketing, and everything in between. I couldn't have done this without you.

To my Savior: Jesus, thank you for continuing to bless my pursuits, and thank you for giving me the opportunity to share my writing with the world. All glory and honor to you!

To my readers: Thank you for continuing this journey with me. Publishing a YA series has been a dream of mine since I was a little girl, and YOU are making this happen for me. As an author, reviews mean everything! I have a request. If you could take a moment to leave a review on Goodreads, Amazon, or Barnes & Noble, it would help my career. I read every review, and it's exciting to hear your thoughts. Your support is invaluable. Thank you from the bottom of my heart.

CPSIA information can be obtained
at www.ICGtesting.com
Printed in the USA
LVHW031715011220
673096LV00041B/682/J

9 781952 112256